SPECIAL MESSAGE TO READERS

This book is published under the auspices of

THE ULVERSCROFT FOUNDATION

(registered charity No. 264873 UK)

Established in 1972 to provide funds for research, diagnosis and treatment of eye diseases. Examples of contributions made are: —

A Children's Assessment Unit at Moorfield's Hospital, London.

•

Twin operating theatres at the Western Ophthalmic Hospital, London.

•

A Chair of Ophthalmology at the Royal Australian College of Ophthalmologists.

•

The Ulverscroft Children's Eye Unit at the Great Ormond Street Hospital For Sick Children, London.

You can help further the work of the Foundation by making a donation or leaving a legacy. Every contribution, no matter how small, is received with gratitude. Please write for details to:

THE ULVERSCROFT FOUNDATION,
The Green, Bradgate Road, Anstey,
Leicester LE7 7FU, England.
Telephone: (0116) 236 4325

In Australia write to:
THE ULVERSCROFT FOUNDATION,
c/o The Royal Australian and New Zealand
College of Ophthalmologists,
94-98 Chalmers Street, Surry Hills,
N.S.W. 2010, Australia

Colin Reed spent some time in the navy before embarking on a career in teaching. Married with children and grandchildren, he now lives in Port Mulgrave, on the North Yorkshire coast near Whitby.

THE FOOLISH VIRGIN

In the beautiful North Yorkshire Dales, a wartime relationship develops between Land Girl Ruth Palmer and captured German flier Holger Fichtmüller. This almost unthinkable affair transcends the prejudices of two nations locked in world combat. Kept apart for more than two years, the couple correspond through a sympathetic chaplain. When, eventually, Holger is transferred to Yorkshire, fortune seems to favour the lovers, despite family opposition. However, as an Allied victory in Europe finally approaches, news of death camp atrocities brings a crisis of conscience to Holger.

Books by C. W. Reed
Published by The House of Ulverscroft:

WRIGHT FAMILY SERIES:
TO REASON WHY
TIES OF BLOOD
ALL MANNER OF THINGS

C. W. REED

THE FOOLISH VIRGIN

Complete and Unabridged

ULVERSCROFT
Leicester

First published in Great Britain in 2002 by
Robert Hale Limited
London

First Large Print Edition
published 2004
by arrangement with
Robert Hale Limited
London

The moral right of the author has been asserted

British Library CIP Data

Reed, C. W. (Colin W.)
  The foolish virgin.—Large print ed.—
  Ulverscroft large print series: romance
  1. World War, *1939 – 1945* —England—Yorkshire—
  Fiction 2. Love stories 3. Large type books
  I. Title
  823.9′14 [F]

  ISBN 1–84395–152–5

Published by
F. A. Thorpe (Publishing)
Anstey, Leicestershire

Set by Words & Graphics Ltd.
Anstey, Leicestershire
Printed and bound in Great Britain by
T. J. International Ltd., Padstow, Cornwall

This book is printed on acid-free paper

But love ye your enemies, and do good, and lend, hoping for nothing again; and your reward shall be great, and ye shall be the children of the highest.

Luke 6, v.35

1

'For Christ's sake, break away!' Holger Fichtmüller screamed to himself, probably aloud, but Helmut, copybook pilot that he was, flew on steadily, into disaster, obsessed with this crazy instruction to hold the formation whatever happened. From his isolated gondola hanging below the belly of the Heinkel 111, Holger could see perfectly clearly the glint of the moon on the water to his right, and the dark blur of the land's edge. Weber's plane was also clearly visible on their left, the night was so fine. Then suddenly a silver bar ribboned the wing with obscene brightness as the plane sliced through the beam of a searchlight. Another came across, held them, blinding in its brilliance, and, all at once, the miniature red clouds of ack-ack bursts flowered below and all around them, spreading like a carpet.

Shells slammed into the underbelly, further back, towards the tail. Holger screamed again, wordlessly this time, every muscle contracting as though he could somehow thus protect himself from these lethal explosives. As though they were aimed especially at him.

1

He felt the bomber lift, flung carelessly sideways, and the intercom was full of screaming voices, procedures forgotten, for long, disorienting seconds, until Helmut's frantic screams penetrated through all the rest.

'Check in! Check in! Shut up, bastards! Franz? Holger?'

'*Ja!*' he yelled, absurdly pleased to hear his name.

They seemed to be losing height in a gentle spiral, but the gunfire was staying all about them. Holger saw the starboard wing, dark above him, flutter, then glow. A large piece of blackness flew past his turret. The engine on that side was stuttering. The plane slewed round again.

The sickness came thickly to his throat, he became aware of a thin screaming, and another babble of voices, until Helmut broke over them, loud and distorted with panic.

'Franz has copped it! I can't keep height. We're banking round inland. I'll go with it. Dawn's coming up. They'll have fighters up in a minute. Keep your eyes peeled, Holger!'

'Are we ditching?'

'Starboard engine's out.'

'Christ! There's a bloody great hole!'

'Get rid of the fucking bombs!'

The voices crackled and screamed in

Holger's headphones, adding to the sense of wildness and terror. The bomber had always seemed such a haven, such a comforting capsule of human warmth in the darkness of the elements, through all their training, the missions they had flown over France and Belgium. Even their latest campaign in Norway had been a cinch. The Spitfires and Hurricanes they had so dreaded had not materialized. Their missions had all been night raids, and even the anti-aircraft fire had been either sporadic or non-existent.

But this. This was different. He had a sudden vision of Helmut's face, glancing laughingly across at him, embarrassed as he himself was in the vast, chilly hangar of their new base south of Stavanger, only two days ago, when the Adjutant had made them all listen to the tub-thumping rhythm of the latest song. A hundred and more lusty young male voices, bellowing out the newly learned chorus. He had joined in, with exaggerated heartiness, head swaying, chin jutting, grinning back at Helmut to let him know it was all a bit of a joke. 'Bombs over England!'

And here they were, falling to pieces in the rapidly lightening sky over their enemy's north-east coast, the river they were searching for not even found, the bombs still lethally nestled in their belly, while below them the whole landscape appeared to be erupting with twinkling, mushrooming weapons bent on destroying them.

'There may be some fire from coastal batteries as you cross.' Holger cursed vehemently the memory of the briefing officer, with his immaculate uniform and dry, slightly bored voice.

All the glamour, the comradeship, even the illusion of security he had felt, vanished around him in the howling dawn as the fragile bits of metal and wood and canvas strained and shuddered to hold the air. 'Are we going to ditch, skipper?' he called out desperately. Helmut didn't answer.

He glanced around him. They had lost a lot of height. He could see the dark patchwork of the land, the undulations of steep hills on the horizon. Behind them now, he had a clear view of the stabbing searchlights and bursting flak. It was thankfully distant. But every second put them further into enemy territory.

He struggled free of the bucket seat, pushing the heavy 20mm cannon away, the barrel tilting down to the right. He pulled on the heavy harness of the parachute, fumbling as he clipped on the straps. It meant he could no longer sit properly at his post, but it might make the difference between life and death in the split seconds of decision.

'Keep your eyes peeled! It's light out there now! I'm going to try to bring her round. We're well inland.'

They banked and yawed sickeningly, and Holger fell, cursing, clinging to the gun handles, kneeling hunched over the seat, while he watched dark patches of trees and paler fields speed past beneath. They were in what looked like a long, narrow valley. The land rose steeply on either side of them. The port engine was screaming now, the bomber vibrating furiously.

'We're losing height! Jettison the bombs! Quick!' Helmut's voice was shrill; Holger responded to the panic in his tones. The plane leapt madly as the bombs dropped. They were very low; he saw the first explode. The black smoke mushroomed up after the dull glow and the muted crump, scarcely heard over the engine roar. Holger mouthed a startled obscenity as a large, ghostly building loomed below. They swept over almost as the second bomb detonated. They'd hit it, surely? What was it? A factory? Barracks? The plane rolled, flipped to its right, and Holger fell heavily against the side of the glass bubble. Helmut screamed in his ear, an elemental howl of pure fear, and Holger clawed madly at the heavy locking-handle of the turret door.

He was trapped! It wouldn't open! He hunched his shoulders against the trap-door above and thrust viciously, bursting through, up into the fuselage, just as the bomber rolled again, turning almost over. A howling chaos of rushing wind caught him, he saw the hatch behind the pilot and the navigator's seat open and he lunged at it. The slipstream caught him, sucked and spat him out, spinning him over and over between pale dawn sky and dark earth, mind jumbled like his body, until one thought screamed into words — 'You're too low! You're too low for the 'chute!'

He yanked the rip-cord, felt the tremendous, snapping jerk pulling at his shoulders, tossing him back. Then he was falling, and yes, he confirmed, he was too low, and he was going to die, the black earth leapt devouringly at him. He did not scream this time, cried out her name softly, weeping for her, for both of them.

'Heidi!'

★ ★ ★

'Heidi! Are you going down to the lake?' Holger flushed as he noticed the sniggering looks the girls with her were exchanging. 'Fraülein Krempel. I'll walk down with you. I'm going that way,' he said stiffly.

6

She grinned back at him, brown eyes flashing, almost as mischievously as all her young charges. 'Very well, Herr Fichtmüller,' she teased. His blushes deepened as he fell in beside her, watching the colt-legged teenagers in their black woollen bathing costumes go scampering off ahead, picking their way gingerly through the grass down to the lake's edge.

He tried to appear relaxed as he strolled at her side, stealing surreptitious glances at her shining, neatly waved fair hair, her slim form in the belted brown dress. Her brown legs looked good, displayed as they were beneath the short hem, which reached only to mid thigh. The tan of her skin stood out against the whiteness of the ankle socks. 'You're not taking a dip yourself?' he asked.

Heidi Krempel laughed. Her voice still held the faintly teasing quality. 'Of course, Herr Fichtmüller! But I'll undress when I get there!'

He knew she was making fun of him, but he didn't mind. She was the best thing that could have happened at this summer camp, and he breathed a sigh of relief that he had not given up his role of youth leader despite the private squirms of discomfort he had felt at being involved in the movement still, at the advanced age of twenty. She was only a year younger, he had discovered, though at the moment, and at others, when she had looked at him with that steady, unfathomable expression in those disturbingly beautiful eyes, he had felt she was mysterious ages older.

'I'll look forward to that!' he answered with awkward daring, his heart bumping.

She giggled, ran ahead of him, towards the margins of the lake, where the younger girls were clustered, squealing and pushing one another like a flock of flamingos. She was already tugging at the thin leather belt, unbuttoning herself at the front, tugging the dress off her shoulders and dropping it from her arms to the ground. She was wearing a black bathing suit, like the other girls, only filling it a darned sight better, he observed, blushing again with guilty knowledge.

Only another week and he would be leaving the camp. And Heidi. But she did not live so far away from his own home in Düsseldorf. Remscheid was only just over twenty kilometres away. It gave him a funny feeling to think of her all those years, growing up, so near. Suddenly, his feelings of eager impatience for the summer to advance had changed. Made him confused all at once. Of course, he still wanted to enlist in the Luftwaffe. His interview was already fixed for the end of August. That was the main reason for his deciding to attend the youth camp at Alsfeld. It would look good, count for a lot, Herr Maurer said. His record as a youth leader would stand him in good stead.

More than anything, he wanted to be a fighter pilot. Everyone was full of their exploits in Spain, and the way that air power would transform warfare. And war was coming, there could be no doubt. You could feel it, the signs were everywhere. Four months ago, Austria had become part of the German Reich, after only two days. The people wanted it, wanted to be part of the new Germanic race, wanted the living space it provided. And the Sudetenland of Czechoslovakia would be next, the territory and peoples stolen from Germany at the end of the last war. They, too, would become part of the Reich, whatever schemes Britain and the other imperialist European powers might try.

Yes, there was a feeling of shackles being thrown off, a new, glorious order coming in, loosening the stranglehold of the Jews and the old-guard power which had kept the people down. Other nations knew it, too. Under their leader, Germany was ready for a new age, and this time they would keep their place in the sun. And Holger wanted to be a part of the glory that was coming.

Only . . . he didn't want the next week to end, he realized, with a shock, as he watched Heidi Krempel's firm body wading confidently out into the still, dark water of the lake. The pale shoulders dipped, the fair head bobbed as she struck out.

'Promise you'll write!' he pleaded, five nights later, as they walked arm in arm, down towards the lake again, leaving the singing and the sparking fire behind them, up on the hill. The August night was clear.

This was their last night at the camp.

She *did* write, agreed to meet him, and in early September a nervously sweating Holger, fair hair slicked down, in best dark suit and polished boots agleam, appeared on the step of the modest, neat house where the Krempels lived. Heidi was almost as nervous as he was, though she was much better at concealing it. She looked very mature, and extremely desirable, in a flowery summer dress, narrow, shiny high heels, and silk stockings. Holger's insides had that melted, empty feeling, he felt red and awkward and ugly, tongue-tied with his admiration.

Herr Krempel was a teacher of science, and Holger was uncomfortably conscious of the fact that Heidi's background was of a superior social status to his own. His father was a foreman at an engineering works in the city. Holger agreed wholeheartedly with the ideal of the sanctity of labour as preached by the Third Reich, but it still couldn't stop his feeling somewhat in awe of Heidi's comfortable home, with its books and magazines, and pictures and objets d'art, and of the beautiful girl herself in her natural setting.

But her parents worked hard to make him feel at ease, listened to him, encouraging him to talk. The crisis over Czechoslovakia was getting into full swing.

'I don't think Britain will be foolish enough to go to war over such a clear issue, do you?' Herr Krempel asked. 'I think Herr Chamberlain knows right is on our side.'

Holger nodded self-consciously. He decided not to put forward his father's simplistic view of the matter. 'Bloody Britain's run by the Jew-boys. Like America! Bound to want to try it on with us some time!'

'We'll be ready for them if they do,' Holger replied now, patriotically.

'Holger's going into the Luftwaffe!' Heidi declared, her eyes shining with pride. 'He's already had his preliminary interview. He's going to be a pilot.' Holger basked in their congratulations. He was pleased, and surprised, when, after lunch, Heidi said casually, 'I want to show Holger my room. My class

11

book and things,' and her parents gave their permission easily, without any provisos or joking hints.

'You will miss me when I go into the service?' he asked presently, when they were alone. 'You'll write to me — every day?' When she finally pulled her mouth away from his, his hands moved downward, rested on the curve of her buttocks, feeling silk glide thrillingly on silk as they hardened, clenching, and she drove the base of her belly with unmistakable heat into the throb of his loins.

2

Ruth Palmer woke in a blind panic, unsure of whether the nightmare crash of sound, the trembling sensation of the creaky old bed having moved, were all part of a terrifying dream she could not remember. For a second she could remember very little, the darkness around her was thickly alien, and she almost called out, 'Mam! Dad!' and reached out for the warm comfort of Julia's body next to her. Then the bed squeaked, she felt the narrow, scooped-out shape fitted to her body, remembered the small dimensions of its metal frame, and knew where she was. Skinnerdale Hall.

She located the small window by the faint edging of dim grey filtering through the blackout blind and the thick curtain. The window had surely rattled vigorously just now in its wooden frame? As she tardily came to full consciousness, there was a dull, deep boom, transmitting itself up through the floor, and the bedframe, as the old stable-building shivered sedately. Ruth was already swinging her feet out into the chill of the August dawn, clawing at the door of her tiny room, running down the steep short, thin-carpeted staircase to the door leading out into the stable yard.

She heard movement, and from across the cobbles, the high-pitched tones of Mrs May, comforting despite their note of shrill panic.

'Is that you, Ruth? What's happening? Have them Germans come then?'

And behind her, the even more comforting, steadier voice of Master Roger, and Miss Felicity. The latter was swiftly at Ruth's side, then brushing unceremoniously past her to open the heavy doors and enter the stall.

'Are they all right?' she asked anxiously, and at once began to talk to the two horses in that mooning, babyish voice which embarrassed Ruth and which she privately thought was so daft. 'There there, my pet. Mumsie's here, look.' Beauty was her own horse. It snorted in grateful recognition. Both animals quietened at once.

All at once, Win May's panic at the prospect of imminent invasion gave way to another, more immediate, concern. 'Good heavens, girl! Go and put something on! You'll catch your death!'

'Oh, I dunno. It's a mild enough night, Mrs May!' Roger Whiteley, clad in his brown-checked dressing-gown, its tasselled cord pulled tightly about his waist, beneath which peeped striped pyjama legs and feet encased in elegant leather slippers, grinned meaningfully, and, for the first time, Ruth realized that all she had on was her thin, pale-blue summer nightie. To emphasize the point, she became aware, also for the first time, of the rough coldness of the concrete stabbing at her bare feet.

Bounding back up the narrow staircase, she hastily hauled on a pair of slacks, stuffing the cotton nightdress down inside them, and pulled one of her thick green sweaters over her wild hair, before tugging on her flat shoes and hurrying down again.

'You're all right, lass?' She felt that instant flow of warmth towards the speaker. Ernie Long was her 'boss', the head gardener at the Hall, the only one of the outside staff left now in full-time employment, and the man she knew better than anyone in her new environment. And so she should, considering the hours they spent together, struggling to preserve the grandeur of the large gardens while converting a great deal of the acreage into a going concern as a market garden. His lined and weathered face was creased further with his concern, his silver hair askew, the ring where his flat cap, for once missing and giving him an incomplete look, rested clearly marked.

He said, 'I heard gunfire earlier. Over towards the coast, like. Then this plane come over — didn't you hear him? He were that low I thought he were coming down on top of us. He's dropped two or three bombs, I reckon. One behind the house there. Made a right mess.' He turned to Roger. 'Where's your ma and pa? I'm off to have a proper look. Made a ruddy great hole in the lawn on the west side.'

'Come through the house,' Win May urged. 'Sir George and Lady Cecily won't mind.'

Felicity Whiteley, dressing-gowned like her brother, decided that the animals were sufficiently calmed to be left, and trooped after the small group across the yard, which was rapidly lightening now in the grey of dawn.

They went into the darkness of the mansion, past the ground floor scullery and kitchen, the butler's pantry and the house-keeper's room, and through the unobtrusive doorway which brought them out into the grand hall, under the wide staircase. A lamp was burning, the blackout curtains at the imposing front doors had been drawn aside. One door was unlocked, off the latch, and they passed through it to the open air.

Sir George Whiteley's corpulent figure was at the bottom of the steps; beside him was

Lady Cissie, delicately groomed, immaculate in silken wrapper, her hair tied up in a silk scarf, not a wisp out of place.

'There's a bloody great hole in the lawn!' Sir George called out in breathy excitement. 'Blown the ground floor windows in. Bits of metal stuck all over the west wall. Like a ruddy pepper-pot!' He led the group round the side of the house, his torch waving, like an eager guide. 'Come and see!'

They stood in awed contemplation on the lip of the shallow crater, stared up at the grey, pocked wall of the mansion, the long, shattered windows of the ground floor, the small squares of their frames hanging twisted, trailing like trellises towards the ground. 'Another thirty yards . . . ' Sir George mused, his voice quieter. He looked up with almost comic incredulity. 'What the hell do they want to drop a bomb on us for?'

'Dropped two or three,' Ernie Long said. 'Up in Harlow's fields somewhere, I'd say. He come over very low. In trouble, I reckon. Just a stray. They'll have been heading further north. Up towards Tees or Tyne mebbes.' Then he remembered, and added quickly, 'Don't worry, Ruthie, love. It'll be all right, you'll see.' And his rough hand closed on her wrist, with real concern.

There was another, more distant crump,

17

then the sky lit up brightly beyond the woods of the estate, up on the high moors, which were standing out blackly against the encroaching dawn.

'What on earth are they dropping bombs up on the moors for?' Roger Whiteley wondered.

'Don't reckon that were a bomb, Master Roger,' Ernie said. 'Look at the sky over there. Summat's afire there all right. I reckon it's that plane that come over here. Must've crashed.'

'There's been a big raid, I should say,' Sir George put in, his voice still aquiver with excitement. 'Going for Teesside. I'd guess.'

Ruth shivered, her stomach giving that odd lurch once more, as it had just now, when Ernie had mentioned the Tyne. The old guilt assailed her again when she thought of her home, and the eagerness and anticipation with which she had left it to come down here, fifty odd miles and a whole new world away.

* * *

'You what? Are you daft or what, lass?' Ruth's father, George, stared at her as if he did indeed suspect that her mental state had become impaired. His reaction was fairly typical of the rest of the household of 18,

18

Roper Terrace, when Ruth announced that she was giving up her job in the offices of the Co-op to volunteer for the Women's Land Army. 'I remember them from the last war,' George declared vehemently. 'A right lot of — '

'George!' Alice Palmer cut in, with firm warning. But her sympathies were entirely with her husband on this matter. 'You can't go giving up a good job like the one you've got now, pet!' she urged. 'After you've worked so hard to get on. This war won't last for ever. It could all be over this time next year and they'll not take you back, you know. Not if you pack it in like this!'

'Mam! They're going to be bringing in this call-up for lasses soon! Then I'll not have any choice where I go! This way, I've got some say in it. And I'll stay at home,' Ruth added craftily. She could be persuasive, too. 'I'll not be sent abroad. And I don't want to have anything to do with fighting!' she ended, with tremulous determination.

'Bloody conchie!' her sister Julia sneered, sparking off her mother's automatic protest at the use of the swear-word. Ruth bit back her retort. She had fought many long, bitter and inconclusive arguments with her sister, and with Willy and Arnold, her brothers, over her pacifist views, which were not popular in the

19

Palmer household. 'Any road,' Julia pursued vindictively, 'this conscription lark's a load of nonsense. How do you know they'll call us up? Look at Willy. He's all right, isn't he?' Conscription for twenty-and twenty-one-year-old males had been brought in almost a year ago, before the outbreak of war, but Willy, who worked with his father in one of the big Swan Hunter shipyards north across the river, had not received his papers yet. His twenty-third birthday had been celebrated just a week ago, on 17 February.

'They need men for the shipbuilding,' Ruth argued. 'It's vital, is that. You can't say working out the divvy in the Co-op is exactly essential to the war effort!'

Her mam bridled immediately. 'You've done real well to get where you are in that office, our Ruth! We're all right proud of you, we are! You cannot toss it away for to go hoiking tatties and working on a farm!' she ended explosively.

Julia sniggered. 'Imagine if she has to milk a cow! She'll run a mile! You're petrified of them!' she said accusingly.

Ruth blushed, felt the prick of tears behind her eyes. She felt very much alone, as she often did these days. 'They train you for that,' she countered defensively. 'You do a two-month training course, down near Durham somewhere. I've found out all about it.'

'She'll do just what she wants, I expect,' Julia said dismissively. 'She always does.' She tossed back the long waves of her black hair, and smiled across at Bill Jameson. 'Fancy taking me to the pictures tomorrow night? Clark Gable's on at the Majestic.'

Stung by the injustice of Julia's quip, Ruth retorted now, 'Why don't you tell her you'll see her inside?' Bill's thin, sensitive features darkened in a typical flush of shyness, and his face was transformed by that startling smile of his. He was far too nice for Julia, Ruth thought, then she blushed, too, as she realized how attractive she thought him.

'Bill's a gentleman, aren't you, love? Not like some of the roughnecks you hang about with, kiddo!' Julia smirked cockily, and Ruth experienced a powerful urge to swipe the grin from her pretty face, a sentiment not in keeping with her pacifist views, yet one with which she was far too familiar.

Her sister was right, though, Ruth conceded. Bill Jameson was a gentleman all right. His manners, the beautiful way he spoke, with scarcely a trace of an accent, in great contrast to their own sing-song Geordie gab. He was their mother's only lodger at present. Ruth could still remember vividly the night he arrived, less than a month before the fateful 3 September, last year. He had stood on the doorstep, dark and handsome in his long navy mac and the peaked cap, with its gold and silver badge. Just like a naval officer, even more so when he slipped off the outer garment and they saw the double row of gold buttons, the single stripe of gold braid around his sleeves.

'Assistant Preventive Officer,' he had explained later, in his diffident manner. 'Water Guard.' A Customs and Excise officer, he had just been appointed to the Tyne, and worked from the offices down on the quayside, practically in the shadow of the New Tyne Bridge. His home and family were thirty miles away, in a village in the south of County Durham.

The family, including Ruth, were rather in awe of him in the early days. All except Julia, of course! She flirted outrageously with him. When Ruth admonished her hotly one day — 'The poor lad doesn't know where to look, the way you come on at him!' — Julia had chuckled with insufferable knowingness.

'What's wrong? Jealous are we, little sister?' The 'little sister' always stung. After all, she was only eighteen months older than Ruth. And twice as daft as far as boys were concerned.

One thing, though. Julia was playing a

different game with Bill Jameson. She was clearly attracted to him. And who could blame her? She was comparatively ladylike in her behaviour towards him, though her flirtatiousness was still glaringly obvious, or so it seemed to Ruth. When Ruth brought this up, during one of their numerous arguments, her elder sister's accusations of 'a touch of the green eye' disturbed her more and more. It wasn't that, she hastened to assure herself. It was just that he was such a nice lad, and so different from the braggardly lot Julia and her cronies usually knocked around with. He even tried to stick up for Ruth, in his shy, quiet way, when Julia and the other family members ganged up in scornful opposition to her anti-war outlook.

That hadn't pleased Julia at all! In fact, it was just as well perhaps that at the beginning of March Ruth was accepted into the WLA and, for the first time in the twenty years of her existence, she moved out of the familial bosom, to the agricultural college on the outskirts of Durham City where the new training courses had been established. It was while she was there that the 'phoney war' finally ended with the German invasion of Norway.

Then had come the excitement of her posting. She had never heard of the village of

Skinnerdale, nestled on the edge of the North Yorkshire moors. 'They need a girl to help out at Skinnerdale Hall,' the drafting officer attached to the college told her. 'These big estates are going to have to convert to market gardens. We're going to have to grow our own food or starve to death, with all these U-boats Hitler's supposed to have.'

She was scared, but excited, too. Living in a mansion! With a real Sir and Lady! She had expected to be sent with several other girls to a farm somewhere. Now she found herself working with the elderly Ernie Long, and a couple of youngsters who came in part-time from the village. And living in solitary luxury over the stables, part of which had been converted years ago to garages for Sir George's motor cars. The upper floor consisted entirely of servants' quarters. Except that the maids had all gone, within a few months of the outbreak of hostilities. Sir George and Lady 'Cissie' had to manage with Winny May, the cook/housekeeper, who had her own sitting-room and bedroom in the main house, and a couple of local girls who came in for a few hours each day. 'We'll have to shut up most of the house,' Lady Cissie proclaimed, with her large-eyed, tragic expression.

Meanwhile, Ruth had not only her own

tiny bedroom, but a large bare sitting-room, as well as a small kitchenette, a lavatory, and a minute bathroom — all to her lonely self. Not that she was lonely. Being alone was a luxury, after the crowded living space at Roper Terrace, and the high old bed she had shared ever since she could remember with Julia. Who no doubt would be even happier with the novelty of having a room all to herself.

And now the war had moved even closer. In fact, it could scarcely get much closer, she reflected, staring down at the raw hole ploughed into the grass, the shattered windows and scarred wall of the house, and once again she prayed earnestly for her folks, suddenly so much more vulnerable in that sprawling urbanization clustered about the banks of the Tyne.

3

Holger became aware of great swathes of pain, cutting into him, all over his limbs and body, while all round him the tumbling chaos of blackness exploded with startlingly loud, cracking pistol-shots. There was a mighty jerk, straining at his armpits and crotch, as his descent halted for a split second, then he plunged down again, and the agonizing cuts to his body continued. All at once, he jerked again, swung sideways, slamming into something so solid it stunned him, and dashed what little breath he had left from his body. It was some time before his numbed senses cleared, and he found himself, amazingly, alive, swaying quite gently, in a pleasant motion, like a child in a swing.

He stared up through the dark foliage to the paling sky. Below, he could see the leaf-mould of the ground passing back and forth between his boots, and he came slowly to realize that he was hanging there, high in the branches of a splendid old beech tree. Its trunk had been the solid object against which he had slammed. The tall shapes of other trees, widely spaced as though in parkland,

26

could be made out. Over him stretched the white 'chute, caught up in the boughs which had broken his fall, maybe saved his life, but which now held him, suspended like a decoration on a Christmas tree, the white silk a marker for his pursuers. They must surely be closing in, after the thunder of the plane and the explosions of the bombs.

Frantically, he clawed at the harness, and thus precipitated the action which caused him more serious injury than any he had yet suffered, for he plummeted down, the folds of the parachute suddenly giving way and tumbling about him. He cried out sharply at the knifing pain which shot through his right knee as he buckled on hitting the sloping ground. He was sobbing as he hauled at the spreading canopy and its tangled lines. With his sheath-knife, he dug furiously at the foot of a bramble thicket, hacking out a shallow hole, which was not large enough to conceal thoroughly the bundled silk, so that he had to stuff the excess back under the tangled creepers. But he daren't spend any more time making a more proficient job of it, and he lurched away, with that same awkward, doubled gait, the stabbing pain from his knee making him whimper.

Think! he urged himself, fighting hard to control the panic. Head upward, that was it.

Away from the farms, from buildings. He could not be far from the coast. Only minutes ago they had been flying over the water; he had seen it in the approaching dawn. If he could hide up somewhere, he could perhaps make it to the shore, find a boat . . .

It was growing lighter all the time. The shapes of the trees, the clumps of bushes, the sky, were all becoming much clearer. Why were there no birds singing? The silence unnerved him. For the first time, he thought of the others, the plane, the illusory sense of comfort, of security, which had been shattered so traumatically, as he was sucked out into the howling night. He began to weep again, tears flowing down his cheeks, but he felt no shame at crying. They deserved that much.

All at once, a hysterical feeling of elation swept over him. The bomber was doomed, already on its final plunge, and, miraculously, he was here, on the earth, alive. He could scarcely believe it! They had been far too low for him to make that jump. My God! They had almost knocked the roof off that bloody factory or whatever it was. And yet here he was, limping along, very much alive! He had a wild urge to yell, fling his arms up, even though the tears were still coursing down his cheeks.

28

As though it were a gift to his crazy optimism, he saw ahead, where the ground was already flattening out a little, the dark shape of a wooden hut, standing in a little clearing. He urged himself to caution, fumbled out, with difficulty, the heavy service revolver. But somehow, already, he knew wildly that the hut was deserted. Out here, in the forest, miles from anywhere, it looked too small, too crude, for a habitation, with its rough timbers, its tar-paper roof. There was a ragged bit of curtain up at the tiny square of its single window, which was distinctly cobwebbed on the inside, opaque with dust. He could see a rough table, a chair. Shelves full of baskets, and other equipment. The door was merely on a latch. And inside — he could scarcely believe it — there was an old striped mattress.

Exhaustion, pain, relief. All these emotions overwhelmed him as he closed the door behind him, and sank with a weary groan on to its musty, welcoming thinness, abandoning himself to the luxury of letting go.

⋆   ⋆   ⋆

He stretched out on the yielding mattress, his senses filled with her fragrant presence in this exquisitely girlish domain. But now her nearness, his aching desire for her, were all one with the depression which folded its clouds about him. How many times had they lain thus, kissing, holding, touching, while he fought the thick, choking urgency of his sexual hunger, so brute-like and alien to this precious room?

Nine months he had been courting Heidi. He was aware of her parents' growing ease and confidence in him, their acceptance, even pride in his achievement. After all, an officer, a pilot in the Luftwaffe, was a worthy suitor for any girl. And now — disaster, falling out of the iron winter sky. To be flung off the course, when he had hardly been up in a plane, let alone seated behind the controls of one of the new Messerschmitts.

It was no disgrace to fail, they told them. Holger wasn't the only one. People had disappeared already, were falling by the wayside every day. In a fit of black despair, he had volunteered immediately, and been accepted, to be retrained as an air gunner. He had taken a desperate kind of comfort from the reaction of one of the older ground-staff members who maintained the training planes. 'Christ! They're a mad bunch of bastards. We'll be hosing what's left of you out of the turret one of these fine days!' He would never rise beyond the rank of sergeant air-gunner, but so what?

The bed creaked as Heidi let her hip nudge companionably against his. 'Daddy says the military still have the old Junker mentality they had in the last war. If your name isn't von Something or Other, they don't want to know you.'

'The Luftwaffe's not like that!' he muttered, not turning towards her. 'I just didn't make the grade, that's all!'

She reached out her hand, feeling even more disloyal at the secret relief she had known when he had first broken the news, for she knew how big a blow he had suffered. With a momentous and noble sense of sacrifice, as well as the tremendous racing of her heart and blood which made her shiver in anticipation, she took his hand in hers, and placed it unmistakably on the cool bareness of her thigh.

He was rough, mad and urgent with his lust, as he knelt, thrusting her over on to her back, tugging her clothing clear before he clawed at himself, unbuttoning, releasing, to fall stabbingly onto her. He hurt her, hurt himself in her tightness, but she clung to him, fingers digging into his shirt, crying out, weeping softly, but proud even as she wept; he wept, too, appalled at the brutality of his action, until, with dazed gratitude, he belatedly realized that she was not horrified, not sick with revulsion at what he had done.

He had been prepared to suffer keen pangs of jealousy and resentment when he joined the newly formed operational unit of Luftflotten 5. Helmut Armin, the pilot, and Franz Weissman, the navigator, were the only officers in the eight-man crew of the Heinkel 111 bomber. But the camaraderie, the bonding, of the air crew far outweighed any differences in rank. Though Helmut and Franz lived and ate in a more privileged mess, off duty as well as on the crew all stuck together. When Holger used the term 'Skip' to address Helmut, as did the others, he found it didn't hurt at all.

They had plenty of opportunity to practise during the first cruel winter. There were far more casualties from natural flying hazards than from the enemy. Dieter Schmidt, the nose-gunner, took particular delight in decrying Helmut's capabilities as a pilot.

'Jesus, Skip! I thought you'd decided not to bother with the undercarriage when we landed this morning! Don't forget, you lot. I'm the first poor bastard to get it when our bloody driver cocks it up.'

'It's all right for you,' Helmut retorted easily. 'Just think how terrible it's going to be for me. I'm the one who'll finish up with his head up your arse!' He glanced at the large pilot's chronometer at his wrist. 'Come on! Whose round is it? I've got a hot date at seven.' He grinned at Holger. 'Why are you still here? Time you were rushing back to the billet to write to the little woman, isn't it? God preserve us!'

★   ★   ★

In the motes of the early sunlight, Holger turned restlessly in his sleep on the old mattress, and murmured his remark about the impressive timepiece on Helmut's wrist. A few miles away, up on the moor, that wrist stuck up, a blackened stump, on which the gleaming watch-face sparkled in a sun-ray. A special constable fought his rising gorge and picked his way through the charred bits of wreckage and the smouldering heather to secure this vital piece of enemy equipment, while his companion called out to the army lieutenant in charge; 'Here's another body over here, sir!'

The lieutenant nodded thoughtfully. 'That makes seven. Search again, chaps. There should be another lying about somewhere. If there isn't, it means one of the beggars is missing!'

4

Ernie Long came out of the doorway of the potting-shed which stood at one end of the first of the three greenhouses stretching away to his left. He gazed at the length of the glass frames, sparkling in the already strong August sunlight. Each square of glass was marked with a curious, broad X, running from corner to corner, in pale, sticky tape. Ruth, and Jack Sanderson and Billy Lambert, the two fifteen-year-olds from the village who came in to help, had spent two days taping them, not long after Ruth had arrived at Skinnerdale. 'Supposed to stop 'em flying about when bombs drop, like,' Ernie told them sceptically.

Ruth nodded. Willy and Arnold, her brothers, had done the windows of Roper Terrace months ago, last summer, before the outbreak of hostilities. All the public buildings back home — and a lot of private houses, too — had been done then. Some of them had sand bags piled high around the entrances. A low, ugly-looking concrete air-raid shelter had been built in the corner of the school yard a few streets away, then, as August advanced and war came inexorably closer, dad and the boys had sweated in the tiny back yard, digging out foundations, then bolting together the strange, curved, corrugated pieces of the Anderson shelter, piling the displaced earth and rubble round the sides, standing back, grimy and proud, while mam inspected it, and sniffed audibly. 'That lot winnat stop a bomb, man!' Next morning, there were three inches of black, scummy water in it.

In the country, things were different. There were hardly any visible signs; the war had been a distant thing, for the towns and cities. Even the gunfire rumbled like distant thunder. That was why the bombs which had fallen out of the sky in the early hours had shaken everyone so much. Destruction had fallen, almost literally, on top of them.

The only casualties had been two of Mr Harlow's cattle, which had been left out in his top meadow, in the mild August night. One had been a messy lump of raw meat, killed instantly by the first of the stick of bombs which had fallen in the pasture. Mr Harlow had had to shoot the second beast himself. It would already be starting to turn into a joke among the drinkers at The Feathers tonight, but at the moment people were buzzing with excitement and alarm.

As soon as she had washed and dressed

properly, Ruth had gone down through the grounds of the Hall to the cottage where Ernie and Maggie Long lived. Already Ruth was very much at home there. She had been surprised, and deeply touched, by the warmth and swiftness of the welcome they had given the somewhat lost and diffident city girl. Colin, their son, was in the merchant navy, on the Atlantic run. It was now more than four months since he had been home, and Ruth could see how worried for him they were. Joyce, their eldest child, twenty-four, worked at a factory outside distant Leeds.

They had offered to put Ruth up at the cottage, but she had tactfully declined. She enjoyed the novelty of being on her own above the stables, in such splendid isolation, even if her 'flat' was somewhat shabby and basic, and, when the weather was really inclement, leaked in places. Besides, she went back to the cottage with Ernie for tea after work every day, and often lingered there for several hours in their easy, pleasant company. She would pop in there in the morning, too, for tea and, unless she was insistent, 'a bite to eat'.

This morning, she had joined them to listen tensely to the news at eight o'clock, but there was nothing beyond a reference to 'enemy aircraft' which had carried out 'a raid over several east-coast towns' and suffered 'several losses from coastal defences.'

'Doesn't sound too bad, does it?' Ernie offered. 'I reckon one of them Jerries crashed up on tops, all right.'

Now, he stood in the morning sunlight, unlit pipe clenched and bubbling softly between his teeth, and nodded at the three greenhouses. 'Good job that bomb fell on yon side of the house. I don't reckon that sticky paper would've stopped them, do you?' He grinned at her. 'Fancy a bit of a stroll, lass? Nice day for it, any road.' Ruth looked at him curiously and nodded. 'I'm going to get on with digging that new pit. I'll set Jack and Billy on it — if they ever show up, that is,' he grumbled. 'Probably won't see hair nor hide of them. Couple of bombs land in a field and folk go on like it's the end of the world!'

Ruth smiled. 'Well, it was a bit of a shock, wasn't it?'

'Anyways, this'll make a nice change for you, lass. You know. Take your mind off things a bit. Up Allerton Wood — top end, getting up toward Skinnerdale Rigg, over on the moor.'

Ruth nodded. She knew the wide area of woodland well, for she often walked that way, on Sundays, or, if she was still feeling energetic enough, after her day's work. It was part of Sir George's land, on the boundary of the estate, and a good three miles from the house and grounds.

'Take the path straight up, from the stile at Barker's Field. About a mile, mile and a half in, over to the right, off the path leading up towards the Rigg, there's a shed. Place they used to use when they were looking after pheasant chicks. Can you give it a good clear-out, like? There's a stack of stuff in there — old baskets for the chicks and so on. Bit of furniture, too, old mattress. Walter Kitching, the gamekeeper, used to sleep up there afore shooting season sometimes. Toss the lot out. Stack the baskets and that outside. They'll send a cart or the lorry to pick it all up later.'

He grunted, pulled a quizzical face. 'Sir George has said this new, Local Defence lot might make use of it. He's in it himself now, is Squire.' He chuckled, shook his head. 'They're on at me to join, with me being in the last lot. Don't know as how they reckon they'll stop them tanks and planes if Hitler does come over. Harry Cole were telling me they were drilling with broom-shanks down in village hall. You know what they say LDV stands for — look, duck, and vanish!'

'You don't have to volunteer if you don't want to!' Ruth said, with such force that Ernie glanced at her with some surprise.

38

'Oh, I don't mind doing me bit, lass. We all have to muck in best we can now, eh? And it looks like things are livening up a bit, and no mistake.'

Ruth was glad to be on her own, and to get away from the Hall and the unaccustomed air of excitement caused by the bomb. Ernie was probably right. There had been the attacks on the south coast and Wales last month, and on the shipping in the English Channel. And now these raids on the north east. As she moved from the rear of the Hall grounds, edging the fields of one of the tenant farms, she could see the village clustered cosily about the narrow, fast-moving river at the bottom of the dale, to her left. Ahead, the ground rose steeply. She could see the dark line of the woodland way above.

Once again, her thoughts turned towards her home and family, and her anxiety over them. How much easier life was for the people with money. The Whiteleys, living in such comfort. Skinnerdale Hall, the beautiful gardens — and all this land she could see on this side of the river, right up to the high moor itself — belonged to them. Fifty miles was not a world away to them. They could be there in a couple of hours, with their motor cars, or first-class train-carriages. Or better still, just pick up the telephone, and there you were. A voice in your ear, as though you were in the same room. She pictured the kitchen at Roper Terrace, wondering what was happening there this very minute. Shaken by the thought of how close to death she had been herself in the grey dawn light, she remembered all at once the acrimonious exchange which had taken place in the bedroom she had shared with her sister last year, just before the outbreak of war . . .

★　★　★

'What you looking like that for?' Julia glowered at her. Ruth was sitting up in the high, old-fashioned bed. She had been listening to Julia's high-pitched giggles as she chatted to the lodger, Bill Jameson, on the landing.

'You've been talking to him like that?' Ruth's voice quivered with indignation as she watched Julia carelessly toss the fawn-coloured mackintosh over the back of the chair. Underneath, she was wearing pink cami-knickers, with suspender-straps attached to her best silk stockings.

'What's wrong? I haven't got a dressing-gown, have I? And I needed to go to the netty. I was just giving Bill that book back he borrered me.'

40

'Lent!' Ruth corrected, and Julia poked out her tongue. 'Aye. And you made sure you stripped down to your underwear first!' Ruth pursued hotly. 'Honestly, our Ju! What is he going to think of you, carrying on like that?'

Julia sat on the low chair in front of the cluttered dressing-table. She stared at the three reflections of herself in the triple mirrors, and smirked complacently.

'What do you think I've been doing then? Giving him a flash or summat? I don't need to do that, little sister. He's keen enough as it is!'

'We could be at war any minute! Maybe even now!' Ruth's voice squeaked a little at the enormity of the speculation. It was late on Saturday night. The previous day Hitler had moved into Poland. If his army didn't withdraw — and there was precious little chance that it would — the British government had threatened to declare war.

'Why should we have to go to war for the Poles?' she had demanded unsteadily. 'We didn't before — with Czechoslovakia!'

'Aye. That's the trouble, lass,' George Palmer had replied bitterly. 'We should've stood up to the little bugger long afore!'

'It's ridiculous!' Ruth exclaimed. 'Who decides we should go to war? Nobody in their right mind would want to get us into this.'

But they were already moving the children out of the cities. Somebody had said that the central station had been packed with school kids, hordes of them, with their cardboard-boxed gasmasks slung over their shoulders.

She felt helpless, her insides heavy and aching, and with a cold emptiness that made her feel sick. At her impassioned words now, Julia gave a hard laugh, tugging the brush through her dark hair. 'All the more reason to make the most of things now, kiddo! We might wake up dead tomorrow!'

* * *

Walking through the sunlit beauty of Allerton Wood almost exactly a year later, Ruth shivered a little as she heard again her sister's challenging words. The anxiety nagged away at her guts. Don't be daft, she reprimanded herself. You were probably in far more danger than anyone in Roper Terrace last night. After all, a bomb had dropped only a few hundred yards away. Anyway, someone would surely have been in touch by now if anything bad had happened.

She looked about her, made a determined effort to shake off her gloomy thoughts. The tranquillity of the scene soothed her, making the events of the dawning seem even more unreal. This would have looked very much the same a hundred years ago, she surmised, and would a hundred years from now, long after these crazy, man-made disasters were over and forgotten.

She felt better with each stride. Presently, she began to search to her right, peering through the widely spaced trees, until, with relief, she spotted the distant, low shape of the hut, and moved confidently towards it.

5

Ruth was surprised at the ease with which the door swung open. Somehow, she had expected it to be stiff, resistant. Ernie had said that the place had not been used for months. Then, a startling smell assailed her, so unexpected she was bewildered, could not at first identify it, until she recalled the sharp, acrid odour of human sweat. Oh God! A tramp! Her nostrils twitched with fastidious distaste as she stepped into the little cabin, all these reflections passing through her mind in an instant, before the world exploded in numbing violence, the hut whirled crazily about her as she was flung headlong to the floor, the breath dashed from her, an agonizing weight in her back, pinning her down, and her face half smothered, pressed into the warm, pungent softness of a mattress.

Terror paralysed her thoughts, left only the vivid, fragmented physical sensations; her stifling contact with the mattress — there was that sweat smell, her nostrils were filled with it. The solid weight jammed across her back was a knee, boring crushingly down. And now the muscles in her left shoulder and arm flared in tearing pain, for her wrist was seized in a vicious grip and being bent up towards her shoulder-blade. Then something brutally hard; round, cold metal, was digging cruelly into the softness of her neck, just above her shirt collar.

'No move! No shout! I shoot!'

Her mind began to work again. The Germans! They must have landed. This was the stuff of nightmares, but she could not deny the reality of the crushing pain. She sprawled there, her head turned sideways, staring along the crumpled folds of the unsavoury mattress to its edge, the dust-covered wooden boards beyond. The rough, angular legs of a table soared up towards the limits of her vision, towering over her, to the brightness high above filtering through the ragged, incongruous flaps of flowered curtain. She found breath to cry, whimpering softly:

'Please don't hurt me!'

All at once, the pressure eased as he withdrew. Ruth was startled to hear a groan, then a sharp hiss of pain, and she turned her head involuntarily, to see a pale, blond man, his face streaked with dirt, and twisting in agony. He shuffled back awkwardly, and her attention was caught, her eyes widening and heart thumping in renewed terror, at the sight of the heavy, sinister barrel lifting and pointing at her.

'You're hurt!' she said. She was still lying there, flat on her stomach, legs spread, left arm still folded up behind her.

Holger blinked in astonishment at the realization that the sprawled figure was a girl. He had thought it was a youth, some young farm-hand. His first reaction, after his amazement, was of great relief. A girl would not prove so fearsome an opponent as a man — or even a boy. He saw her eyes, wide, dark — helpless with her fear. They were awash with her tears. He could see the glistening runnels on her cheeks. She was pretty — her face was brown, tanned with the sun. All at once, a vivid picture of Heidi emerged, at the summer camp at Alsfeld, two years ago. It jarred him.

He lifted the revolver, waved it menacingly, saw her wide-eyed reaction. He stared at her clothing. No wonder he had taken her for a boy. The clumping heaviness of her boots served to emphasize the slenderness of her ankles and calves, encased in thick stockings, whose tops were turned down, folded over the stiff, corded breeches. Was she a horse-rider? She was wearing a green jersey, out of the top of which he could see the turned-down collar of a khaki shirt, very masculine-looking. Was it some kind of uniform? Perhaps she was part of this new Defence Volunteers force the desperate Britishers were trying to form. A sudden, renewed burst of fear came to him. There might be others.

'By your own?' he barked, waving the gun.

Most astonishing of all, then, in the midst of the fear gripping both of them, she smiled. A little, fleeting, totally involuntary grin, but it transformed her, subtly changed the atmosphere. To his own surprise, he felt himself smiling sheepishly in return.

'English no good, *ja?*'

He had been quite good at school. When he had joined the Luftwaffe, his interest had been revived by the language classes they were made to attend. 'You may all be in London very soon,' the elderly teacher had told them. Most of the others had laughed, treating it all as a joke. What's English for 'How much for short time?' and that sort of thing. But Holger had really tried, reading through his phrase-book at night in his bunk. The trouble was, there had been so many new, exciting things to learn. Matters of life and death.

His eyes met her scared gaze. He could see the dying remnants of that suddenly flashed smile there. Something passed between them. He felt a strange, almost-shiver.

'You're hurt,' she said again and slowly lifted her dark head, raised her body from the mattress.

'No move! Take off the boots! Lie!' He waved the gun.

Slowly, she bent and unlaced her boots, slipped them off. Though she was shaking, she was surprised at her degree of control, the manageability of her fear now.

'It's all right. I'm on my own. By myself,' she murmured, and wondered immediately, Why on earth did I tell him that? He could shoot me now, knowing there's no one else about. Or worse. She dismissed her shameful conjecture as swiftly as it had come. Of course he wouldn't do anything like that to her. And then she was startled yet again by the strength of her conviction.

'I am Luftwaffe. Air Force. My plane — it damage. I jump.'

'Oh yes! Last night! The bombs — that was you!'

'The bombs we must lose,' he answered quickly. 'We come down. Crash, I think.' He stared intently, his head came forward a little. 'You know?'

She gave a little shake of her head. 'No.' She remembered Ernie's words, the way the sky had lit up over to the west, up on the moors, and was suddenly reluctant to tell him about it. 'Only the bombs. They just missed the Hall. The house. Where I live.' She saw the instinctive flicker of relief as he concentrated on her words. It registered powerfully with her. He was glad. Glad that their bombs had missed. Had failed to do any serious damage.

'Ah! Miss. Goot!' His strained face relaxed a little. He was handsome, she thought, in spite of the dirt, and the lines of care and pain and shock stamped on his young features. There were several seconds of silence, then he said abruptly, 'I am Holger Fichtmüller. Your name?'

'Ruth. Ruth Palmer.'

'Are you married?'

She gave a shy laugh, shook her head. 'No, no.'

He smiled in return. 'I also. Not married. I have — er — friend. Girlfriend. We will marry.'

She nodded. 'That's good.' The significance of what he had just said, in the dramatic abnormality of the present circumstances, struck them both at the same time, hovered painfully about them. She could think of nothing to say, was touched by the desperately vulnerable look which came over him.

After a while, he said, 'I not hurt you. We stay. At night I go. For coast. Find boat.'

'But — you're hurt. Why don't you let me go? Get help? You'll be looked after.'

'Nein!'

She flinched at the vehemence of the German word, and again he looked oddly apologetic. 'It is my — er — how you say?' He pointed, and she told him. '*Ja*. Knee. I land in a tree.' His smile came again, boyish, lighting his face. 'I fall down from tree. Hurt my knee.'

'Can I look at it? Perhaps I can help. Strap it up, or something.' He stared at her, startled by her offer. 'I promise I won't run away or anything. I give you my word on that!'

He understood the solemnity of her pledge, nodded. Then he looked embarrassed. 'My — er — clothing.'

'I've got two brothers. One as old as you.' All at once she appeared unafraid as she knelt briskly in front of him. 'Come on. I'll give you a hand. Let's get these great boots off.' He groaned as she managed to draw off the lined flying-boots. He unzipped the front of his grey overalls, and, with her help, struggled out of them. He groaned again as, gently as she could, she fought the right leg down over the swollen knee joint. Underneath, he wore a collarless uniform shirt, and the grey serge trousers, held up with thick, white canvas braces. 'Come on. Pants and all.' She turned away, kneeling there, and heard him grunting and gasping, the rustle of clothing.

'Ja. Is good.'

She turned back to him, started to smile at the incongruity of his sitting there, primly clasping his shirt flap between his legs, the pistol still in his grasp. Then she saw the hugely swollen, badly discoloured kneecap, and she let out a soft exclamation of dismay. 'It looks bad. Like — it's twisted or something. You need a doctor.'

'No! You find — how you say? Tie — with cloth.'

She noticed the other bruises, the deep lines across his thighs, which looked as though they had been whipped.

'My God! What's that?'

'I come down in tree. I think is like that all over body. The — branch. Yes?'

'Yes. You need them seeing to. You need them cleaned up.' He gazed at her, his blue eyes holding her so intently she felt herself blushing deeply. The silence was charged. 'What is it?' she whispered at last.

'There is barrel with rain outside. You bring water. I wash. You make tie the knee.' As she made to rise, he put out his left hand, grabbed her wrist. 'You give word, *ja*?'

51

She looked back at him, equally solemn. Her eyes carried just a hint of gentle reproach. 'Yes,' she whispered. He simply nodded, let go of her wrist. She saw him settle back.

There was a chipped enamel bowl in the sink and she took it with her. The rain barrel, with its folding wooden top still in place, stood against the side of the hut. She blinked, as though startled at the perfect ordinariness of the bright scene around her. She was taken aback at how weak she felt, the trembling, jelly-like quality of her limbs. Run! a voice screamed in her head. Run! By the time he gets to the door you'll already be too far away for him to hit you. She didn't know if that were true. Then a quieter, insidious, voice told her, He won't shoot you anyway. You know he couldn't. With a kind of anger, she swiftly dipped the old dish into the scum-covered surface, and hurried back inside.

She found some old bits of cloth, pulled down and shook the dusty curtains to add to them. She turned her back, listened to his wincing gasps as he awkwardly tried to clean himself, until she could stand it no longer, and turned round with an exclamation of impatience.

'Let me do it!'

She had time to register the slim beauty of his frame before her compassion at the sight of the raw weals. Then farce took over as he cried out in shock, grabbed for the gun on the shelf near the sink, then grabbed to shield himself from her.

'Don't be daft!'

He kept still, even when she bent, and dealt with the wounds on the lower back, and thighs.

'Right!' she said briskly. 'Put your shirt back on and let's get that knee seen to. Though I still think I shouldn't touch it. It needs a doctor. It's been put out, I think.'

He tried to straighten it himself. She could see he was racked with the pain. She felt sick with sympathy, her hand shook as she obeyed him and bound the swollen joint tightly with the wet cloths. His face was paper-white by the time she finished, but he nodded, and said, '*Ja*. That is good now. It keep it strong.' He strove with touching modesty to hide his body as he scrabbled back into the clothes. He even wrestled his feet into the thick socks and heavy flying-boots before he leaned back against the wooden wall of the hut, with a sigh of weariness.

She gazed at him, her face stamped with her concern. 'You can't walk on that knee.

53

We're miles from the coast here. You can't go anywhere.'

'I must try. It is — how you say? Duty.'

Her dark head shook. 'You're mad! How can you? You're crippled. By yourself. You've done your duty. You're lucky to be alive. You got out of that plane. That's enough, isn't it? You've got to stay alive now. Your girlfriend. What's her name?' He told her. 'Heidi wouldn't want you to go on risking yourself!'

'Your people. They say they shoot us. When they catch.'

'Rubbish!' Her face was alive with her indignation, and her urgency to make him agree. 'You'll be put in a camp. A prison camp. They won't hurt you. You'll be able to write — let Heidi know you're all right. I'll make sure.'

'No!' His mouth was thin, the outline of his jaw tight. 'I tell you. Give you *my* word also. I will not you harm. But you must stay with me. Until the dark.'

'They'll be out looking for you. And for me, if I don't turn up soon.'

'Where is your home? Is it near? Your father and mother . . . '

She told him about herself, and he listened with eager interest.

'They call us land-girls.' She shrugged, pulled a self-deprecating face. 'They make all kinds of jokes about us. Say bad things.' She gestured at the light brown breeches. 'I think it's the uniform and everything. The menfolk don't like to see the women in trousers. They think we're — shameless.'

'But you — er — you join. They not make you?'

She nodded shyly. She didn't look at him any more, could feel herself reddening, but she felt compelled to go on. 'They say that girls will be made to join up soon. The forces. I don't want to. To be part of the fighting. I don't believe in it. It's senseless! Killing each other — like animals!'

She stared at him helplessly, all at once the enormity of what he was, what he did, lying obscenely between them. A dealer of death. A bringer of destruction to thousands of homes, of families. It appalled her.

'We bomb only the military targets,' he said, as though he read clearly her thoughts. 'The factories for the war, the shipping. We do not want war. You force us!'

'Nobody wants the war!' she cried passionately, waving her hand in frustration. 'But here you are! Trying to blow us to bits and — and we're trying to shoot you down, and . . . '

The shocks and tensions of the eventful day, begun so long ago with that fearful blast

55

which had jerked her from sleep, and which had led to her tenderly bathing the wounds of a naked and beautiful enemy, caught up with and overwhelmed her. To her own horror, she felt her throat close, a huge sob shake, then erupt from her, and she dissolved into a cascade of weeping.

'*Nein! Nein!*' He was struggling, moving, and Ruth felt herself plucked by the shoulders, lifted, and she was clinging, her head on his chest, his arms about her, drawing her into him, a hand securely cradling the back of her head. She could hear the rumble of strange foreign words, like soft caresses, and shook with weak relief in the warmth and comfort of his encircling embrace.

6

'You took your time, lass. I thought you'd got lost or summat.' Ernie pulled off his cap and wiped at the sweat shining on his brow. His iron-grey hair was flattened to the shape of his skull, the little silvery wings sprouting to mark the lower edges of the cap's cover. The mid-afternoon sun was strong. 'We shall have to give them a good watering tonight,' he said, nodding at the long rows of green vegetables.

'Eh, Ruth! You've missed all the fun!' Jack Sanderson, the more extravert of the two lads, called out excitedly. 'That plane! Jerry bomber! It crashed up beyond Riggs, over towards Ledham. We've had old Reece and his men here! And some army toff and all! They wanted to question us.'

'*Captain* Reece to you, son!' Ernie cut in, with mock severity. Mr Reece, a retired army officer and small time 'gentleman farmer', had a comfortable eighteenth-century house, and a spread, across the river from the Hall, on the eastern slope of the dale. With his military background, and active interest in local affairs, even though he was an 'in-comer' of a mere ten years' standing, he was a natural choice to take command of the new LDV force. There were many privately enjoyed jokes in the village, muttered behind hands of course, at the prospect of Sir George, 't'squire', having to take orders from such a Johnny-come-lately.

But Ruth was staring intently, oblivious to the grins. 'Why? What's the matter?'

'They reckon there might be a Jerry missing. From that plane!' Jack told her, wide eyed with self-importance. 'There's only seven bodies in the wreck. They reckon one might've got out, like. Parachute. They were asking us all if we'd seen owt. This officer bloke is warning everyone to keep a look-out. They're doing a search of the village now. Outhouses and that! They looked all round this place.'

'I told them none of us has seen owt.' Ernie peered at her. 'What's up, lass? You look right mithered. Don't fret yourself. No Jerries round here!'

'They've got all the other bodies!' Jack insisted, revelling in the goriness of his speculations. 'I bet they were a right mess, eh?'

'Bloody good job, too!' Billy asserted patriotically. The boys laughed. Jack punched his companion, then lifted his hand, stiffening the palm to imitate a plane, and mimicked the increasing whine of the bomber's final plunge, his hand diving downward, to the final cacophony of the explosion which blew out his red cheeks.

'For God's sake!' Ruth's voice startled them all with its shrill intensity. 'They're dead, aren't they? It's not a bloody joke, you know!'

Her depth of feeling, as well as the use of the swear-word, shocked them. The two lads gawped at her. There was an awkward little silence. 'Look,' Ernie said, with rough gallantry. 'You'll be a bit tired after that walk down from woods. Why don't you go back to the stables? Have a bit of a wash and that. Make yourself a cuppa. Come down to the cottage later on, then we'll come up and do watering, when the sun's gone. All right?'

Ruth's mind was whirling with disjointed images and emotions as she made her way quickly up through the grounds, skirting the wing of the Hall which still bore evidence of the bomb-blast, and the lawn scarred by the raw new crater. She hurried through the courtyard, where a line of washing was stirring gently, into the cobbles of the stable yard, and her own front door.

Upstairs, in her little bedroom, she quickly

stripped off to her underwear, intending to have a cold-water wash at the sink in the tiny recess across the way. All at once, she recalled Holger's nakedness, the smooth, warm feel of his skin, the smell of him, as she had bathed those dark weals. She sank down weakly on the edge of the creaking iron bed, the tears starting, her hands twisting together in her lap.

She must be mad! What on earth was she doing? She heard again her own shocking tones, hushed, aware of the enormity of her words. 'Listen. You stay here. Stay inside. I'll come back later. This evening. I'll bring some food. A bandage.'

'Some clothing, please!' Holger urged, gesturing at his uniform.

'All right. But you stay here. Promise?'

He nodded. They stared at each other solemnly, both startled by their commitment. She was still dazed from the feel of his arms around her, the comfort she had found from letting go, leaning on his strength. She was frightened, but determined now.

'I don't understand — about the war and everything. Why you're fighting. But I know how I feel! I know how wrong it is! All this killing! I'm just — ordinary. I just want to get on with my life. All of us . . . '

She stopped hopelessly, and he came

forward again, very slowly reached for her once more.

'You are good girl, Ruth. Beautiful girl.' She saw his mouth, watched it come close, fascinated, and quite helpless. Then suddenly her own was lifting, eager, open, she felt the pressure of his lips, hard on hers, demanding, and she didn't mind, her body trembled with the urgency of her feeling. She was breathless, gulping hugely when the kiss ended, and they clung, shaking, together. She had never kissed like that, with anyone . . .

★   ★   ★

'Happy New Year, Ruth. Seems a heck of a lot to ask for suddenly, doesn't it?'

She could just make out the thin, serious face, as Bill Jameson bent slowly, hesitantly, his mouth coming close. It was meant to be a friendly, brotherly peck on the cheek, but she knew, in spite of his diffident manner, he wanted more. And so did she. As the first seconds of 1940 ticked by, she thrust her mouth, lips closed, tightly and inexpertly against his, felt his start of surprise, then his arms came up around her, their pressure increased, and their bodies strained together briefly through the thick layers of clothing. His mouth softened on hers, seemed to come alive, wonderfully, and she shivered while they clung together, oblivious to the cries of 'Happy New Year' all around them, the spilling of light, strictly against blackout regulations, as the doors of Roper Terrace opened then swiftly closed to admit the muffled figures of those who had spent the last shivering minutes of the old year on the front steps.

Number eighteen's door opened, and Julia's perfume wafted out. Ruth and Bill sprang guiltily apart.

'Howay! You're supposed to knock you know! Not stand canoodling with our Ruth on the doorstep! You get back, our Ruth, and let him get in. *He's* the first foot! Happy New Year!'

Julia flung herself into his arms, her lipsticked mouth open, searching. Ruth, blushing in the dark, heard the passionate grunt from deep within Julia's throat, and turned away, hot with embarrassment, still giddy from the kiss she and Bill had exchanged. The passage was full of figures, all wishing one another happy new year, hugging, pumping hands.

'Got your coal? Your bread and salt? Let the lad get in, Julia, for God's sake!'

Mam ushered them all in from the cold night, to the front room, where the fire glowed and the ceiling light shone through a thicket of hanging paper-chains and sprigs of holly.

Ruth caught Julia's eye, saw the bright, hard challenge in her stare, the aggressive tilt of her sharp face.

'Well, little sister — Happy New Year, eh? You did a grand job of keeping Bill warm outside. No wonder he forgot to knock to be let in!'

Ruth moved in close. 'Happy New Year, Ju!' She bent, felt Julia's slim frame remain absolutely rigid. There was not even a token move to return the kiss which Ruth gave her on the cheek.

'I think they gave you the wrong Bible name,' Julia murmured. 'If you were a feller, I'd call you Judas!'

Inevitably, any talk of the future centred around the progress of the war, or, rather, the lack of it over on the western front. Julia wasted no time in moving on to the attack.

'Our Ruth doesn't think they should be there at all, do you, little sister?' she sneered, referring to the BEF in France. 'She'd rather they all just refused to fight and went to gaol as conchies! If she had *her* way, Hitler would be marching through the streets of London now and we'd all be out waving our little swastikas!'

'That's not true!' Ruth felt her face glowing, felt a constriction in her chest, a thickness that made it hard for her to express her emotion. 'That's not fair! I don't think anything of the kind! I hate what Germany's done. What they're doing! It's just that I don't think — '

'You don't think anyone should stand up to them!' Julia pursued with relentless contempt. 'And what do you think would happen if we don't? Eh? Look at Poland. He's not going to stop for nothing! Least of all for a bunch of namby-pambies saying, 'Come on now! Don't be such a naughty boy. Get off home with you!' You silly bitch!'

'Language!' Alice cut in automatically, while her husband threw up his hands in disgust.

'Will you two lasses shut up? You were bad enough when you were bairns! Like a couple of alleycats, the pair of you!'

It was after two before Ruth got to bed. In spite of her winceyette nightie, a pair of thick socks, and the old ginger-beer bottle filled with hot water, she felt the freezing cold of the bed. Even though she was seething with anger at her sister, she wished she would get herself up to bed. But no! She'd be taking full advantage and lingering in front of the fire with Bill, who seemed lamentably short of his usual common sense where Julia was concerned. And mam and dad were hardly any better, letting the couple sit up till all hours, on their own. She tried to stop her vividly disturbing imagination from dwelling on what might be happening in the fireglow.

She was jerked awake by a wicked little punch to the region of her kidneys before Julia fitted her icy form with supreme selfishness into the curve of Ruth's back.

'What do you think you're playing at?' Even as she squeezed her, Julia's voice continued vindictively. 'Just keep out of the way as far as Bill and me are concerned, all right? I don't know what you're up to, acting like butter wouldn't melt. Well, it won't work, kidder! I'm warning you!'

'Is that right?' Goaded into renewed rage, Ruth jabbed her elbow back, and was meanly pleased by her sister's soft gasp of pain. 'You two engaged or summat, are you? I've heard nothing about it. Not from him, any road!'

'Not yet!' Julia replied with grim determination. 'I'm just telling you, that's all!' She flounced dismissively round, dragging most of the warm bedclothes with her.

Ruth lay there, choked with rage. Her eyes stung with tears whose wetness seeped onto her eyelids. She smarted once more with injustice at her sister's scathing attack in front of Bill. Making out that just because Ruth was against the senseless violence of war, she was some kind of traitor. But she was sure Bill understood, and even sympathized to some degree, even if he didn't entirely go along with it. She thought again of that kiss, the uncertain, hidden suggestion of it, the hint of powerful emotions . . .

★　★　★

Now, eight months later, she thought of it again, and was appalled when she compared it with the embrace she had shared with the German. There had been nothing uncertain, nothing hidden, about the blaze of passion that had flared. Raw, naked — naked as his bruised, beautiful body, which she had viewed with such breath-catching wonder. She was a traitor now all right. No mistake about that, either. She was about to set out again, in secret — to meet with the enemy, to take him food, clothing — she was even planning details of how she would take him one of her uniform shirts — they hung loosely enough on her, he should be able to get into them — and a pair of Ernie's overalls which were hanging in the potting-shed. Maybe a pair of Wellington boots, too, if she could get away unseen with them.

An act of outright treason. Except that to her he was no longer the enemy. Never had been, from the moment he had released her, and she had seen him, his face haggard with pain and with fear. So young — just like her brothers, or Bill. And contrite, concerned for her own fear, in spite of the dangers surrounding him. Twenty minutes later, she was on her way, terrified that she would meet someone in the mellow evening before she could get safely into the wood beyond Barker's Field. They would be curious in the extreme about the large sack slung over her shoulder, which took two hands to support, and which banged about uncomfortably at the backs of her thighs. She made it over the stile, and into the beginnings of Allerton Wood. She moved cautiously, very aware of the boys' excited talk of the LDV's search of the village and its environs.

She was so confused. It wouldn't be so bad if she could be absolutely certain that what she was doing was right for her conscience. But she was far from that. Holger had been flying over to inflict death, perhaps on hundreds. In fact, but for a matter of yards, and seconds, she herself might have been a fatality. And, apart from that, what she was abetting him in was probably the worst thing possible for him. He needed medical attention. She was convinced he would not get far without it. Also, the longer he remained at liberty, the greater the danger when he was finally apprehended. There was far more risk of injury, or death.

She was in a turmoil of indecision all the while, as she strode panting through the lengthening shadows of the wood. Somehow, she must try again, urge on him the necessity of giving himself up. She would guarantee his safety, speak to the forces of law and order herself. But even those forces carried weapons, could deal out summary, violent death, were rightfully empowered to do so.

She was vastly relieved to see the hut silent and undisturbed. With a frightened glance behind, she hurried forward, pushed at the door. 'Holger!' she whispered, stopped on the threshold, sickened. It was empty. Then she gave a smothered scream as he appeared right behind her. She dropped the sack, sobbed out his name. 'God! I thought you'd gone!'

'Ruth! You come back! *Liebchen!*'

7

She watched his fair head dip, the wolfish movements as he crammed in the food she had brought him, and ached with compassion for the ugly, desperate need she saw there. He glanced up quickly, his cheeks pouched, his jaws noisily chewing, and gave an embarrassed little smile. His shoulders shrugged in a tiny gesture of apology.

'No! It's all right. You must be starving,' she said quickly, as though he had spoken, and he nodded gratefully. 'I'm sorry it isn't more. You need something hot.'

'No, no! Is good. Very good.' He pushed the last piece of the brown crust into his mouth, which bulged again. He grinned and pointed, his head nodding comically as he chewed, then he swallowed, exaggeratedly, and sighed to indicate his pleasure. 'You make?'

She shook her head. 'No! My friend.' She pictured the tins, laid out in Maggie Long's hearth, the wonderful smell filling the cottage as the new loaves swelled and cooled. What would Maggie think of her now?

'Listen,' she said urgently. 'That knee's

69

worse.' It was true, although he denied it. He couldn't move it now from the angle at which it was set, couldn't flex it at all. He wouldn't let her remove or retie the cloths she had bound around it earlier in the day. 'You can't move. If you won't let me get help, at least stay here for tonight. And tomorrow. Maybe it will be easier . . . ' Her voice faded away uncertainly. She felt herself blushing, her eyes dropped from his.

There was a pause, a hesitancy which was charged with significance, and she knew he was struggling with his own conflicting thoughts. 'I make trouble for you. Is better for me to go. In dark. Perhaps with — er — how you say? Stick? I can go.'

But she could hear the doubt in his tones. And all at once, her desire for him to remain was urgent and overwhelming. She knew that deep down she could not believe in the possibility of his successful escape. There were people out there looking for him, aware of him. They would surely find out that she had tried to help him. She didn't care — perhaps tomorrow she would tell them herself, bring them to him before any more danger befell him. She could hardly understand her own motives, why it should matter so much. But she knew it was desperately important to her.

'They'll have patrols out,' she said urgently. 'In the dark — it could be dangerous. At least you're safe here. For the moment.'

He gave a weary sigh, leaned back on his elbows on the mattress, nodded in grateful surrender. He patted the rumpled space beside him. 'Come.' He put out his arm, and though she blushed again, fiercely, she moved at once, stretched out beside him. Startlingly, his next words echoed the confusion of her thoughts. 'Why you do this for me?'

'I told you!' The hint of conflict was in her voice. 'I don't like - I don't believe the war . . . ' She moved, her whole body stirred with a depth of feeling she could not express, and with the complexity of the storm of emotion she could not properly understand. 'You're hurt — and alone, and . . . ' She had been going to add the word 'frightened', but stopped herself just in time. He was a warrior. A young male. It didn't matter what his beliefs or nationality. No young man would like such an unpalatable truth.

She felt his arm about her shoulder, and he drew her in to him. 'It is like — how you say? I cannot believe! You are so good girl, Ruth, so beautiful. It is — ach!' Her head bounced violently as he shrugged in his frustration with his inadequate English. 'You know! Like plan! Like *Gott* God . . . '

She knew what he was striving to say. Fate. Divine providence. The words flew through her mind. 'Maybe it's God's way of saying — of showing us how senseless, how stupid, this war is. How daft we all are — to be fighting like this.'

The passion of her words held them both, he felt the muscles in his throat move to utter his agreement, grunted as he choked them off. He was deeply moved, and shaken, by his sudden confusion. He was in the land of his enemies, the land he had wanted to conquer. This girl was his enemy. An Englisher. He might have killed dozens of her compatriots. Had come close to killing her last night! The very thought terrified him, made him clasp her to him fiercely, his mind racing in even greater conflict. Why did he feel so close to her, why did he wish to echo her heartfelt condemnation of the war between them?

For a split second, he had terrible difficulty in relocating a sense of time, his mind a frightening blank. August! Of course! August 15. No, no. That was yesterday. The day of the raid. This time yesterday evening, they had been clambering out of the truck, the bomber waiting there, dark, but comfortingly massive, on the grass. They were chattering wildly, laughing hysterically at everything, to cover their fear, that tight, sick feeling in the guts. They shivered, too, but were glad to blame that on the chill of the Norwegian night.

His mind shied away from the terrible memory of his last fear-crazed minutes in the plane, but he was unable to stop himself from blurting out, 'The plane. The bomber. You hear?'

He knew at once, from the way she was tensed beside him, that she had. Her voice was hushed, unsteady. 'Yes. It crashed up on the moor. You were so lucky, Holger! No one else got out.'

'They know? For sure?'

'They found seven — bodies. In the wreck.'

He nodded, swallowed hard. The faces of Helmut, Franz, Dieter, the others, paraded before his mental vision. He tried to take in the numbing reality of their violent deaths, vividly imagined the smashed, charred remains. They would know them only from the identity discs, maybe not even from them. 'That's why I don't want anything else to happen to you!' Ruth declared passionately. 'You see — you were the only one to escape. It's important — '

'*Ja.*' He nodded again, savagely, reliving his panic, his plunge from the doomed bomber. He should have stayed. Helmut was still there, flying the crippled plane. The others

— Holger began to shake. Appalled, he felt his throat seize, a huge spasm shake his lungs, and the sobs burst from him. God, oh God! The tears were wet on his cheeks, his shoulders heaved, but he couldn't stop himself, he wept like a child, desolately.

Ruth wept, suffering his pain with him. She turned, gathered him in her arms, and he turned, too, lost, needing her, and she was full of love, and hurt, mothering him to her. Somewhere, at the back of her mind, with a shameful defiance, was a sensation of physical pleasure, too, at the feel of his face pressing into the softness of her breast, his hair beneath her cupped palm.

They lay together for a long, long time, holding each other, until the spasms of his weeping died, and the hut was in the deep gloom of the last of the daylight. He moved, at last, gently disengaging, sitting up and groping about him, in his clothing, for a handkerchief, blowing his nose noisily, not looking at her.

'Pardon me, yes? Not good — '

'Yes, good!' she cried, startling him, reaching out to put her arm around his neck, pulling him down to her briefly again, in a friendly hug. 'It's good. You needed that. So many things have happened to you. For me, too. There's never been anything like this before.' They both understood, knew how uniquely close this strange meeting had brought them. 'You're exhausted. You must sleep. It's all right. I'll keep watch.'

They lay together, arms about one another, in that strange cocoon of innocent intimacy. He did not sleep much. Instead, heads touching in the dark, they talked. About each other, about their homes. Holger talked of Heidi's coming birthday celebrations, of how he had hoped to be able to go on leave, to get married. He stopped abruptly. His plans had been delayed because of this newly active phase of the war — Operation Sealion, the invasion of Britain. And because, much to Luftflotten 5's surprise, the stubborn British had actually attacked the airfield at Stavanger, with a force of twelve Blenheims. True, all of them had been destroyed or damaged, but the raid was a salutary reminder to them that this war would not be a one-sided affair, as the German propaganda machine had proclaimed.

He did not think it wise to mention any of this to the girl who was lying beside him. The war had nothing to do with them. It was outside the strange, capsuled intimacy of their world inside this hut. 'For you,' he asked, 'there is someone? Boy friend? I cannot believe — you tell me no.'

She gave a little laugh. 'It's true, though. No one fancies me — likes me. Not *that* much, anyway!'

'Never?' His voice rose, to mark his disbelief. 'How old you are?'

She laughed again, even more embarrassed. 'I'm just a couple of months younger than your Heidi. I'll be twenty-one in October — the 26th. And never been loved! Shame, isn't it?'

'*Nein!*' She felt him shake his head vigorously, his arm tightening companionably about her. 'I not believe. Is not possible! Girl like you — so beautiful!'

She giggled. 'I know. It *is* hard to believe, isn't it? Mind you, there was one lad. But that was when I was twelve! He used to walk me to school. But since then, nobody!' She gave a theatrical sigh, and his arm tightened yet again, his cheek came to nuzzle against hers.

'Then it is I. I love you, yes?'

She gave another laugh, shoved him playfully, her hand on his chest, for all the world as though they were any lad and lass sparking about, then suddenly the underlying meaning of his words seized them, catching them unawares, and it was no longer a joke, no longer absurd. 'I think is true,' he continued starkly. 'I know you — close, I think. *Ja?* Is like — for long time . . . '

He was right. This was not, could not be, any normal relationship. This feeling of intimacy which bound them, this isolation, was so far from the norm, it felt as though a lifetime had been crammed into the raw intensity of the few hours they had shared. They were lying together, in each other's arms. On a mattress. Sharing the night. She had never done such a thing, had blushed even to imagine it. And suddenly she was afraid, truly afraid, of the powerful wave of emotion she could feel, the strength of the sensation which made her turn her body towards him, answering his questing embrace even as she gasped out her startled, 'No!' before his mouth cut off her protest, and she was straining to return the passion of the kiss, thrusting against the body and limbs pressing against hers.

'Excuse! Pardon me! Forgive!' He remembered the word he was seeking. 'Sorry! I very sorry. Forgive me.'

She was still trembling, sniffled softly. She quickly smothered her weeping, dabbing at her cheeks with the back of a hand.

'Yes, yes,' she answered quickly. 'It's just — I was frightened. It's not your fault. It was me, as well as you.'

She stopped wretchedly, wondering if he would understand, scarcely understanding herself. She reached for his hand in the gloom, found it, clasped it tightly, and held on. He returned the firmness of her grip. She felt safe once more, the strange bond once more uniting them, and she was not sure whether she was glad or sorry.

★   ★   ★

'I'm pregnant, Ruth! I'm going to have a baby! I haven't told anybody. Just you.'

Ruth, bewildered by the disclosure, privately wondered why Julia had chosen to confide in her. Unthinkingly, she said, 'Oh, Ju! How could you?' Julia's neat, dark head went down again, and Ruth stared at the delicate shoulders, the slim waist, quivering with the storm of abandoned weeping. In spite of the many, many times she had been infuriated by her sister's supreme selfishness, Ruth was deeply stirred with compassion. She sat on the edge of the bed and tentatively put her hand on the heaving shoulder. 'You say you haven't told anybody? When's it due? Who's the father?'

The head came up again, wildly, the glittering eyes staring at her with wounded contempt. 'Bloody hell! What do you take me for? Bill, of course!'

'What? Yes — I just thought . . . ' Ruth

nodded inadequately, fought to keep the shock from her features, wondered why the name should have thudded into her like an unexpected blow, leaving her numbed, sick with dismay.

Julia was still gazing at her with that expression of bitter incredulity. 'You know, you can be a right nasty little bitch! You think I'm some kind of tart or summat? I've never looked at anyone else since — for ages!' She gave a choked snort of disgust, went back to her sobbing once more, her head buried in her arms, while Ruth sat there, in dumb misery. She continued to pat awkwardly at the quivering shoulders. She wished vehemently that she hadn't come home. And to think she'd been so eager, agog with excitement at the completion of her training, dying to tell them about her posting to Skinnerdale Hall, to show off her new uniform. She might have known Julia would find some way of stealing her thunder.

But not this. Ruth felt a rush of guilt. The poor girl was clearly almost out of her mind with worry. And no wonder. Tentatively, Ruth explored her own secret hurt, surprised herself at the extent of her pain on learning who the father was. Why should she be so disappointed, why did she feel so let down, betrayed, by the fact that it was Bill who had got Julia pregnant? Her sister had set her cap at him almost from the moment he had appeared in Roper Terrace. By the time Ruth had left to start her WLA training, back in February, Julia and Bill had been 'going together'. So why should she feel so shocked?

Her conscience stabbed her, as she remembered the New Year's Eve kiss, the look she had intercepted at times, the warmth of his gentle smile. You were keen on him yourself — hoped he might be keen on *you!* she attacked herself. If only Julia, with her ruthless determination, would give him half a chance. Well, Ruth thought, helpless at the resurgent bitterness, you've obviously had your wicked way with him now, big sister! Somehow, she couldn't think of Bill as anything other than the manipulated innocent in this relationship.

But then the raw ugliness of Julia's grief smote on her conscience again, and she was deeply ashamed of her uncharitableness. There was nothing assumed or melodramatic about her sister's anguish now. She must be feeling very lonely, and very frightened, to confide in Ruth like this. And who could blame her? Ruth herself quavered at the thought of her parents' reaction to the catastrophe. A sudden doubt struck her.

'Does he know? Bill? Have you told him?'

'No! How can I, man?' Julia swung round, glared at her tragically. 'He'll think — I mean . . . ' She hesitated, threw a tortured look at Ruth, and rushed on. 'It was my fault, really. More than him. I wanted — I told him it'd be all right. I didn't know — I wanted him that much!'

Ruth flinched at the abandoned quality of Julia's sorrow, the tormented sobs which shook her again. The passionate nakedness of that last sentence hung frighteningly between them, making Ruth's face burn with shaming acknowledgement. Then compassion took over once more. 'Come on, love.' She took hold of the thin arms, moved to tears herself. 'It'll be all right. He's a good chap. The best. You love him, don't you?'

'Oh, I do, Ruth! I really do!' They were hugging each other, Julia buried her wet face in Ruth's breast. 'He's wonderful! Listen!' Her fingers dug into Ruth's shoulders, her dark eyes, eloquent with both pain and hope, held Ruth's imploringly. 'I can't tell him! Can't bring myself — he'll think I've done it all on purpose! Just to make him — you'll tell him for me, won't you, Ruth? Please! He thinks a lot of you. Tell him how I feel about him. How much I love him! Won't you?'

★ ★ ★

'No, no! I can't!' Ruth whimpered. She started awake, heart racing.

'Ssh! Is good. No fright.' Holger was clutching her tightly, she was returning his grip with equal force, burrowed into him, beatingly aware of his body pressing on hers, his hold of her.

'Oh, I'm sorry! I was dreaming. Must've dropped off.' She felt his face pressing into her hair, his lips nuzzling kisses on to her brow, and she blushed, not wanting to end their warm embrace, and feeling that she must. As gently as she could, she disengaged herself, moving her hip slightly so that she broke the contact, rolled on to her back. 'What time?' She looked at the curtainless square of the window, saw the grey of dawn seeping its dim light through. 'I'll have to go,' she whispered apologetically. Her stomach felt sick and empty, appalled at the new day and its problems.

She sensed his own similar feeling as she stirred again, sat up stiffly, her muscles aching. Her skin felt stretched and taut, her body under her clothing prickly and moist. She thought with longing of the sink back at home, the all-over wash she would treat herself to. She massaged her toes inside the thick stockings. They felt cold and cramped, too, even though she had taken off her heavy boots soon after she had lain down. She pulled the boots towards her, slipped her feet in, and tied the laces. 'How's the leg?'

She could see how difficult it was for him to move at all, despite his brave smile. 'Is good, I think. Better, you say. *Ja*?'

She nodded, gazed solemnly at him, her face, creased and tired as it was, looking extremely young. 'You can't go anywhere on that. You know you can't. What are we going to do?' She had a powerful urge to be in his arms again, folded down once more.

'I stay here again. Tonight I go.'

Despair closed her throat; she hugged him tightly, feeling the tears fill her eyes, trickle down her face. 'I don't want you to go.'

His hand came up, to stroke her wild hair, his lips pressed a kiss upon her temple. 'You so good girl,' he whispered. 'I forget never. Never!'

All at once, her mind was clear. 'We have to find somewhere — somewhere safe!' she murmured urgently. 'You stay here! Keep very quiet. I'll come back soon. I'll bring food. Promise me you'll stay?' He nodded, grabbed her to him and once again they clung together. She gazed at him intently, then forced herself to move quickly away, through the door.

She made her way along the edge of

Barker's Field, and into the grounds of the estate. As she approached the wide gate which led into the stable yard, she saw a clustered group of men there, recognized the dark arm-bands of the LDV, which was all the uniform they had, except for their leader, Mr Reece, who still had his military uniform from his days as a captain in the regular army. He was wearing it now, complete with Sam Browne and swagger-stick. There were two lighter patches on his lapels where he had removed the insignia of his former regiment, but the three cloth pips at the shoulders were still very much in evidence, though his captaincy was Acting Only at the moment.

She did not need to ask what was afoot, for Harry Cole, who had one of the estate smallholdings and was a particular chum of Ernie's, caught her eye, and was clearly bursting to impart his news.

'They've found a parachute up in Allerton Wood! Buried like! We're off up there now to search for him!' To her horror, he brandished a long scythe menacingly.

'Right! Fall in, men, and pay attention!' Captain Reece reddened a little underneath his officer's cap. 'We're just waiting for Sir George, then we'll be off, so listen carefully.'

Heart thudding, Ruth immediately turned about and went out through the gate again.

She had to warn him. She thought of the comfortable, unmartial Harry Cole, and his murderous gestures with the scythe. She broke into a run, back down the path leading through into Barker's farm. Oh God! she thought in panic as she ran, toiling along the narrow, overgrown path at the edge of the lower field, which was ready for harvesting. Where could she hide him? What could they do?

Her breath wheezed noisily, her body was soaked with perspiration as she forced herself up through the gentling slope to the hut. She saw the group of figures stood about the door, and though she was exhausted, she spurted ahead, her heart wild with her panic. Holger was stretched out on the ground in their midst. She could see two or three khaki figures, and the dark blue of police uniforms, but she took no heed, her eyes on the outstretched form dressed in Ernie's overalls.

'Holger!' Weeping, she bent down, flung herself at him, clung desperately to him.

An outraged voice snarled something, and she was torn away from him. She caught a swift glimpse of Holger's eyes, pleading, tossing her a silent message as he spewed a string of curses at her in his own language, then spat in her direction.

'Crazy woman!' he yelled, and someone hit

him hard across the side of his head.

She screamed, flung herself forward again, half over him. 'Leave him alone! He's injured. Can't you see? Leave him!' She wept desolately, and the group stood in shocked silence, slowly taking in the scene, before someone, more gently this time, lifted her by the shoulders, pulled her away a little.

'There there, lass. He's all right. Don't take on.'

There was a grinding, intrusive noise, as a grey military truck made its careful way down through the spaced trees from the upper, moor side. A young lieutenant seemed to be in charge.

'Let's get him in the truck. Easy now.'

Ruth recognized PC Lawrence from the village. He and another policeman bent, helped Holger to his feet, then made a seat of their linked hands as he slipped his arms about their shoulders for support.

'Don't hurt him!' Ruth said again, trying to get near. The soldier who was holding her gripped her more tightly by the upper arms, and she twisted, trying to break from him, so that he was forced to tighten his grip even further.

'Come on, miss. Don't be daft!' the man muttered, kindly enough. Holger's face looked all the paler for the streaks of dirt which covered it. The blond head turned, gave a very slight shake, and, again, he tried to flash a silent message to her, then he was being taken away, she saw him diminishing, saw him being lifted carefully over the back of the canvas-covered truck.

The soldier, who was with some difficulty holding her, gratefully surrendered his charge to one of the policemen. 'Behave yourself!' this constable ordered, more sternly. Ruth's teeth rattled from the strength with which he shook her. 'You're in enough bother!' His ominous words, and the vigour with which he delivered them, had their desired effect, and Ruth subsided, weeping in anguish as the lorry ground slowly away again. She couldn't see anything of Holger, only the two khaki figures sitting at the tailboard of the labouring vehicle, which slowly weaved its way back up the slope.

★　★　★

'I think you'd better tell us exactly what's been going on, young lady!' Sir George said, with heavy emphasis. Ruth sat there, on the edge of the upholstered chair, with its uncomfortably high, round wooden arms encircling her like some medieval torture instrument. They were of highly polished, richly dark material, with a delicate, pale yellow pattern painted on them. They looked thin and fragile, as though they were too elegant for everyday, robust sitting on. She hunched uncomfortably, her arms resting on her knees. Her head was throbbing, she felt weary, all cried out. She guessed the truth couldn't harm Holger now, so she told it, haltingly, aware of the growing atmosphere of cold hostility.

'You stupid girl! Giving aid and comfort to the enemy! You know that's treason in time of war?' Captain Reece's voice beat into her.

She nodded, without looking up. 'It didn't seem — he was just a boy, who was hurt. Frightened. I wanted to help him.'

'You spent the night up there alone with him?' Sir George's tone was eloquent in its condemnation, and all at once, deeply shocked, Ruth realized what his words implied. Her face stamped with her outrage, she didn't answer. 'He might have killed you!'

'He wouldn't! Didn't!' she cried passionately. 'He's not like that.'

'Only because you were protecting him! And those clothes he was wearing — Mr Long's overalls. You stole them for him. Took him food. You should have handed him over to the authorities!' Sir George glowered righteously. 'You realize you could go to prison for this? For a very long time, my girl!' His curving belly, more pronounced in the tight-buttoned, thick tweed waistcoat, quivered with indignation. He glanced across at a tall, bald-headed individual in a dark suit. 'What do you think, Inspector? What's going to happen to her?'

'Is there somewhere where she can be kept, for the moment. Here, sir? We need to pursue a few more enquiries.'

Sir George came and stood right over her. She found herself staring at his heavy brogue shoes, the thick green stockings leading up to the hanging bags of his plus-fours.

'Stand up, girl.'

She gazed dully into his ruddy features, still glowing with his outrage. His grey eyes pierced her.

'Do we need to waste manpower placing a guard over you? Or can I trust you to give me your word you'll remain in your quarters? You won't do anything else stupid?'

She murmured her assent, feeling like a guilty schoolgirl, conscious more of the ridiculousness of the situation than any sense of shame. 'What about work?' she asked humbly, and Sir George grunted derisively.

'I'll tell Mr Long what's happened. If he hasn't heard already! I don't suppose he'll be very keen to have you around, in view of what you've done.'

His words got through to her, and she felt the tears well up, so that she was glad to escape, trooping out head down, with PC Lawrence following embarrassed in her wake, back across the bright morning hallway, and out past the kitchen and the butler's pantry, to the scullery and the back door leading out to the yard.

She paused at her front door. 'Don't do anything daft, lass, will you?' She shook her head, shut the door quietly at his nod, then fled, breaking down in a fresh outpouring of grief, up the stairs to the lonely solace of her room.

8

'Eh, lass! What have you been up to?'

She had been convinced that she could not cry any more, that her tear-ducts had been squeezed dry by the volumes she had shed since the events of the morning, but at the sight of Ernie's grizzled face, and the concerned gentleness of its woeful expression, Ruth flung herself forward to the comfort of his arms and his overalled chest. Awkwardly, he patted at the heaving shoulders, his nostrils tickled by the unruly brown hair clouded about his face.

'I didn't mean — he was hurt. All alone. Just a lad. Like — like . . . ' Like any of ours, she had been going to say, but didn't. Who would accept that at these momentous times? Even Ernie's silence on her behaviour seemed like a condemnation.

The gardener had been the first person she had seen since her internment in the flat, and she was touched by his visit, which was entirely of his volition. He quickly made it clear that, although he thought her action had been supremely foolish, he did not consider it at all criminal. Soon, though, there was equally clear evidence that others disagreed.

Not long after Ernie had left, and she had forced herself to eat a thick tomato sandwich, washed down with recklessly sweet tea in her favourite, inelegant enamel mug, she heard the sound of a vehicle's engine and its abrupt cut-off. She glanced down through the small, white-framed squares of her living-room window, into the cobbled yard. Her heart leapt as she saw the dark green of an official car. She recognized the bald head of the inspector who had questioned her earlier. There was a younger man, in army officer's uniform. She raced down the dark narrowness of the stairs, opening at their first knock.

They did not greet her, and she flinched at the coldness of the policeman's steady gaze.

'This is Lieutenant Newman,' Inspector Norman said. 'We've some more questions. We thought you'd prefer it here than at the police station at Whitby.' She knew he was trying to frighten her. And succeeding, too, she acknowledged as she padded back upstairs ahead of them, in her stockinged feet. She had dressed in her uniform once more after her wash earlier in the day. She didn't know why, really, except that it gave her some measure of comfort.

'Where's Holger — the prisoner?' Ruth asked, as soon as they were back in her room.

'That's no concern of yours,' Inspector Norman told her, with blunt hostility. He took the sole armchair, waving the lieutenant to the battered, two-seater sofa. Ruth turned the hard wooden dining-chair from the cloth-covered table to face them. She thought suddenly of the print in the hall of her school back in Gateshead. The richly dressed, silken children facing the line of darkly sombre, seated men. *'When did you last see your father?'* Miss Andrews had said it was called. Ruth felt like a guilty child. She stared at her toes in the thick woollen stockings, curling on the worn pattern of the carpet.

'Now then. Tell Lieutenant Newman everything. From the beginning.'

Ruth stumbled through her tale, aware that she had already related every detail to the inspector. The lieutenant kept interrupting, with questions she could not answer, about Holger's military duties, his unit, the plane he flew. 'I don't know anything about that!' Ruth cried emotionally. 'I just wanted to help him!'

'You're very free and easy about confessing!' Inspector Norman cut in. 'I told you! Aiding and abetting the enemy in time of war is a very serious offence. Very serious! You could be locked up for the duration, girl! You realize that?'

'He wasn't — isn't the enemy. Not to me.

He's just a boy — injured . . . '

'Why did you steal the clothing? Bring food for him?' the inspector pursued. 'You were helping him to escape, weren't you?'

Ruth shook her head hopelessly, the tears starting to fall yet again. 'It wasn't like that! I just thought — in his uniform — somebody might shoot him — on sight. I wanted him to give himself up. He was scared — scared they would — harm him.'

'You a Nazi, Miss Palmer? Ever been a party member?'

Ruth gaped in horror at the inspector. 'No! Of course not! I wouldn't give — '

'Just wondered,' Inspector Norman went on calmly. 'We can easily check, of course.'

She blushed, looked through her tear-blurred vision at her fingers, twisting in her lap. 'I was thinking,' she murmured reluctantly, 'last night — while I was up there with him — that I would get help this morning — make them promise not to hurt him. Bring someone to the hut.' She felt guilty and disloyal to Holger, and her feeling was made worse by the inspector's sneering tone.

'Oh yes! Looked like you were hotfooting it back to warn him when you arrived at the hut this morning!'

'I've told you! I didn't want him hurt! I . . . ' She shook her head again, lapsed into silence. The only sound for a while was of her muffled weeping.

Lieutenant Newman's voice was tinged with embarrassed sympathy. 'Well, not a lot of harm done, as far as I can see. Perhaps it turned out for the best, Miss Palmer keeping him holed up like that for a while. As it was, he didn't put up a fight, did he?

'Could've gone off half-cocked, running about with that ruddy great gun of his. Of course,' he went on hastily, 'it was a darned silly thing you did, miss, not letting us know right away. But — well, a case of misplaced sympathy, I think, eh, Inspector? Officially, we wouldn't want to take it any further. Least said soonest mended. Not good for morale if a big thing was made of it.'

'Not up to me as far as the civil authorities go,' Inspector Norman announced severely. 'Have to see what HQ have to say.'

They stood, and Ruth rose, too, digging in the pocket of her britches for a handkerchief and blowing at her reddened nose.

'Can't you tell me where he is?' she asked softly, humbly, and the lieutenant spoke swiftly over the inspector's glowering frown.

'They took him over to Northallerton, to the police cells. They were going to get a doc to look at his leg. He'll be shipped off to a military gaol somewhere after that.' He shrugged, added, with a hint of reproach, 'He'll be looked after. By the book.'

She nodded gratefully, followed them to the head of the stairs. The inspector turned.

'You just stay up here, in your room, understand? You should still be locked up, really. It's not over yet, by any means.'

Ruth lay unmoving while the daylight faded, and darkness seeped in to fill the little bedroom. The sounds from across the yard faded too, eventually, and still she stayed there, hunched, facing the wall, aware of her body's growing chilliness under the thin sheet.

★ ★ ★

Ruth felt her cheeks grow warm. 'Get dressed and go down!' she said tersely. 'He's waiting. In the front room. Mam's still out.'

'You're a grand lass, our Ruth!' Julia turned, let the nightgown fall down over her slim frame, and planted a boisterous kiss on Ruth's lips. 'I'll never forget this!'

She grabbed the blue quilted housecoat from the back of the door, pulled it round her as she moved out to the landing.

'Aren't you . . . ?' But she was gone, racing down the stairs, and Ruth sat down on the bed, expelling her breath in a gusty sigh. Why did she suddenly feel like weeping? Surely she should be flooded with relief, the way that her sister obviously was? And who could blame her? Not that Ruth had been in any real doubt from the very beginning that Bill would do the right thing. Of course not. So why did Ruth feel that she had just performed one of the most painfully embarrassing and shameful acts of her young life?

The worry and concern in his eyes had stabbed cruelly home when she saw how selfless and warm that concern was for her. 'I've got to talk to you, Bill!' she'd said, and everything had shown so eloquently in that look he had given her, the way he had come straight to her, his hands automatically reaching out towards her. It hurt so much to realize that he had absolutely no idea what she was about to tell him, that he thought the trouble he saw reflected in her face was for herself only.

'What is it, Ruth, love? Tell me.'

'No, no!' She blushed fiercely. 'It's not — it's our Julia. She's going to have a baby!'

He was stunned, she could tell at once. And for one split second — the only time she ever saw it — in the naked look that passed between them, she saw the dismay, and it hurt her more than anything else that happened in the days that followed.

'Oh God! Why didn't she tell me? It's my fault. I mean — I'm the father. Where is she? Why couldn't she tell me? The poor girl!'

'She was scared. She didn't — she thought you might think she'd done it on purpose. She told me all about it. She said it was as much her fault. She doesn't want you to feel that you're being forced into anything. She really means it, Bill! She — thinks a lot about you.' Why can't you say it? Ruth lashed at herself. Somehow she forced herself to go on. 'She really loves you.'

'Oh God! The poor kid! Where *is* she?'

Ruth caught at his wrist as he made an involuntary movement towards the door. 'Listen, Bill! Are you sure? Are you absolutely sure? She means it. She doesn't want you to feel you have to do anything just for her sake. There are ways round it.'

Her own eyes misted as she saw the depth of pain, the wounded reproach in his gaze. 'You surely don't think I'd let her down?'

She knew he was waiting, how important her answer was to him. She shook her head. 'I know you won't.' Her fingers were still on his wrist. 'Do you really love her, Bill?' He nodded. She saw, and felt, his eyes tear away so painfully from hers. 'Wait here,' she muttered faintly. 'She's upstairs. I'll tell her to come down.'

Later that night, Bill and Julia faced her parents together. George was working overtime as usual. It was after ten when he got in, his face stained and grey with dirt and weariness. His reaction was every bit as violent as Ruth and her sister had feared.

'You filthy little bastard. Worming your way in here with your posh voice and your gannins on. Taking advantage!' He rounded on the chalk-faced Julia. 'And you! You stupid little bitch! Could you not see what he was after, eh? Have you no sense?'

Ruth waited a few moments, then, tying her dressing-gown firmly about her, came down to enter the fray in the kitchen.

'For goodness' sake, dad! What's the good of yelling? That's not going to do any good, is it?'

'Oh, aye? We've not done enough yelling by the look of things! And what about you? Put you up the spout and all, has he? Nothing'd surprise me in this house, I tell you!'

His ugly words fell like a lash across Ruth, and for seconds they were all shouting, leaning forward, stiff with hate, until the quiet firmness of Bill's voice pulled them up short.

'I want to marry Julia as soon as possible, Mr Palmer.' He turned to include Alice in this address. 'We love each other very much. I'll be proud to have her for my wife. I'm sorry — deeply sorry — for what we've done. I'll take good care of her. And I'd like your blessing. But whatever happens, we're going to get married.'

'Come here, lad!' Alice burst out, throwing her arms wide and crushing him to her before she burst into fresh, noisy tears. 'You shut your gob!' she said to her husband. 'And get that whisky out! We've got summat to celebrate!'

Much later, Ruth woke to feel her sister's body fitting into hers, her hands coming round to hug her tightly to her. Ruth felt her face burning fiercely in the dark at the contact of Julia's near naked frame, and the visions that spun tormentedly through Ruth's helplessly vivid imagination.

'God! I just can't believe it!' Julia's breath stirred the hair on Ruth's neck, her lips tickled the sensitive skin. 'I'm the luckiest lass alive, I reckon! And isn't he just about the most gorgeous bloke in the world, eh?'

★ ★ ★

Ruth sighed, turned, kicking her leg free of the clinging sheet. She sat up, blinking at the strong daylight streaming in through the window, instead of the customary thick gloom edging past the drawn blackout curtains. After she had washed and break-fasted on toast and tea, she dressed carefully in her uniform. She was determined that she would not remain meekly imprisoned in her quarters for another interminable day, but she did not have long to wait before there was a tap at her door. One of the young village girls who came in to help with the cleaning of the Hall was standing there.

Normally very friendly, the youngster did not look at Ruth as she delivered her brief, rude message. 'Sir George wants to see you right away. In his study.'

In spite of her efforts to calm herself, Ruth's legs quavered, and her stomach heaved when she knocked on the heavy oak door, and entered at the gruff summons from within. Sir George was sitting, tweed suited, at his desk. 'You're a very lucky girl!' he declared, without preamble. 'Both the police and the military authorities have decided not to prosecute you for your disgraceful conduct, though, as a member of the bench, I've been asked to inform you that your actions have been both foolish and disloyal. They could have had the gravest conse-quences. You could have been facing a sentence of lengthy imprisonment. I don't need to tell you how deeply disappointed I am personally that you should have let us down so badly. I only hope you've learnt your lesson.

'I've been in touch with your superiors. You're suspended from duty pending their investigation. It's best that you return home for the moment.' He held out three pound notes towards her. 'This can be deducted from any future settlements. It'll help to get you home and so on. I'd like you off the place today. Mrs May will come and have a look at the flat before you leave. You can leave the key with her. If necessary, we can forward anything you can't take with you today. That's all.'

He turned away with cruel emphasis. Ruth found her way to the door. Her boots clomped on the polished wooden floor of the hall as she made for the door leading back through the kitchen. She saw the bright flash of a dress, caught a shimmering glimpse of Felicity Whiteley's slimly pretty form coming down the wide staircase.

'Filthy little traitor!' The words were like a cut across her shoulders as she made her escape.

9

'Ruth! What the hell are you doing here?' Julia was standing in the hallway, wearing a cardigan over her flowered pinafore, whose gay front bulged in a pleasing little pot to indicate her fifth month of pregnancy. 'I wondered who on earth it could be coming in the front door like that.'

Thankfully, Ruth dropped the kitbag she had been balancing precariously on her aching shoulder, and lowered her suitcase. She swallowed hard. 'Where is everybody?'

'Mam's round at Aunt Ginny's. Dad and Willy are still at work. Bill's on two till ten — or till he gets in, whenever that is!' She scowled fiercely. 'I've hardly seen him since the wedding!' She stared suspiciously at Ruth. 'So what's brought you back all of a sudden? Seeing as how you couldn't even get time off for your own sister's wedding!'

'It's a long story.' Ruth's voice shook with emotion, in spite of her best effort. 'I'll just make a pot of tea.' She was glad to delay her explanation even for a few minutes as she made her way along to the kitchen.

By the time her mother, then the rest of the

family, had returned, Ruth had got the worst of her weeping fit over. Their disbelief, then dawning consternation, mirrored that of her sister, to whom she first broke the news of her disgrace. George Palmer summed up the general feeling in his roundly delivered pronouncement:

'You daft beggar! You could be put in gaol, lass.' He stared bitterly round at all of them. 'Just make sure nobody round here gets to know what's happened, otherwise we'll be getting our windows put in, or worse.' He glared at Ruth. 'And you'd better pray your secret never gets out, lass, or they'll have you tarred and feathered on your own doorstep!'

'I did nothing wrong, I know that!' Ruth muttered defiantly.

'Aye? You should've been here two nights ago when we were all crouched in the shelters and the bombs were falling!'

Ruth had already heard how unsuccessful the raid had been from the Germans' point of view, and how little damage had been inflicted, but she made no answer to her father's angry words. She was so weary and unsure of herself. She had never felt so lonely and alone. Even her own family were against her. Arnold, just two weeks past his seventeenth birthday and already taller than his older brother, Willy, grumbled bitterly when his mother announced, 'You'll have to go in with our Willy.' He had been delighted at Julia and Bill's wedding at the end of May, for it meant he could move into the small bedroom at the front of the house, which had been Bill's former room. With all the overtime at the yard, and with Bill's continued contribution to the household budget, it had been decided that the need for another lodger to take his place was not pressing. Now Ruth's unexpected return to the nest had shattered Arnold's newly won independence.

'Why, you can hardly expect our Ruth to climb in between Julia and Bill, can you?' Alice Palmer told him irritably.

'Pity she didn't do that a few months back!' Arnold muttered rebelliously, earning an even sharper response from his mother.

'Watch your mucky mouth, you! You're not too big for a clout, mind!'

Ruth made do with a quick wash out in the scullery before heading upstairs to make up the bed in the little room. The last time she had been home, Bill had been sleeping here. She blushed at the thought as she folded away her uniform and slipped her cotton nightie over her head. He had not yet come in from work, though it was after eleven. She thought of the more familiar room across the landing, which she had always shared with Julia, and the wide double bed which the married couple now occupied.

When she switched out the light and groped in the blackness for the narrow single bed, she suddenly recalled the musty old mattress in the hut, the feel of Holger's arms about her, and the warmth of his body pressing close to hers. She was dismayed at her awareness that she had not thought of the young German for hours. What right had she to feel so sorry for herself, when he was so friendless and alone, perhaps in fear of his very life, locked up in some miserable prison cell right now? Desperately, full of guilt and tender remorse, she began to pray for him.

* * *

'You can give us the names of your crew members,' Lieutenant Newman said, striving to keep the irritation out of his voice. 'If only so that their families can be informed. You know they were all killed, don't you? Surely you want their families to know? Yours will be told that you're a prisoner of war.'

Holger stared back at the officer. His knee was throbbing painfully again, but he knew the doctor had taken good care of him, and the nurse had bound it carefully.

'Torn ligaments,' the doctor had said, prodding knowledgeably at the swollen, discoloured joint. 'He'd better rest up for a few days before you move him.' They had put him in a high-ceilinged, bleak room, in this civilian hospital, with a soldier, complete with 303 service rifle, to guard him. At least it meant taking up some military time and duty, he consoled himself, when they could ill afford it. And more so in the days to come, when the operation against Britain really got under way. He told himself again that he must be ready to seize any opportunity to escape, as soon as his knee eased up a bit. Before they shut him up in a proper prison.

He had been steadfast in refusing to answer any questions which might be of help to the British authorities. Though he had to admit that this young lieutenant was far from belligerent in his attitude. After a suspicious pause, Holger decided that he could with honour give the names of the rest of the crew, and did so, while the lieutenant painstakingly wrote them down. 'They'll be given a decent burial, you have my word,' Lieutenant Newman said. 'A military funeral, I expect.'

'Can I attend?' Holger asked at once, and the lieutenant frowned.

'I shouldn't think so,' he said honestly. 'In any case, it'll probably be better if you keep a low profile. Now that these air raids have started, I don't suppose you chaps will be too popular in these parts.'

Holger was surprised, and considerably relieved, when the officer stood to indicate that the questioning was over. He had expected a much harsher interrogation. Perhaps that would come later. Maybe they were just softening him up. He must remain on his guard at all times. He remembered Ruth. Her face appeared vividly in his memory, and he felt ashamed, then confused. They were not like her. She was unique. These people were his enemies. He was surrounded by them.

A tall girl, heavy-hipped and plain, in an ugly uniform, brought him his food. It was lukewarm, and bland, but he ate it all. He had to keep his strength up. It was his duty. Then the guard, in his ill-fitting khaki battledress, came and sat in the hard chair against the far wall, and gazed at him with unhostile curiosity.

Despite his discomfort, Holger's thoughts kept returning to Ruth. He had been very worried about her, wondering if she would get into trouble. He had done his best to make them think that he had somehow coerced her into helping him, but he doubted if it had worked. He had even spat and sworn at her outside the hut, but it had not done much good. He recalled how she had flung her arms around him, her tears. He could feel in his tunic pocket the photograph of Heidi, which the lieutenant had allowed him to keep, along with her letter, though doubtless it had been carefully translated first. He was startled at the depth of guilt he felt when he thought of Heidi, and of his family. It was foolish, he argued with himself, to feel so guilty. But it was not only because of Ruth. He was haunted still by those final moments in the plane, the secret but agonizing charge of cowardice he brought against himself, despite all the arguments he could present to deny it. You should have been there, on the list of the dead, with the others, the accusatory voice ran on in his head.

★   ★   ★

Herr Krempel's respectably middle-class status as a professional meant that the comfortably modest house in Remscheid had a telephone, so that Holger's mother was able to call them directly. Heidi knew as soon as she was called by her father to the front hall. She felt her stomach lurch hollowly at the solemn expression on his thin face. Then she heard the trembling voice in her ear, the clipped effort made by Frau Fichtmüller to hold back the tears as she gave her the news. Heidi was not so restrained, or so brave.

'Nein!' She began to sob harshly, tearing, ugly sounds, as the words drove into her.

'We've received notification from his squadron. The plane's missing. It was reported hit, over the enemy coast. They've heard nothing more.' There was a painful pause, and Heidi heard the smothered sigh. 'We can only wait for more news. And pray.'

'What'll I do?' she asked her parents bewilderedly. It was her twenty-first birthday in a week's time. She was still hoping that Holger would surprise her by managing to get leave for the great event, that he would tell her when he could get leave for their wedding, under special licence. Somewhere at the back of her mind, she kept telling herself she should be braver, should be able to feel the nobility of grief, the dignity and pride of his sacrifice, but she was helpless against the overwhelming despair. She sobbed wildly, hysterically, lost like a child, until exhaustion took its toll and she actually fell into a dream-haunted, whimpering sleep, there on the sofa, in the comfortable room, where the sunlight filtered strongly through the curtains she insisted should be drawn.

'He may be all right, alive,' her mother

said, when Heidi woke, her face puffed and ravaged with sorrow, but the fair head shook with weary certainty.

'He's gone, mummy. I've lost him.' Frau Fichtmüller's words came back to her, and she nearly screamed aloud in her elemental rage. 'We must pray.' Pray? Curse you, God! she cried inside herself. And curse this whole bloody war, and curse the Führer who had led them into this madness! I hope we lose! I hope all the young men die! She was shocked deeply by the extent of her blasphemy, her anger, but, again, she could not help herself. She lay back, and the tears began again, falling silently this time, unheeded.

Her mother brought some medicine, a mixture of laudanum, which sent her into a drugged sleep for most of the following day, from which she woke periodically with a feeling of unreality, aware in the first moments of consciousness of a leaden despair without understanding why, until memory flowed dully back. So the sense of unreality, of being cut off, continued when, late the following night, she heard her mother's shrill cry, then her weeping as she came racing upstairs and into her room.

She flung herself across the bed, tears pouring down her cheeks, and clutched at Heidi. 'He's all right, darling! He's alive! He's

111

a prisoner of the British!' Then Heidi *did* pray, fiercely, that this was not part of her dreams that had plagued her.

It took a long while for the truth to sink in. When it finally did, guilt and penitence engulfed her, along with her gratitude, and as soon as she was alone, she got down on her knees by the side of her bed, her body torn with convulsive sobs, her head pressed against her folded hands on the coverlet. I'm sorry, God! she wept. Thank you, oh thank you, for giving us this second chance. For keeping him safe for me! I'll never doubt you again. Nor the cause for which they were fighting, she vowed.

The next morning, she woke very early, and went to take out her Young Girls' League uniform, which had hung untouched in her wardrobe for months now. She was ashamed as she remembered her doubts, her private discomfort at the notices she had seen down by the park — *Jews are not wanted here.* She had even expressed those doubts to Holger, but he had laughingly distracted her, changing the subject to talk of their own personal future.

Well, she would prove worthy of his sacrifice now! She would make him proud of her. She had seen the posters encouraging young people like herself to support the war effort by working on the land. *Faith and Beauty Scheme for Girls*. She would go into town this morning and volunteer. Holger was safe! Though of course, he was enduring terrible hardships as a prisoner, she reminded herself guiltily. But at least he was alive. And in a matter of months, England would capitulate. Perhaps even sooner, for everyone was waiting for the announcement of the invasion. Even that stubborn fool Churchill would see how impossible it was to resist German might. Then Holger would be home again, a hero, feted and handsome in his flier's uniform!

They could have a proper wedding. Not a hurried affair at the registry office, but at a church, with bridesmaids and bouquets. And a white wedding-dress. White for purity. She smirked with childish defiance at her reflection in the clouded mirror as she ran her bath, and quivered with sharply disturbing desire as she lowered herself into the warm, scented water.

10

They heard the faint wail of the siren a minute before the slide came up trembling on the screen. *An air raid warning has been sounded. If you wish to leave the cinema please do so as quietly as possible.* There were a few ironic cheers. Hardly anyone moved, as the beam from the projection box shone palely through the darkness, picking up the swirling wreaths of smoke, and the Hollywood escapism took over once more.

Ruth felt movement beside her. Julia's knees banged against her as she grappled with her coat.

'Come on. I'm off. There's not just me to think about now, you know. There's the bairn.' Ruth heard Bill's whispered words of apology from the seat beyond as Julia stood.

'Why, it's all right, man!' a protesting voice called out from behind.

'Sit still!' someone else hissed, and there were several shushes.

'Excuse me!' Julia replied loudly, and trod on Ruth's toes. For a second, Ruth considered stubbornly remaining seated, but reluctantly she surrendered, and got to her feet, muttering her own apologies as she edged along the crowded row to the aisle. 'You stop if you want to!' Julia snapped, now that it was too late. She clutched tightly at Ruth's arm as they groped slowly up the wide, shallow steps, whose edges were picked out in white canvas piping. The door at the back of the hall opened, the heavy curtain swung aside, and they made for the rectangle of light gratefully. A few more shadowy figures joined them, and Ruth blushed anew at the muttered comments from the rest of the audience, who were staying put.

'Bloody mad lot!' Julia said witheringly, when they were out into the dimly lit foyer. 'They'd rather get blown to bits than waste their shillings. It was a right load of tripe anyway!'

The night sky along the river and over towards the coast was lit by the sweeping fingers of searchlights, then the thunderous flashes of the ack-ack batteries opening up. Julia whimpered with fear

'Let's get into a shelter! There's one in Duke Street.' She grabbed at Bill's hand and tugged him along, breaking into an awkward run.

'Hey! Take it easy, Ju. Slow down. We'll be all right.'

'I think we should get back home,' Ruth

advised quietly. 'Dad's out with this fire-watching. There'll only be Mam and our Arnold in.'

'They'll be all right. They'll be in the shelter by now.' Julia rounded on her angrily. 'You can do what you like! Bill and me are going to the shelter!'

Ruth felt the anger flowing through her, not so much at her sister's selfishness, which was no more than she expected, but at Bill's indecision. Why didn't he tell her not to be so soft? And why did it upset her so much? she asked herself miserably, as she trudged in their wake. What had it got to do with her how he behaved towards his wife? But, she had to admit, she hated to see the way he kowtowed to Julia, the way her sister was so ruthlessly dominant in their relationship. It was embarrassing, horribly so, eating away at his manhood, his self-respect. She didn't deserve him, Ruth thought, and was immediately pricked with guilt.

But Bill *was* so different. He was the only one who had not condemned her outright for her action in helping the German, and he showed real concern for her. 'What will happen now?' he had asked her, and she warmed to his caring.

She shrugged. 'I expect they'll sling me out. There's nothing I can say, is there?

Nothing that any of *them* would understand, any road!'

'Don't let them get you down,' Bill answered. He reached out and put his hand on her arm, just above her elbow. She felt the strong grip of his fingers pressing her flesh, and she flushed with pleasure at his touch. 'You didn't do anything wrong. You don't have to feel guilty.'

His words meant so much to her. 'I don't. He was just a lad — you know?' He nodded, and all at once she wanted to fling herself into his arms, the warmth of his tenderness filling her. Her throat tightened, the tears stung at the back of her eyes, and for a long while she could not trust herself to speak. Increasingly, over the days that followed, that warmth of feeling, and the sense of unexpressed intimacy between them, disturbed Ruth more and more. She had no right to feel like that. Not about her brother-in-law.

She resolved that she must do something to get away, and she took a tramcar over the high-level bridge to Newcastle, and to the regional office of the WLA. After waiting for more than two hours, she was eventually shown in to stand before a motherly figure behind an impressive desk, who belied her appearance by coldly and clinically expressing her disgust at Ruth's action. 'I really cannot

117

see that you have any future in our organization,' she concluded. 'You're not the sort of gel we want at all. I'm recommending immediate dismissal. You'll hear in a few days.'

To her horror, Ruth could make no answer. Instead, she dissolved in tears, and was led weeping away from this formidable presence, where a harassed-looking, bespectacled woman, also in uniform, comforted her, sat her down and gave her a cup of tea, before coming up with a solution for which Ruth could only gaze at her with tearful gratitude.

'Look, I'm afraid I can't do anything about the decision. That's HQ's business.' She sniffed eloquently. 'But what I can do is get you transferred. You can start right away, if you want to. Ever heard of the Timber Corps? No, I thought not. It's a new set-up, all female. Forestry work. It's vital. I don't know if you're aware of it, but Britain is just about the world's largest timber importer. Ninety per cent of what we need comes from abroad, or rather, used to. We need timber for all kinds of things — railways. And for the mines. Pit props. If we can't find enough to keep us going we'll go under. It's as simple as that.'

The woman took off her glasses, peered

through narrowed eyes at Ruth while she cleaned her spectacles on the hem of her green jersey. 'We've got to make use of all the woodland we can lay hands on. And there's plenty of it scattered around the country, most of it on big private estates. That's where the Timber Corps comes in. We're desperate for recruits. How about it? You can stay up north if you wish. Loads of work. There's a group starting training now. Are you in?'

Ruth nodded. 'Thank you, ma'am.'

★   ★   ★

'Eeh, our Ruth!' her mother fussed. 'What with all these raids starting and everything! Will you be all right?'

'She's not daft!' Julia sneered. 'She's off back to the country, isn't she? She'll be well out of it, living the life of Riley again! Don't go making friends with any more Nazi airmen though, will you? You might not be so lucky next time!'

Lucky? Her thoughts had often dwelt upon the German, despite her own predicament. She didn't even know where he was. And she didn't know who she could ask to find out. Nor if they would tell her, in any case. He had probably forgotten all about her by now. She remembered the snapshot he had shown her, his fiancée. Heidi. A pretty girl. Would she know by now that he was safe? Of course she would. She was probably writing passionate letters to him every day. She could imagine how much they would mean to him, how overjoyed he would be, how he would treasure each one. Suddenly, at the start of a new and uncertain phase in her young life, she was seized with a fierce longing to see him once again.

★　★　★

Holger stayed in the small hospital in Northallerton for more than a week, before he was transferred to the detention quarters at Catterick military camp, where he was kept in virtual isolation, apart from the medical orderlies who inspected his knee, and the guards. There was a narrow exercise yard, high walled, but with a barred gate at one end, through which he could stare across a vast parade ground framed by long rows of identical, single-storey huts. In the distance, khaki-clad squads marched to and fro. No one came near. After forty-five minutes he was taken back to his cell, with the prospect of another seemingly interminable day stretching ahead of him, the pale green, glazed brick walls closing in, and the small arched window, high above the narrow bench-bed and far beyond his reach, permanently blacked out, with shutters and a heavy black drape, to seal in the light from the bulb, under its ugly white, institutional shade. A light which was never switched off, day or night.

He was given no paper or books, except for a bible, which he spent hours reading through, struggling with the seventeenth-century English. The guards simply ignored his questions, or his attempts to strike up a conversation. He tried pacing the confines of the cell. Five paces to the steel door, with its small shutter which clicked open then screeched shut again every half-hour, day and night. Five back to the wall, and the chipped enamel bucket which was his lavatory, and which stank even before he used it. Though even carrying that out to swill down at the sink at the end of the corridor, before he was permitted to wash in a small bathroom, became a welcome ritual to herald the start of another day.

He worked backwards, from the day of the mission, hoping that he had calculated correctly, and began to keep a calendar, making minute marks on the brickwork beside his bed with his thumbnail. Both in the yard, and in his cell, the pain in his knee severely inhibited his ability to exercise. He limped badly, couldn't straighten his leg, or put any weight on it, and he began to fear that the damage was permanent. He was afraid of adding to the injury, and so was forced to spend long hours resting on his bed; staring at the walls, and the high, grubby ceiling.

'I wish to write letter. To my family. My girlfriend.'

The duty guard said nothing, did not even meet his gaze. Holger had to restrain himself from grabbing hold of the fellow, from screaming at him, or, worse, begging. 'I have right.' The guard turned away, the door clanged shut.

Again and again, Holger kept seeing Ruth's face in his mind, kept on wondering about her, recalling the feel of her, the sweet smell of her presence close to him. He dreamt of her one night. They were in the hut, and her mouth was open, wet and inviting, her breasts strained against him through their clothing. He woke, the light high above dancing and stabbing at him, his brain reeling, his body afire with his excitement, the throbbing ache of his arousal. The light beat down on him from the ugly walls, he felt an intolerable weight pinning him down on the hardness of the bench until he could scarcely breathe.

The weight became the burden of his despair.

He groaned, turned, full of self-loathing, on to his side, facing the wall, pressed his palm on the cold roughness of the bricks, felt blindly for the tiny notches he had made with his thumb. How many? Ten? Twelve? There may be hundreds ahead before he was free. He vowed he would stop. No more. Better to let the days and nights roll together into a formless misery. Guilt assailed him again, and desperately he tried to conjure up Heidi's face, Heidi's body. Tried to recall every detail of how it felt to make love, torturing himself by his failure to do so. When he strove to call up her face, the face of the English girl seemed to superimpose itself, like a misty photograph, so that the features beneath were no more than a blur, an impression which he could not clear, no matter how hard he tried.

11

'Bit basic, isn't it?' The small-featured, dark-haired girl gave a wide grin as she bounced on the creaking iron bedstead next to Ruth's, and one of a row of eight which ran along one wall of the long wooden hut. Eight more faced them on the opposite wall, across the rough wooden boards of the floor. Between each single bed stood two simple wooden lockers, about three feet high, consisting of a plain top, an open recess with a shelf eight inches below, then a cupboard with a key already in its lock. Despite its length, the room looked crowded as the sixteen new occupants chattered eagerly, unpacking and stowing away their things in the severely limited space available.

The slightly prominent teeth of Ruth's neighbour, whose tips showed when she smiled, added to her appearance of cheery ingenuousness. Ruth was glad that she and Irene had managed to get next to each other in the barrack-like hut. They had already struck up an easy friendship during the very brief time they had spent together. Ruth guessed how important relationships would be in this uncomfortably public life style, and there were already several among the batch of trainees she had decided it would not be all that easy to get along with.

They were all from the north, but clearly from varying backgrounds. There had already been some unkind banter — Irene had come in for some of it because of her noticeably refined accent — 'Hey! You don't half talk posh, doncher? Real toff, aren't you?'

'I can't help the way I talk, can I?' Irene had answered robustly, with that engaging grin, though she had since kept a wary eye on the girl who had accosted her, an amply built blonde in the 'glamour puss' tradition, Norah Graham, who was already emerging as one of the dominant personalities of the group.

'You'll have to show us the ropes,' Irene remarked, while she and Ruth bent to put away their folded clothes. 'You knowing this area already.'

Ruth nodded. She was still astonished at the irony of the circumstances which had brought her back here, to the very place she had left in such disgrace only a few months previously. She had been stunned when Miss Dyer, the Assigning Officer, had told her, 'You'll be going back to north Yorkshire. Where you were working before, I believe. Or near there, anyway. We've set up a camp at

Allerton Woods. It's part of Sir George Whiteley's estate, at Skinnerdale. There's loads of work there. Enough to keep us going for the duration, I should think. There'll be about twenty of you, working with a bunch of foresters. On the job training. Best kind there is! It'll be useful to have someone who's already familiar with the area — I expect you'll be glad to get back there, won't you? It's a beautiful spot.'

Ruth could only nod bewilderedly. Surely Miss Dyer must be aware of the circumstances of Ruth's transfer? She was about to speak up, to declare the impossibility of her returning there, when something made her hold back. Perhaps she might release a whole new hornets' nest of troubles by her objection. She had been amazed, and gratified, at how easily her recruitment into the Timber Corps had been arranged. If she spoke out against her posting, who knew what might ensue? And the prospect of conscription for girls loomed ever larger. Ruth was fiercely resolved that she would never allow herself to be a part of the armed forces and the fighting machine. More than ever now, since she had become involved with Holger Fichtmüller. Besides, in spite of her embarrassment at the idea of going back, she felt a measure of defiance. Why the hell shouldn't she? She'd done nothing wrong! Not as far as she was concerned. There was almost a kind of justice in it, she told herself righteously.

However, it didn't stop the whirling anxiety in her stomach as the now familiar beauty of the countryside began to reveal itself during the train-ride back along the Esk Valley, and when the party alighted at Skinnerdale, she was glad that the blustery, overcast day allowed her to pull the wide brim of the brown felt hat low over her face, and to shrink down into the high, rough collar of the unflattering khaki greatcoat which came almost to her ankles. She recognized the station master, Mr Wyatt, and his wife, who had gathered with several others to watch with interest the arrival of this large contingent of young females.

They did not linger, fortunately. A rather dapper-looking man, of middle age, and with a receding hairline which emphasized the nut-brownness of his complexion, smiled somewhat uncertainly at them. 'I'm Harry Guy. I have the pleasure of being in charge of you lot. I hope we'll get along fine. You're not in the army, so we don't have any getting into ranks of threes and marching, and all that rot. Just listen for your name and as I call it out, shout out and get aboard the lorry there.'

The ride soon became a bumpy one, after the lorry had swung over the hump-backed stone bridge across the shallow river, and ground up the long hill out of the village, on the northern side. The track leading into Allerton Woods had been considerably widened since Ruth's departure in August, to allow the passage of timber lorries in and out, and they drove for several miles, into the heart of the forest land, before they reached their new home.

Not that they had a chance to appreciate the scenery during the ride, for the lorry was canvas-covered, and they had sat facing inboard, in bouncing, knee-jostling intimacy, on the narrow wooden benches. This added a touch of drama to the first sight of their destination when they clambered awkwardly from the high tailboard of the vehicle. 'Bloody hell!' Norah Graham declared feelingly. It was a sentiment echoed by the vast majority when they beheld the low wooden hut, its planking still rawly smelling of creosote. It rested on four brick pillars, at each corner, so that there was a space of about three feet from the floor of the woodland. Wide wooden steps led up to the double doors, which stood open to the chilly breeze.

But, inside, a wood-burning stove at one

end of the room was already well alight, and presently, with all sixteen occupants installed, a good number puffing away on cigarettes, the temperature rose, and a homely fug was created. There were a few protests when Irene Beasley struggled to open the stiff window between her and Ruth's bed.

'Here! Don't let the cold in!' Norah Graham called.

Irene flapped her hands at the billowing clouds of blue smoke from the Woodbines and the Park Drives. 'Don't panic!' she grinned. 'It's only fresh air. It won't kill you!'

'Eh! You're not on your daddy's yacht now, you know!' But Irene continued to smile broadly, and the blonde girl, after a speculative glance in her direction, let the matter rest.

★ ★ ★

Most of the girls were from humble backgrounds, and were quite used to living in crowded, cheek-by-jowl conditions back home, but none of them was used to the Spartan quality of the camp. The kitchen, or galley as they learnt to call it, was a canvas affair. The hut which would be their dining-room and recreation-room was still being built, so that trestle-tables had to be set up and then dismantled in their sleeping-hut for their meals. By the time they turned in for the night, the atmosphere was rich with an assortment of aromas, from the smells of stale food to the cigarettes and the fumes from the stove, which burned day and night.

The latrines, also behind canvas walls, were crude long-drop affairs, with corrugated-iron roofing and sections for individual stalls. It was not a place to stay longer than necessary, particularly as autumn gave way to winter, and the wind howled icily through, while the rain and sleet rattled above.

There was at least a wooden structure for their ablutions, and plenty of hot water from the boiler which was fed with a seemingly endless supply of logs, but most of the girls were shocked at the primitive nature of the bathroom, with its duckboards and metal washing basins, and the chummily communal row of showers. Even in the humblest homes, the weekly bath was a private affair, and the idea of appearing naked in front of colleagues even of the same sex was not greeted with enthusiasm. Ruth was surprised to find that one of the least self-conscious in the matter of communal bathing was her friend, Irene. 'At school, we always had to share baths,' Irene told her, with her customary grin.

'Blimey! What sort of school did you go to

then?' one of the others, who had overheard, asked, and Ruth realized just how privileged Irene's background was, for she had attended an exclusive girls' boarding-school.

'My folks paid for the privilege of having me bullied, half-starved, beaten, and generally terrorized, in conditions hardly better than a gaol!' she declared flippantly.

There were three galvanized iron bath-tubs as well, for which there was fierce competition, and, often, lengthy queueing. It took a while for all of them to get used to their new life style. Two duty cooks were assigned daily on a rota basis to assist the taciturn male catering manager who was responsible for feeding them. The pair also had to clean the mess-hut and the ablutions. Some made a better and more willing job of it than others, but gradually they began to settle into a more cohesive unit. Despite the onset of a wickedly wet winter, which wreathed the woodland in smokily damp mist, where every bare branch dripped icily and the ground turned to a soggy mush with the consistency of wet tea leaves, they spent almost all the shortening daylight hours out of doors, learning their new craft, labouring clumsily under the patient guidance of Harry Guy and his small, dedicated band of professional foresters. The girls were glad enough to spend the hours of darkness in the insulated fug of their hut, resting weary limbs and, in most cases, muscles which ached from unaccustomed use. They played cards, or wrote letters, or flicked through magazines, or listened to the wireless set and grumbled at the unreliable reception from the tall, domed, fretwork cabinet, which was rarely switched off until lights out at ten o'clock

An expectant silence fell over the company at nine o'clock, when the impassive tones of the announcer would read out the news. London had been under nightly attack for the past two months, but the capital was not the only city to suffer from the 'blitz'. On November 15, they heard that Coventry had endured a heavy raid the previous night, with 'numbers of civilian casualties'.

'And I bet that's not the half of it!' Norah Graham declared darkly. 'They don't tell us half of what goes on!'

'Probably just as well,' someone else observed philosophically. 'Probably shit ourselves if we knew what was *really* happening!' Though Ruth still winced inwardly at the startling crudity of some of her comrades' language, she was becoming used to it. The next remark, however, set off an uncomfortable train of private speculation.

'I just wish one of them Jerry bastards

would be shot down round here! I'd tear the bastard's bollocks off with me bare hands, I would!'

Norah laughed indulgently, and reached out to ruffle the short, spiky black hair of the speaker. Beryl Mills had attached herself to Norah as her own personal acolyte and skivvy. But it was not this relationship which occupied Ruth's thoughts so disturbingly. Beryl had unknowingly unleashed some painful reflections in Ruth's mind with her belligerent comment.

Holger Fichtmüller had figured a great deal in her thoughts during the intervening months. Often, she had wondered how she could find his whereabouts, longing to get in touch with him, but lacking the necessary knowledge or the will power to do anything practical to achieve her goal. She had also worried a lot, in spite of her earlier bravado when she had learnt she was returning to the area, about meeting up with local people, and, increasingly, how her companions would react to her history when they heard about it, as they surely must.

But, during the weeks they had so far been at the camp, no one had been to the village of Skinnerdale, which was only five miles distant. In fact, Kilbeck, up on the moor, 'the tops' as the higher, heather-covered countryside was known locally, was much nearer, less than three miles away. Several of the foresters were billeted there, so that there was always a lift, at least one way, in the lorry after work, should any of the girls have sufficient energy left to make the trip. On the first Saturday, when work had finished at midday, a group of girls had hitched a lift, then walked back in the dark, with tales of the wild time to be had at the village's only inn, The Shepherd and Shepherdess.

'We gave some of the old codgers a heart attack nearly by walking into the public bar,' Norah chuckled. 'But never mind. We've even been invited to make up a team for a dominoes' contest! I tell you, we'll never stand the pace!'

Sundays were completely free, apart from the two detailed for duty-cooks. The girls could lie in as long as they wished, and breakfast was a late and leisurely affair. Thick slices of bread were toasted at the stove, and many of the participants lay back in bed, still in their night-clothes, and munched and sipped at the steaming mugs of tea in decadent luxury.

'I'm off to church,' Irene announced. 'Fancy coming, or are you a heathen?'

Ruth was surprised at the number of girls who dressed themselves in their civvy

'Sunday best', except for the standard issue gum boots, which were necessary for the long walk up through the woods to Kilbeck. They carried their shoes crammed into their shoulder bags, or as paper parcels tucked under their arms. Almost half the squad were heading either for the parish church of St John's, or the Wesleyan chapel.

'I thought you'd be C of E,' Ruth teased, and Irene grinned back.

'Not like you, peasant! I'll see you after the service, all right?'

They were made to feel welcome, and after the morning service were surrounded by the village women, eager to involve the newcomers in the social life of the nonconformist community. Some of the younger males, red faces scrubbed and shining, and hair brilliantine-slicked, looking awkward and raw-limbed in their dark suits and glowing Sunday boots, hovered on the fringes, mostly tongue-tied but awaiting a providential chance of conversation. Ruth made her excuses. 'I'll have to go. My friend's waiting for me.'

Ruth saw the groups standing about the doorway and the porch of the much more impressive Anglican church. Irene waved to her and came down the path to meet her. Weathered gravestones leaned at odd angles on either side. On some, the sandstone had worn away so much the inscriptions were undecipherable.

'Hey! Come and have a look at this!' Irene said animatedly. She took Ruth by the arm and pulled her along, staggering slightly over the tussocky grass, leading her among the graves towards the far wall, lined with low, tough looking trees. 'See?'

A wave of powerful emotion swept over Ruth as she stared at the glaringly new, large slab of marble stone, and the words which seemed to leap at her, so clearly and blackly etched.

⋆ ⋆ ⋆

Here lie interred the remains of the crew of FL-S, ST TS23, Heinkel IIIE, which crashed nearby, August 1, 1940, with the loss of all on board:
U/Lt Helmut Armin
U/Lt Franz Weissman
Sgt. Dieter Schmidt . . .

As she read the seven names, so unfamiliar and yet so painfully close, and thought of the eighth, who, by God's grace, was not there, Ruth recalled in every detail the sound, and the feel, of Holger's anguished sobbing as he clung to her. Her throat closed, her eyes misted, and the slab dissolved into shimmering indistinctness,

'Good heavens, Ruth! What's the matter? You're white as a sheet! What is it?'

The tears already spilling down her cheeks, Ruth stared helplessly at her friend, then her shoulders heaved in a great sob, and she turned away to gaze out at the sweep of the dark, winter heathland, and the high, limitless expanse of the sky above.

12

'Welcome to the arsehole of the world, friend! Don't worry about our brave guards here — they're just passing through!'

In the roar of laughter that greeted the speaker's words, Holger glanced quickly at the two English soldiers who had brought him across the bleak, grassy surface of the small compound to the barrack hut from the commandant's office and admin block. It was obvious from their stiffly glowering expressions that they knew the remark was derisory, even if they couldn't understand the language. To Holger, the sound was like the sweetest music, for it was the first time in almost three months that he had heard German from a native speaker.

He had begun to think that he was doomed to spend the duration of the war in virtually solitary confinement. He had remained on his own at the military camp in Yorkshire for day after day, week after endless week, with no human contact other than his dour captors. A medical officer had come twice to examine his knee, which Holger was afraid might be permanently damaged. The pain had lessened considerably, though his activity was still restricted, and he could not straighten his leg properly. Eventually, he had been given a walking stick. He tried to do without it, struggling to restore full use of the joint by a programme of exercise, the hope of escape still emblazoned in his mind.

The move came with absolutely no warning. He had almost no personal belongings other than the few items of clothing he had been issued after his capture. He had been allowed to keep his flying-suit and his boots, and had eventually been given half a dozen cheap paperback novels. Also some writing-paper and a pencil, so that he was able to write to Heidi, and to his parents. 'One letter a month,' a sour-faced sergeant had warned, and anyway, the paper was rationed to a few sheets only.

'When will I receive mail?' Holger asked repeatedly, to be answered always with an indifferent shrug.

With his few items stuffed into a small haversack, his heart thumping with excitement, and renewed hope, he had been bundled into a lorry, to find himself, after a short ride, at a wayside halt. With hands manacled at his back, he glanced around, trying in vain to discover where he was. His two guards refused to answer any of his questions, and his excitement became tinged with faint alarm. He strove to reassure himself. If they had not intended to keep him alive, they would not have waited until now to execute him. Or perhaps there was to be some mockery of a trial? He had overheard one of the guards one night say to a colleague, 'I see London copped it again,' and he had guessed that the fellow was referring to an attack. Perhaps most of the cities were in ruins now — perhaps he was to be made an example of?

They changed trains at a large railway station, clearly in an important town. Uniforms were everywhere, but there was no visible sign of damage. He searched in vain for a clue as to his whereabouts. His escorts kept him at one end of a long platform, well away from the main station concourse, though even the sight of other people in the distance was reassuring. Then he noticed, on the back of the long, green wooden bench on which they were sitting, letters showing faintly through the paint which was meant to obliterate them: YORK. He tried to recall the maps they had studied. Surely that was somewhere well to the north of London? Yorkshire was where the plane had crashed. Ruth had told him so. Ruth! As always, when he thought of her, he felt his heart quicken;

he saw so clearly her face, her eyes, filled with tears of compassion for him.

All the long and freezing hours of darkness were spent travelling, sitting on the dusty wooden floor of a guard's van, chained to the bars of a window above his head, among the piles of luggage, most of which seemed to be military kitbags, and large sacks of parcels. Then another lengthy wait on a freezing, rain-spattered platform, away from the other travellers, until two schoolboys approached, and stared curiously.

'Clear off, sonny!' one of his guards said warningly, but the boys continued to hover, their eyes growing wider. 'Hey! He's a Nazi, isn't he?' Their accent was thick and strange, Holger did not properly understand them. Two railway officials joined them.

A plump, freckle-faced man in a porter's uniform came up close. The placid features contorted, and Holger recoiled with shock as the man puckered up his lips and spat in his face. 'Ye bastards, ye! Bombing innocent wee wains and womenfolk!'

The soldiers urged them firmly away. 'They are English?' Holger asked. He was shaken by the encounter. Perhaps his escort felt sorry for him, for one of them answered.

'Naw, he's Scotch, Fritz. You're north of the border now, mate! Bonny Scotland! And you can fucking have it!' he added feelingly.

It was mid-afternoon before Holger finally arrived at his destination, a hastily converted camp on Scotland's north-east coast, near Stonehaven. The bleak huddle of huts, surrounded by a barbed-wire perimeter, was actually about two miles inland from the coast itself, and a similar distance from the village, in a windswept glen that led up to the inhospitable moorland of the Grampian Highlands. In spite of his weariness, and his relief at having reached his journey's end, Holger's heart sank at the bitingly cold, mist-shrouded desolation. It was doubly heartwarming, after a thankfully brief interview with the camp commandant, an elderly major who was formally correct if somewhat remote, to find himself hearing his own language and to be surrounded by a dozen of his countrymen, after all this time.

Quickly, he introduced himself. One of the British soldiers who had brought him across — the one with two stripes on his arm — grinned unpleasantly. 'We'll soon have to get a bigger place for you lot, if we keep knocking off your planes like this!'

The one who had welcomed Holger in such forthright terms, a tall, youthful-looking individual with the fuzz of a new, blond beard, returned the smile challengingly.

'Do not worry, corporal. The boots will soon be on the other foot, *ja*? You will be our prisoners then!'

'My boot'll be up your arse if you don't watch it, Fritz!'

'Please! I have told you! My name is not Fritz. He thinks all Germans are called Fritz. I am Wolfgang — to my friends, that is!'

The corporal swore pungently, nodded at the wooden bunks. 'There's a blanket there somewhere, unless one of these thieving bastards has pinched it. Make yourself at home. You'll be here a long time, laddie!'

★ ★ ★

During the walk back, down from the moor, through the dank silence of the forest, Ruth told Irene all the details of her encounter with the German boy.

'He was really sweet,' she ended, somewhat lamely, and blushing as she spoke. 'And scared, too. He tried not to show it — you know how they are — but I could tell. Ever such a nice lad. He showed me a picture of his fiancée, told me all about her, and his family and everything.'

Irene was glancing at her speculatively. She was secretly astonished that such a quiet, conventional girl as Ruth appeared to be should have behaved in such a startling manner. She was shocked by the confession, yet instinctively found herself responding to Ruth's honesty. She was her friend now, she could not find it in her to condemn her foolish behaviour.

'Weren't you scared? I'd 've been petrified! A German!'

Ruth shook her head. 'It wasn't like that at all. The war — all that — it didn't seem to count.' Her face took on a determined look. 'I want to find out what's happened to him. Where he is. I want to write to him.'

'I shouldn't think they'll tell you. I mean — they won't be very keen on it, will they? He'll be in prison somewhere, won't he?'

'I don't even know who to write to. Where to start,' Ruth murmured, so forlornly that Irene immediately felt a deep sympathy.

'Well, I suppose you'd start with the War Office. There must be some branch that deals with prisoners of war. I'll ask my dad for you, if you like. He knows about that sort of thing, I should think.'

Ruth turned to her and caught hold of her hand. 'Would you? Really? I'd be ever so grateful, honest!'

Being confronted so powerfully with the

evidence of the momentous events of the summer, Ruth determined to go ahead with the plan she had been putting off since she had returned to the area, and the following Saturday, after lunch, she begged a lift with the manager, Mr Ross, who, she knew, rode his motor cycle into Skinnerdale and left it at the station to catch the train into Whitby, where he lived.

'Ruddy nuisance, this petrol business!' he told her, nodding for her to climb onto the pillion seat. 'I could be home in half the time the train takes! But I can't get hold of coupons for love nor money! Climb on, that's right. Put your arms round me. Hold on tight!'

Ruth tried to ignore the jeers and lewd comments of the girls who were watching as she obeyed. She was glad she had not got dressed up, but was wearing her slacks and solid work boots.

He dropped her at the entrance to Barker's Farm, through which she could pass into the grounds of the Hall without going up to the lodge and the main entrance. It wasn't sneaking in through the back door, she assured herself. It was much quicker this way to reach the Longs' cottage. Nevertheless, she was quite relieved when she negotiated the yard without meeting any of the tenant farmer's family, and she stepped out along the tree-lined path in the direction of the Hall.

Maggie Long was in the kitchen and let out a cry of startled delight. 'Ruth, love! By heck! This *is* a surprise! What's happened? Have you come back to work then?'

She was invited to 'get your coat off' and sit down. She was touched that she was still accorded the familiarity of the large kitchen-table, and not led through to the 'front room', which was reserved for Sunday visitors.

'Ernie's up at the garden. Where else? I've told him, he might as well take his bed up there. He's got another lass working for him, but he misses you summat rotten, I know he does!'

A tall girl, with yellow locks peeping from a towel, and with another draped over her shoulders, suddenly appeared in the door-way, with a curious smile. A silk slip showed beneath the towel, and she wore a short skirt so tight that it clung revealingly to her amply curved figure. Maggie gave a good-natured exclamation of disapproval. 'You're out of the wash-house at last, are you? You've not met our Joyce, have you? She's home on leave for the weekend, from Leeds.'

'Hello again.' Joyce grinned, as she came in and sat opposite. She began rubbing her hair vigorously. 'We having a pot of tea then, Mam?'

'Give us a chance! I've just put the kettle on! I hope you've left some hot water for your dad. He'll be back in a minute.'

Joyce worked at a large aircraft factory outside Leeds. 'We're working all the hours God sends,' she told Ruth cheerfully. 'All the overtime we want. You don't want to bother with this Land-Girl rubbish! Get yourself to the factories! They're crying out for lasses! You can make a fortune!'

'I'm not on the land any more,' Ruth said diffidently. She told them what she was engaged in now.

Joyce chuckled. 'Aye, I heard about you getting the boot from here. You were quite famous, I believe!'

'Joyce!' Maggie remonstrated. She looked flustered, and her tone was one of irritation. 'Ruth doesn't want to be reminded about that, thank you!'

'It's all right, Mrs Long!' Ruth answered hastily, though her cheeks were red. 'I don't mind. I know I did nothing to be ashamed of,' she added defensively.

'That's not what some folk round here reckoned!' Joyce laughed unrepentantly. 'Not that I'm one of them,' she went on easily. 'I wouldn't dare! Not round here! Me dad would give me a thick ear! Not to mention me mam! You've got a right pair of champions in these two!'

13

The girls crowded round the deep cardboard box. 'Here we go! Come and get your new titfers!' Norah Graham, who had been appointed Section Leader, was pulling out the piles of green berets, which were to replace the felt hats they had previously been issued with. 'And there's these to go with them. You just pin them on. Real flash, aren't they?' She pointed to the brown cockades, which had come with the berets. She caught sight of Ruth. 'Sorry we haven't got any swastikas for you, Palmer!'

'Funny!' Ruth snapped, She had so far got away lightly, she acknowledged, thanks largely to Irene.

'It's no use saying nothing and just waiting for them to find out,' Irene had argued forcibly. 'You've got to get in there first. Beat them to it.'

She had initiated things the next day, as they were all gathered round the table for the evening meal.

'You didn't know our Ruth was famous round these parts, did you?' Irene announced importantly. 'A bit of a heroine, actually. I only just found out.' Everyone was all attention, eagerly demanding details.

'Seems our Ruth found a Jerry airman. The one who baled out of a bomber that crashed up on the moor last summer. Damned near dropped a bomb on Skinnerdale Hall before it came down as well! She looked after him. Even bound up his wounds for him, like a proper little lady of the lamp. Made sure he turned himself in all nice and quiet, without doing any harm.'

The girls were all agog, pressing Ruth for more details, adding to her embarrassment, but she soon came to realize that Irene had been extremely wise. Her version, which made Ruth sound humane and not at all unpatriotic, became the accepted one for her colleagues, successfully counteracting any subsequent tales which might come from other sources.

'You must be barmy!' Beryl Mills taunted meanly. 'Helping a bastard Nazi!'

Again, it was Irene who quickly opposed this belligerent view, which had drawn one or two nods of agreement. 'Listen. I've got a cousin, and an uncle, who are in the forces. I only hope that if they're ever taken prisoner somewhere, they meet someone as decent as Ruth here!' There was a far more vigorous confirmation from her listeners. Since then, any criticism had been confined to a few supposedly joking snide remarks such as the one now passed by Norah.

Morale was generally on the up. Christmas was near, and the girls had just learnt that there would be leave. Half of them would go on leave from 23 to 30 of December, the other half leaving on the 31 and reporting back for the morning of the 6 January. 'See if you can sort out for yourselves who goes when,' Harry Guy told them. 'If not, I'll have to do it for you.'

Even the news was not quite as glum as it had been earlier in the year. Despite the air raids, it was beginning to be clear that Hitler was not going to bomb Britain into submission. The fact that we weren't simply sitting back and taking it, but were carrying the fight to German cities, and those of occupied Europe, with our own bombing offensive perhaps helped to convince him of the folly of using poison gas as a weapon. That had been one of the greatest fears in many people's minds before war broke out. In the North African desert, our armies had just begun a campaign which was having great and rapid success against the Italians. People did not speak in optimistic terms of a quick victory, but the bulldog spirit, personified in the jowled and craggy features of the prime minister, was proudly and steadfastly defiant.

The girls, like the rest of the population, had smaller, more personal tragedies to contend with. They spent a lot of their free time in the evenings trying to make do and mend. One girl looked up from her bed a few nights before the first group went off on leave. She was darning a pair of pink panties.

'These'll be round me ankles before I've gone five yards!' she grumbled. Knicker-elastic was as rare, and almost as precious, as gold.

Norah Graham laughed lewdly. 'Don't worry, kid! You won't have them on long enough to worry when that lad of yours gets hold of you!'

A startling apparition, swathed in a towel over its crimped hair and wearing the long army greatcoat as a dressing-gown, rose dramatically from one of the beds at the far end of the hut. The eyes stood out in huge white saucer-shapes from the dark green mask of the face. Walking stiffly, it headed for the heavily curtained doorway and the bleakness of the bathing hut.

'Christ! I hope you can get that stuff off, Glad!'

The apparition spoke, trying not to move the muscles of her face, which was coated thickly with the Fuller's earth pack. 'Probably peel off me skin with it. Here goes!'

*　*　*

'You look fine, Ju. Honest! Wonderful!' Ruth lied convincingly. Her sister was enormous. Her face looked puffed up, a blotchy red, with a pronounced double chin, and her breasts were a pillowing mass, resting on the huge bulge which rose directly beneath them. She moved about with a slow motion reminiscent of a diver under water, her gait a rolling waddle as she moved from staircase to chair to table. Ruth had hoped that the great event would have been over by the time she came home for leave. 'It'll be a Christmas baby', mam had written optimistically, in one of her last letters. Ruth had the distinct impression that everyone would be relieved when Julia at last gave birth, her patiently suffering husband more than most.

'He won't be around when it does come!' Julia moaned. 'He's always at work anyway. There can't be that many ships coming up the Tyne! I think he'd rather be out the way, if you ask me!'

'I've told you, love,' Bill remonstrated plaintively, when she upbraided him yet again in front of the newly returned Ruth. 'We've

153

got to cover Shields as well now. They're coming in in convoy nowadays — '

'I bet it'll be tonight,' Ruth said brightly. 'Hang on till after midnight and see if you can have the first baby of the new year!'

'Oh God! I hope not! They'll all be drunk as lords, I bet!'

Though the imminent birth had the whole household gripped with its tension, there were other problems which added to the strain. The day before Christmas, Willy had received the buff coloured OHMS envelope informing him of his conscription into the forces and ordering him to report for a medical the following week.

'I thought you were exempt?' Ruth said, when they gave her the news.

'Looks like they've got enough joiners at the yard!' Willy shrugged philosophically. 'You could've fooled me, mind. They're still giving all the overtime we can manage.'

The family had all changed into their best things for the New Year's Eve celebrations. The kitchen, and the rest of the house, had been given a thorough cleaning — Ruth had sweated away all day, helping Alice — as part of the traditional preparations.

'Mucky tonight and you'll be mucky all year!' Alice declared. 'You want to shift yourself and all!' she snapped irritably at her

154

eldest daughter, who was settled stubbornly in the worn armchair which her father would occupy when he came in from work. 'Might get things started. We'll have to dose you with castor oil if you don't get going soon!'

Arnold was proud to be selected as 'first foot', though he tried to be as nonchalant as he could about it. Willy went out to keep him company during the last minutes of the old year, and while the family waited in the warmth of the front room to let them back in again, Ruth's memory dwelt all too vividly on the last year's ceremony; the intimacy — and the kiss — she had shared with Bill.

The sirens didn't go. 'Perhaps Jerry's celebrating and all,' Willy grinned. Nobody stayed up long after midnight. They were hoping to enjoy the luxury of an uninterrupted night in their beds, and besides, the menfolk were in at work in the morning, despite the public holiday.

'I won't get a wink of sleep, I bet,' Julia sighed. Ten minutes later, Ruth could hear her snoring, loudly and unattractively, through the thin walls. Ruth was still awake when she heard Bill quietly let himself in, at about one-thirty, and, on a sudden impulse, she quickly rose, pulled on her dressing-gown over her pyjamas, and padded downstairs and along the passage to where the light showed under the kitchen door. She caught a faint but unmistakable whiff of spirits as soon as she entered. Bill was helping himself to a nightcap, and looked round with startled, comic guilt. 'Oh! Sorry! Did I wake you?'

'No, it's all right. I couldn't sleep. I'm not used to sleeping on my own any more. There's sixteen of us in our hut.'

He grinned, raised his glass to his lips. 'Fancy joining me?'

'No, thanks. I'll put the kettle on, though. That fire's still warm.' She looked more closely. He was flushed, his eyes brilliant, his smile a little lop-sided. 'You look as if you've had a few.'

He nodded, gave a smile of complicity, and winked. 'They had a bottle in the wardens' hut. Navy rum. Somebody's lad had brought it. It's been quiet. So we stayed and had a few. Oh — Happy New Year, Ruth.'

'Happy New Year.' He had moved towards her, his arms coming up, then he stopped, caught in indecision, and she moved forward, into his embrace. She raised her face towards him, smelt the drink on his breath as they both paused, very still, their faces only inches from each other. He kissed her, gently, on the lips, kept his mouth against hers, and she felt her response, knees and thighs touching, arms tightening about each other. She moved at last, laughing shakily, gasping a little. She moved further away from him, jerkily, distancing herself.

He sat down in George's chair, bending forward towards the red embers of the fire behind the solid mesh of the guard. He grunted softly. 'Here we are again, eh? Remember last year? Outside?' She nodded, and remained silent. 'Did you get what you want? Any of your wishes come true?'

'Not really. And what about you?' Their eyes met, and she wished she could take back her words. Her blush deepened. His smile was a wry one. It faded quickly, and she saw the expression of tension return.

'Listen, Ruth. I'm thinking of joining up. The navy, if they'll have me.'

She stared at him, wide-eyed, appalled. 'You can't! Bill! You don't mean it! The baby! Julia!'

He gazed up at her helplessly, shrugged. 'I know. I don't want to — but I feel — bad. About not going. I ought to do my bit.'

The trite phrase made Ruth quiver with anger. 'Don't be so bloody daft! You'll be no good to your bairn a dead hero.' Urgently, she moved close, put her hand on his shoulder, standing over him. 'You're doing your job here. It's where you're needed. Where your family needs you! Think of them first, before yourself!'

He looked up again, with that sad little smile, and put his hand over hers where it rested on his shoulder. She had a sudden violent desire to pull his head into her body, to hold and feel him tightly against her. 'You're a lovely girl, Ruth,' he murmured softly. 'Even if you have learnt to swear in that barrack room of yours! You're going to make some lucky young man very happy one day.'

* * *

Julia went into labour in the early hours of 4 January, the day before Ruth's leave ended. Contrary to his wife's gloomy forecast, Bill was present, not even out fire-watching. The sirens had sounded, and Julia had waddled down to the sloping cupboard under the stairs, which had been cleared of most of its junk, and a bed-chair rigged up permanently for her exclusive use, while Bill crouched awkwardly on a low stool at her side — a position occupied by Alice when he was not there.

Julia had managed to fit herself into the siren suit, over her winceyette nightgown. It was stretched to its limits. Her dressing-gown was draped over her shoulders. She had given up attempts to tie it at the waist. She was cocooned in a nest of blankets, the edges of which Bill tried surreptitiously to draw over his knees against the biting cold. She complained about pains, and pressure, but she had been doing that for weeks now. However, a dozing Bill was startled when her hand clawed at his shoulder suddenly, and she gave a loud wail.

'Christ! I've wet myself! Fetch me mam! Quick! Go on, you gormless lump!' she added, blubbering, when he gaped at her. 'It's me waters!'

The others were swiftly out of the shelter in the yard, the rumble of the distant anti-aircraft guns ignored at this new crisis. Arnold was dispatched at full speed round to Mason's. The taxi man had been alerted almost daily for the past fortnight. 'It always has to be at night!' he grumbled, but he was turned to and parked outside the Palmers' front door in fifteen minutes.

Julia, changed and padded, lumbered the yard or so across the frosty pavement, clinging with painful tightness to Bill's arm. In his other hand, he clutched the bulky bag containing all the para-phernalia she had been instructed to bring to the maternity hospital. 'Dunno why she couldn't have had it at home!' George muttered grumpily. He didn't see the withering look, which was all Alice had time for as she climbed into the cab after Julia and Bill.

Ruth stood among the family group waving off the hooded lamps which swiftly dwindled into the darkness. She found herself subconsciously playing along with the sudden divide which had widened dramatically between the sexes. Julia had done nothing but snap and snarl at Bill between her groans and whimpers of pain, while mam had treated the male members of the family with equally fiery contempt. Ruth felt the same tendency in herself to bark impatiently at her dad, and Willy and Arnold, as though, somehow, the men were responsible for all the discomforts and danger, and pain, associated with this natural process. As she went back inside the darkened house, Ruth acknowledged the unfair bias of her emotions. As far as Julia and Bill were concerned, Ruth was pretty sure that it was her sister who had led in the dance. Which was why it was doubly unfair that Bill should be seen as the perpetrator of all evils in the jaundiced view of his wife. Not that it's got anything at all to do with you! Ruth reminded herself severely. Again, she felt that painful twinge of conscience over her feelings towards her brother-in-law. It's just that he's such a nice lad! she defended herself stoutly. She was almost convinced.

She thought about the pain and the fear Julia would be enduring just now. She mocked at herself when she discovered she had placed her hands protectively over her belly. She even thought she felt a sympathetic spasm or two deep inside. What would it be like? she wondered, then felt her cheeks grow warm, and a spasm of a different nature seize her as she wondered about the process which started off such a chain of events as Julia was experiencing right now. Would she herself ever find a man with whom she would want to find out for herself all these mysteries?

Holger Fichtmüller. The name bobbed to the surface of her mind. Don't be ridiculous! she scolded herself, scandalized at the license of her thoughts. Her cheeks were even warmer now. Partly to divert herself, she made a mental note that she must chivvy Irene up. Her friend had written to her father about how Ruth could get in touch with the young POW. So far there had been no reply to the query. Perhaps Irene would return from leave with some information for her. Ruth found herself looking forward to her return to Allerton Woods the following day. And that in turn made her feel guilty again at her wanting to be away from her family at this momentous event in their history.

It was late afternoon before the news came at last that Julia had given birth to a girl. 'Five and a half pounds, poor little mite!' their mother told them, on her return from the phone box two streets away. 'She's had a rough time. And such a tiny bairn and all! I thought it'd be a strapping great lad the size our Julia was.'

Ruth visited briefly that evening. Julia looked haggard. Ruth tried to keep the shock and dismay from her face at the sight of the muddy, yellowish complexion, the deep rings of exhaustion around the heavy eyes, which seemed to fill with tears every few seconds.

'I'm that sore!' Julia murmured tragically, with an aggrieved glance at Bill, who looked suitably wretched.

Ruth looked down at the dark tufted, wrinkled red orange of a head on the sheet of the bassinet. They had long ago decided on the name Angela for a girl. It was a miracle, Ruth thought emotionally, as the sleeping face screwed up in a fleeting acknowledgement of the awesomeness of life. She glanced across at Bill, her eyes misted with tears. A boy next time! she almost said, before she remembered the weary figure of her sister, curiously flattened beneath the sheets. A boy like Bill. Like her brother, Willy. Like Holger Fichtmüller. To grow into one of the young

162

men so obsessed with killing one another. Welcome, little niece. I'm glad you're a girl, after all. Let's hope you can bring a little sanity into our world. We need it so much!

★ ★ ★

The girls trooped wearily into the hut after their hard day's work felling, and stripping off, the branches from the thick trunks. It had been a day of blustery showers, and, in spite of their oilskins, they were cold and wet.

'These effing gum-boots are effing useless!' Norah Graham declaimed. The girls all suffered from sodden feet. Their woollen socks were soaked, their toes whitely crinkled and dead-looking, and they vied with one another for a place near the stove, so that they could sit with their limbs propped on the guard, which was festooned with their socks and other, more intimate, items of clothing. The hut soon reeked with the pungent smell of drying wool.

There was a buff envelope for Ruth. 'At last!' she breathed excitedly, her hand trembling a little as she tore it open. She felt a wave of disappointment, like an obstacle in her chest, at the severe brevity of the War Office's reply to her request concerning Holger Fichtmüller. *It is not in the interest of national security to divulge such information to the public at large*, the lieutenant who had answered her wrote. And it was decidedly unpatriotic of her to ask, was the implied meaning behind the official wording.

Irene grimaced sympathetically, and shrugged. 'It was worth a try,' she said. Ruth nodded.

That night, the hut was buzzing with the cheerful news from the North African front. The Allies had advanced further along the Mediterranean coast, and taken a town called Tobruk. Ruth's heart ached as she lay in bed later, and listened to the chit chat, and bursts of profane laughter around her. She could not get her mind off the young German. It pained her so much not to have any idea of his whereabouts, or to be unable to picture his surroundings. Probably not so different from hers, she speculated, with a wry inner smile. She hoped he was with his fellow country-men, and wondered if he felt as lonely as she did right now.

14

'Oh no! Not another billet-doux from that girl of yours!' Wolfgang Deist grinned at Holger, who was stretched out on his bunk, holding the envelope reverently in his hand, savouring the seconds of sweet anticipation before he opened it. Over the thick, grubby white, rolled neck of the sweater, Wolfgang's beard curled in undisciplined profusion, the fine blond hairs glinting in the winter light. 'I won't get a wink of sleep tonight for the creaking bed-boards!' he complained, 'I wish you'd pack her in. It's so bad for your health, dear boy!'

'Jealousy will get you nowhere,' Holger answered, enjoying the familiarity of the exchanges. Already, in a few months, he felt that he had known his companions a lifetime. He was one of the veterans now — most of them were, in Hut B-1, for they had stayed together, while new arrivals turned up almost daily. There were now four long huts identical to this one to house other ranks POWs, and two for officers only — a prisoner population of close to one hundred and fifty.

Letters came regularly, usually at intervals

165

of two or three weeks. This was the fifth he had received from Heidi. The others were at the back of his shelf, all numbered and stood in chronological order. He did not like to dwell on how thick the wad would be before he got out of this place. Perhaps there would be more than his narrow shelf could take.

He remembered his joy, and sadness, too, when the first batch had been brought to him. Letters from his parents, as well as Heidi's almost hysterical outpouring of love, and relief — and passion, for she was thrillingly, shockingly, uninhibited on paper. As she had been in real life — immediately Holger chided himself, glanced ashamedly at the small photo of the smiling girl pinned now beside his bunk. He had to keep on reminding himself that she was real — that the world was still there, waiting for him, that one day he would return to it, for, despite his guilt, Heidi had metamorphosed into some kind of fantasy figure, like the legendary Jane, whose exploits in the British daily paper he and his fellow prisoners chuckled and lusted over as fervently as their guards.

He kept on telling himself that he would get out soon. He was determined he would get in on one of the escape plans with which the camp was constantly buzzing — so far, with entire lack of success, he had to admit.

The trouble was, the officers had set up a committee — even in here, rank and military regulations took precedence. And though he had been privy to several schemes, he had been told by the committee that he could not be considered as a possible candidate to go 'over the wire', because of his gammy leg.

'You should think yourself lucky!' one of his new comrades said to him. 'You've come through it. You could've been lying there up on some English hillside with your mates! And if you got back home, they'd only send you up again. You'd be bound to buy it some time or other!'

His words had made Holger think again of the pretty English girl who had been so good to him. She had told him the same thing. She kept bobbing up in his thoughts, at all kinds of times, catching him unawares with the power of emotion she aroused in him. When he started to get mail, he hoped, foolishly, that somehow she might write to him. Which in turn gave him an uncomfortable feeling of guilt whenever he received a letter from Heidi, brimming as it did with her passionate love.

Christmas had been particularly bad, though they all made a brave effort to bolster one another's spirits. For a couple of days, they all mucked in, officers and men ate together, played together, relaxed. They had a carol service, and put on an impromptu concert — he had even taken part himself in an 'I say I say I say' routine with Wolfgang. Holger had been the straight man, feeding him the lines so that Wolfgang could deliver the punch. It had gone down well, and Holger had surprised himself with his facility for clowning, and the enjoyment he got from it.

But there was no disguising the heartache, and the misery, of being prisoners, that lay inescapably beneath all their show of spirit. Heidi's Christmas letter had come two weeks into the new year, but she painted a vivid picture of home, and the festivities — and her loneliness without him. The intensity of it, the eroticism, only made the pain of their separation worse. Perhaps she was bitterly disappointed at his letters, with their stilted phraseology. He found it very hard to express his deepest feelings in words. He had when he was with her, and it was equally difficult on paper.

But he still thrilled with pleasure, and anticipation, whenever he saw the familiar script on the envelope, and he settled down now, in that private world, cut off from the noise all about him. He scanned quickly through the opening, the news of family and events outside their love. She had joined the Faith and Beauty Scheme for Girls, was back in uniform, she joked. She was working on a farm outside Remscheid, travelling home by bicycle each evening. Tenderly he read her lively descriptions of her work and work-mates.

Her letters were like a diary, sections headed by different dates, so that when she posted off a letter each week, it was a thick tome. Holger wondered what the censor made of it all — especially the last part, which she usually completed in bed, on a Sunday evening.

When he had finished reading this latest missive, the weight and helplessness of his imprisonment was like a suffocating physical burden, the comfortably predictable repartee of those about him suddenly insufferable, jangling his nerves, and he moved abruptly, swinging himself down from his topmost bunk. He was almost glad of the stabbing pain in his knee as he stomped towards the door.

'See? What did I tell you?' Wolfgang called mockingly after him. 'Keep an eye on him, somebody. He's going to try and jump the wire. Those bloody letters!'

'Jump? He'll be able to pole-vault over now!'

He slammed the wooden door savagely on the burst of laughter. The sky was a monochrome grey, spread low with the threat of more snow. Beyond the wire, the slope of the glen rose whitely, to where it disappeared in the wintry haze, which seemed to enclose the camp, adding to the sense of entrapment. The quality of light was a poor twilight, even though it was not yet mid afternoon. They would be having the final roll-call soon, then they would be locked in for yet another interminable evening.

Holger had felt more and more at conflict with himself since his capture — and his miraculous escape, he had to acknowledge. It all seemed inextricably tied up with Ruth, the English girl, who had assumed such significance in his mind. Her vehement stance against the war, her sadness, and horror, at all the killing, the wastage of life, intruded more and more upon his innermost thoughts. And, with it, her refusal to condemn him, to look upon him as an enemy. And all that in spite of the fact that he had unknowingly come so close to being part of the machinery that had so nearly destroyed her, and others around her.

'Hullo there! Not much of a view just now, is it?'

Holger was startled out of his reverie. The

English army padre who was attached to the camp appeared at his side, joined him in his pacing of the perimeter. 'It'll warm up a bit when this next lot comes down'. The priest nodded up at the low ceiling of cloud.

'Yes, sir. That will be good.'

The army chaplain, Michael Bates, was quite a popular figure at the camp, one of the few Britishers to whom the POWs responded with open friendliness. He had intervened several times with the authorities on their behalf, had helped them out with their Christmas celebrations, wheedling little extras and privileges from the stiff-necked CO. He had even started informal English classes, which had been very well attended, until they had been abruptly terminated. They all knew why. One of the officers' orderlies had been lurking about the admin block and had heard the CO say sarcastically to the priest, 'They'll be inviting you on to their blasted escape committee next, Padre!'

Michael Bates nodded towards the official envelope which jutted from the breast pocket of Holger's tunic. 'News from home, eh? Everything all right? Are you married, by the way?'

'*Nein*. I have girlfriend. Fiancée, yes? We should have married in August.'

'Bad luck. Never mind. I'm sure she'll wait.'

'I hope.' There was a pause, then Holger spoke, on a sudden, powerful impulse. 'Father — '

'No, I'm not that sort of priest,' Michael Bates smiled. 'Padre will do.'

Holger nodded. He coloured. 'Padre. I would like you help. There is girl. A British girl. Ruth, is her name. Ruth Palmer. She help me very much. When my plane crashed. She look after me — was very kind. Bind my knee, bathe my — er, wounds, yes?' Bates nodded, looking at him with interest. 'We talk. A long time. She was like — a friend to me. Very close. Then, when they catch me — I never have chance to say thank you. I would like to know — she is all right. I would write. But I have not address. When I ask later, no one will help.' Holger grimaced. 'I think they not like — me to write to British girl. Not good.'

Bates grunted, nodded understandingly. 'Yes, I can imagine it wouldn't go down too well with the powers that be.' He reached into the inner pocket of his battledress and pulled out a battered-looking black note-book, full of bits of paper stuck in its pages at various intervals. 'You give me all the details you can. Where it happened. Where you were shot down. I'll do what I can. Now. What was the name again?'

★ ★ ★

'Glad to see you're back in circulation again. Sorry I couldn't get in to see you in the cooler. They're getting pretty strict these days.' Michael Bates smiled sympathetically. They paced fairly briskly round the edges of the open space which served as exercise area and parade ground, for the April day, though sunny and bright with spring promise, was chilly, the breeze boisterous. The padre noted that Holger was limping quite badly. 'Leg playing up?'

Holger shrugged. 'No chance for exercise in the cells.' Four of them had been confined for two weeks in the bare brick room measuring twelve feet by nine. The three-tiered wood and metal bunks affixed to each wall effectively reduced the space available to move around into a narrow path no more than three feet wide. There was no furniture in the cell, no shelving, no washing facilities. The lavatory was a stinking enamel pail with a lid. They were allowed out for half an hour each day, to an enclosure which ran along one side of the low brick punishment block and was itself no more than a few yards in width,

173

bounded by a high fence of wire mesh topped by strands of barbed wire. The rest of the time they sat or lay on their bunks, and chatted, or read, or brooded.

Holger had been afraid they would not be allowed to take any reading matter into the cell, and was hugely relieved when no one took away the two battered paperbacks, already disintegrating, which he had crammed inside his jacket just before the guards had bundled them roughly out of the hut. It had been a madcap scheme from the start, Holger had known. More an act of defiance against their captors than a serious effort at escaping. So it had seemed to him, at any rate, though it had been given the go-ahead from the committee.

Wolfgang and another of the members of Hut B-1 had hidden themselves in the roof of the showers, and attempted to scrape a way out under the wire, after dark. Holger and the others had managed to disguise the absences at the roll-call in the evening, by creating a diversion with a mock fight, and other horseplay. Though the would-be escapees had successfully negotiated the first trip-wire, they had been caught scrabbling at the earth at the perimeter fence. A burst of automatic fire dangerously close to their crouching figures had alerted the whole camp to their capture.

174

Subsequent investigations had revealed the part played by their comrades in the escapade, and, as a result, eight had been detained in the punishment cells.

'It was not bad,' Holger told the chaplain philosophically. 'It was warmer than the hut, and it gives me the chance for reading. My English is better, yes?'

Bates nodded. 'Deist and his pal can count themselves lucky. If they had got out, they might well have found themselves lynched. Your blokes are still giving us a bad time.'

Holger smiled. 'Be careful. You should not bring such good news. And in Africa. This man Rommel. He is giving headache, I think?'

Bates glanced quizzically at him. 'All the latest news, I see.' He grunted, gripped his unlit pipe in his teeth. 'I think our lords and masters are more concerned about the threat from our own government. I suppose you've heard about the latest budget? Income Tax up to fifty per cent! Not that a poor old army padre needs to worry about that.'

Around them, others were walking, singly or in pairs. Several, in singlets and shorts, were running obsessively round and round the bare patch, their faces shining with sweat, their eyes glazed, unseeing.

'I'm afraid I haven't got anywhere with that

query about the girl. I eventually got a reply from the place she'd been assigned to. Skinnerdale Hall. Very grand. But the estate manager told me she'd been given the sack. The local squire didn't take too kindly to her fraternizing with the enemy. I haven't given up, though. I've written to the national HQ in Whitehall Place — London. They might be able to give us her home address.'

Holger could not disguise his disappointment. 'But this place — of her work. They could not give her address?'

Bates laughed ruefully. 'I'm sure they could. But I was a little too honest, I'm afraid. I mentioned you, wanting to thank her and so on. I should've been a bit more devious. The tone of the letter was decidedly snooty.' He interjected a note of enthusiasm into his voice. 'Anyway, how's your own girl? Heard from her lately? I expect you're glad to be out of the cooler, start getting your mail again. And writing too.'

'Yes, of course.' Holger wondered if the priest had noticed his embarrassment. He actually felt as though he were blushing. 'Heidi is very well. She is also working on a farm. And my parents — they are well, too.'

'Give them my regards when you write,' Bates said easily.

Holger stared at him. 'I'm sure you know they read our letters. Before they send them.'

The padre nodded, his grin broadening. 'Maybe they'll shoot me, eh?'

★ ★ ★

'Eh up, Palmer! Here's your mate!'

Ruth's eyes were stinging against the wreathing smoke which came from the brushwood fire, but she recognized the slim form of Felicity Whiteley, who was mounted on Beauty and dressed in the usual black hacking-jacket and jodhpurs. The rain clung in beads and dripped from the brim of her cute riding-hat. A few yards behind her came the lumbering Clydesdales, in single file, led by the girls who had been assigned as their handlers.

The rain, a fine, penetrating drizzle, had set in soon after they had started the day's work. They were miles from the camp — it had taken the girls almost an hour to get there on foot — and they had grown increasingly miserable as, despite their oilskins, the rain had soaked them through to the skin. The girls had been stripping the trees which the foresters had felled, working with the crosscut and the bushman saws, until arms and backs ached and their hands were blistered.

Then they had to dig trenches in the peaty earth around the piles of brushwood before it could be burnt, in order to avoid any chance of starting a forest fire. 'Never mind, girls! At least you'll have a chance to warm yourselves,' the head forester in charge of the small gang of men had joked, before they collected their tools and haversacks, and headed off towards the distant track and the waiting lorry. The men were not required to keep on working during such rainy conditions and would be paid 'wet time' for the rest of the day. The girls were afforded no such luxury.

'Not bloody fair!' Beryl Mills whined, watching the men leave with a sarcastic wave. 'And another thing! We're only supposed to work fifty hours a week. They should pay us overtime now we're working longer.'

'What you going to do, Gyppo? Go on strike?' Norah Graham grunted. 'Come on! Let's get these bloody fires lit! Old Shortarse is right. At least we can warm ourselves!'

Even the fires were difficult to get going, but eventually they succeeded, and huddled in their dripping capes to eat their late snack-lunch. Irene sniffed suspiciously at the pale smears on the thick slices of bread.

'What on earth is this?'

'Don't ask! Looks like summat you step in!

And this ruddy wheatmeal bread! Why can't they give us white?'

At this point, Felicity Whiteley appeared, guiding her horse carefully down the slope between the trees. Ruth's colleagues were already well aware of Sir George's daughter's antipathy towards Ruth, and her condemnation of Ruth's involvement with the captured German airman.

'The horses can't work any longer in this!' she called out in her well modulated tones. 'It's too dangerous. They're slipping about all over the place. We're taking them back to the camp.' She had halted, climbing out of the saddle. Ruth was meanly pleased to see that her clothing was heavy and sodden with the rain, her breeches darkly stained with water about the thighs. She was shivering visibly and came across the shallow trench, to warm herself at the now crackling fire.

'You in the Corps now, then?' Norah asked bluntly, nodding at her civilian garb.

'No,' Felicity answered stiffly. 'Not yet. Attached, as it were. I may be going into one of the services soon.'

Several of her listeners bridled at the scarcely hidden dismissiveness in her cultured voice. It rankled with many that the WLA was not considered to be part of the women's services, particularly as more and more girls were beginning to be conscripted as Land-Girls. The Timber Corps now had its own distinctive insignia, apart from the beret. The badge on the arm of the jersey consisted of two crossed axes, and above them was the shoulder flash, with the word, 'Forestry' written on it.

'They don't even give us proper kit!' the girls grumbled. 'These bloody baggy breeches and stinking socks! And there's room for three in these dungarees!'

'What do you mean?' Norah had grinned mockingly. 'They've given us our blackouts, haven't they?' 'Blackouts' was the name popularly bestowed on the generously sized regulation knickers, two pairs of which had been issued to each individual, both because of their colour and the material from which they were made.

Ruth was one of the few who did not grouse about the WLA's status, however. She was quite content not to be associated with the more belligerent auxiliary services, such as the ATS, or the WAAF, or the WRNS, though she did not express her sentiments aloud, except during the course of her confidential chats to Irene. She was sensible enough to know that her pacifist point of view would not gain much sympathy at the present time.

Felicity Whiteley had backed up against the fire, and already her clothing was steaming gently. The others stood well back from the blaze, holding the tossing heads of the great beasts, whose bridles jinked softly. Normally, there would have been a great deal of vociferously impolite badinage between the handlers and the other girls, but they were inhibited in Felicity's presence. Official status or not, they clearly behaved with untypical deference in her company. Only Norah seemed truculently determined not to be awed by Sir George's daughter. As for Ruth, her wet toes were curling with deep embarrassment inside her sodden gumboots, and she kept her head down, avoiding looking at the slim figure. But Felicity's next words suddenly captured her wholehearted attention.

'I see your Nazi friend is still trying to keep in touch. It must make him feel good to know he has such a close chum over here.'

Ruth flushed. She stared piercingly at the haughty girl. 'What are you talking about?'

'Don't pretend you don't hear from him. He even had the cheek to try and use the Hall. They got a letter from the estate office asking about you. Some idiot padre or other asking after you on his behalf.'

'Where is he? What's happened?' Ruth's

unsteady tone betrayed her agitation.

The pretty face curled in contempt. She gave an elaborately casual shrug of her shoulders. 'Goodness knows! Daddy just mentioned it in passing. He thought it was an infernal cheek of the fellow, and I must say I agree.'

Ruth stood. Her dark eyes showed her hurt. 'You knew I was here! Why wasn't it sent on? Why didn't you let me know? How long ago was this?'

Felicity made a gesture of impatience. 'Oh, I don't know! Days ago! I told you — Daddy mentioned it, that's all. He sent it back, I think. Somehow I don't think he's in favour of British girls communicating with Huns!'

Ruth was breathing heavily. She could feel her chest tighten, and she fought to keep the quaver out of her voice. Her fingers curled, and she had a wild and powerful urge to push the girl in front of her backwards into the blazing fire.

'You're a nasty little bitch!' she managed quietly.

'How dare you?' Felicity brimmed with righteous indignation, but she edged away from the fire, stepping back a little from Ruth. 'I won't have you speaking like that! You of all people! You're — '

'I thought you said you were going back to

camp!' Norah bludgeoned in. Her tone was quiet, too, none the less intimidating, and Felicity took another step, further away. She turned, striving to make a dignified with-drawal. She stepped across the wide trench, her elegant riding boots squelching in the mud, and moved over to her horse. She swung lithely up into the saddle, then glared down at them from her lofty height. 'It's a pity you're not in the real army! A bit of discipline wouldn't come amiss with you bolshie lot!'

'Tarah, your ladyship!' Norah bowed, tugging at the damp blonde hair at her brow.

'Come on, girls!' Felicity piped shrilly. 'Be careful. Not too tight! Lead them slowly.'

'Aye, go on! Do as miss tells you!' There were a few catcalls and sniggers as the band trooped off, then a chorus of relaxing laughter at their departure. Ruth did not join in.

She squatted again, surprised at how shaky she felt, and pent-up inside. Her eyes were moist and she had to swallow hard. 'I can't believe it. She really is a stuck up, wicked cow!' she murmured to Irene.

'She's only trying to get your goat,' Irene answered. 'Succeeding too, I'd say,' she added shrewdly.

Ruth acknowledged the truth of her

friend's remark. She was shaken herself at the depth of emotion she felt. All this time he had not forgotten about her. Had maybe been trying to get in touch over the past months, just as she had been. It made her feel warm inside, rekindled that special closeness she had felt between them. Then came the ache of desolation at the realization of how close he had come, and yet had failed.

'Cheer up!' Irene said encouragingly. 'You can call in at that office, can't you? They must have an address, surely, even if they've sent the letter back. Somebody must have it somewhere.'

* * *

Though there was a steady breeze blowing, the bite had gone out of the wind on this fine early May day, so that Ruth was quite warm when she entered the grounds of the Hall. She had to pass the ornately gabled lodge, and by chance she saw Mrs Burridge, the wife of the estate manager, playing with the children on the front lawn.

'Afternoon. Is your husband in? I'd like a word.'

Mr Burridge appeared almost as she spoke. His face, always sombre, with its narrow structure and drooping black moustache, assumed a frown of severity as he recognized her.

'Ah, Miss Palmer. What is it?'

She tried to keep her tone unhurried and calm as she explained.

His brow furrowed as though he were trying to recall a forgotten detail. 'Yes, we did get a letter from some army chap. We told him you were no longer working here. No, we didn't pass on your home address. It wouldn't have been right. Not without your consent.' He smiled in mean triumph, and she wanted to smack his face.

'Surely you knew I was back in the district? Up at Allerton camp?'

Again, the sneering smile. His shoulders rose, appealing to reason. 'I'm afraid not. It was only afterwards — Miss Felicity mentioned it to me the other day. No, I'm afraid I can't remember where this army fellow was writing from. We do get a fair bit of correspondence these days, as I'm sure you'll appreciate. Sorry I can't be more help. Don't know much about what they do with Jerry prisoners. Can't say I'm all that interested, either,' he added pointedly.

15

'Clothes rationing is starting next month. They're going to issue coupons, just like food.'

Irene was reading her letter from her mother, and made the announcement from her bed, on which she was sprawled in her flapping shirt-tails, her bare legs much in evidence. There was a chorus of groans and indignant exclamations, which Norah Graham cut short in her forthright manner.

'Fair enough, I reckon!' She nodded towards Irene. 'It's only toffs like Beasley here who can afford to buy anything decent nowadays. Look at the price of stuff! Same with rationing! At least folks get their share of proper grub now. When there's anything to get!' she added broodingly. Personal rations had just been cut again, for food supplies were at their lowest due to the German U-boat successes.

'I'll have to get Mummy to lay in a stock of undies,' Irene offered provocatively, anticipating quite correctly the reaction.

'Aye, you do that!' someone called drily.

Several of the girls had already been reduced to fashioning their own brassieres and other garments from the plentiful supplies of cheese-cloth which Mr Ross was able to pass on to them.

'What for?' Norah declared challengingly. 'Nobody's going to see them, are they? Unless you're doing a turn on the quiet for old Harry Guy! I must admit, he's looking a bit knackered these days!'

Ruth had been for a quick wash before supper, towards which the girls were beginning to move. The dining- and mess-hut had been in use for a considerable time. There was another accommodation hut almost completed. It was of the new Nissen variety, with the curved walls of corrugated iron. 'Bloody freezing in winter!' the girls opined. They were waiting eagerly for a new batch of the Corps to arrive. More than twenty of them, Harry Guy had told them, and with the luxury of a four-week training-course under their belts. 'Huh! Be able to show us how to do the job properly then, will they?'

Towel still round her neck, Ruth picked up the mail from the bottom of her bed. She was surprised to see her sister's writing on one of the envelopes. She glanced at the other letter hurriedly, the envelope also handwritten, in an unfamiliar scrawl. She turned it over, and her heart began to race as she read the name on the back of the envelope. *Capt M. Bates, Chaplain.*

She was shocked to discover how badly her hands were shaking, how weak her knees felt. She sat on the edge of the bed. Irene had risen, and was hauling on the baggy bottoms of her plum-coloured siren-suit, tucking her loose khaki shirt into the elastic of the waistband.

'Come on, slowcoach! Grub up!' She put her hand on Ruth's shoulder, stared down at her. 'What is it? Nothing wrong?'

'Eh?' Ruth looked up vaguely. 'It's a note from that army fellow. And there's a letter from him — from Holger. That German lad,' she added unnecessarily.

'My God! Really? What's he say?' Then Irene flushed, recollecting herself. 'Oh, I'm sorry, Ruth. I didn't mean to be so rude! I'll push off. See you over in the mess!' She left hurriedly.

'It's all right!' Ruth called after her. 'I'll tell you when I've had a chance to read it!' But Irene had already fled, appalled at her own lapse of good manners. Ruth turned back avidly to the sheets on her lap. First she read the chaplain's short note.

Dear Miss Palmer,

I'm enclosing a letter from Holger Fichtmüller, a German POW at the camp which is part of my jurisdiction. He's been trying for months to get in touch. He told me about the circumstances of your meeting, and how kind you were to one of our enemies. I must say I was impressed, and agreed to help him right away. I hope with some success, at last. I gather from the reply I got from Skinnerdale Hall that your efforts were not much appreciated, and that you paid a quite heavy price for them. I only hope that the milk of human kindness, of which you have more than your fair ration, has not been soured by your experience.

The National HQ of the WLA put me on to the Timber Corps, with the result that I now believe you will eventually get this letter, and the enclosed. It would be easier if you conducted any correspondence through me at the above address, if you don't mind. If it's considered a deception, it's in a good cause. I'll make sure Holger gets your reply, if you write one. I do hope you will. It will mean a lot to Fichtmüller, who is a good chap, and not the monster we should, according to our zealous patriots, regard him as. He is bearing up well, and in reasonable health given his circumstances, but I'm sure he'll feel a lot better for hearing from you.

Best wishes,
Michael Bates.

Her heart still beating rapidly, she turned to the carefully folded note, which was not sealed in an envelope.

My dear Ruth,

I hope you remember me still, your friend, Holger. No one reads this but the priest, Captain Bates, who is such good friend to me and finds you for me.

I have tried long time to reach you, now I am so happy. Thank you for all of the help you give me. It seems so long time ago now, yes? I am very sorry for the trouble I make for you. Captain Bates tell me that you are sent away from your work. Now you are in other place, I think, but you work still on the land. That is good.

I think of you so many times. I cannot forget the night we spend together. We were such close good friends, yes? I am in far place now, in Scotland. Very cold, but now I think beautiful when summer comes. Please write to me if you can. I want very much to hear from you. Do not think of me bad things. I know the bombings go on everywhere, but remember you say the war is not for us. It does not come in between us, yes? I pray that you keep safe.

Your true friend,
Holger Fichtmüller.

The lettering blurred as she stared at the piece of paper, brushed at her eyes, then read it through again, slowly. She wanted to start answering him right away. Then guiltily, she saw Julia's letter beside her, tossed aside on the counterpane. Her brain was whirling, her emotions too highly charged to deal with it now. She pushed the bundle of correspondence to the back of her locker, slipped her feet into the soft canvas shoes, and went out quickly into the almost darkness, crossing the yards of gravelled earth to the noisy laughter and the clatter of the dining-hut.

It was quite late when Ruth returned from the dining-hut, which doubled as a recreation space when the evidence of the evening meals had been cleared away. Irene looked up with anticipation, for she had passed a boring evening so far, listening to the wireless, reading through old *Home and Country* magazines, and half-heartedly joining in the conversations eddying around her. The dark-haired girl had already changed into pyjamas and dressing-gown, though it was not yet nine o'clock. She greeted Ruth's arrival with some relief, but swiftly noted her friend's air of dejection. 'You look glum,' she said tentatively. 'I'd have thought you'd be over the moon, hearing from your Jerry chum. You were full of it earlier. What's wrong?'

'This bloody war, that's what's wrong!' Ruth answered, with such vehemence that Irene gazed at her tensely, waiting for her to elaborate. Ruth gave a long sigh that was dangerously near a sob. 'You're right. I was feeling so good. Then I read my letter from home.' Irene did not speak, but continued to wait attentively.

Ruth sat wearily, slipped off her shoes and lay propped back on her pillow. She indicated her small pile of papers, on top of the locker beside her. 'I've had a letter from my sister. My brother-in-law's gone and volunteered for the forces.' She shook her head, gave vent to a sound of disgust. 'The bloody idiot!'

She recalled the hysterical paragraph in Julia's large, rounded, childish hand, which had leapt out at her with the force of a blow, then the whining, martyred tone of the rest of her letter. Yet again, for all the miles that separated them, Ruth felt the overwhelming urge to dig her fingers into her elder sister's hair and shake and slap her until she squealed for mercy. The injustice of her moaning made Ruth's blood boil. At the same time, she felt a sense of frustration and anger towards Bill that was like a choking phlegm in her throat.

Why oh why did he have to become a part of all this huge madness the world was gripped in, that made decent, honest fellows like Holger Fichtmüller and her brother-in-law set out to kill each other? Though, sadly, she felt that she could in large part answer that question, at least as far as Bill was concerned. He had that inbred sense of honour, of outmoded romantic chivalry which was still contained in stirring phrases like 'doing your bit' and 'answering the call'. And which made him and those like him suffer pangs of guilt if they didn't go rushing off to fall for the flag, even though she could hardly imagine a less bellicose person than gentle Bill.

Add to that, the supreme selfishness and blind complacency of Julia, who had always treated him with an attitude of lenient contempt, and the assumption that she must be the centre point of his existence, by natural right. Ruth had no doubt that his position of subordination had been made far worse by the arrival of baby Angela. Though she had not been there to see it, Ruth could imagine all too clearly the extent to which Bill would have been pushed further and further back in his wife's thoughts and attentions.

As though to highlight the foreboding of her own private concerns, someone called for urgent silence, and they listened, stunned, to the measured tones of the news reader announce the loss of one of the Royal Navy's proudest capital ships, the battle cruiser, HMS *Hood*, sunk with 'it is feared, heavy loss of life', in the Denmark Straits.

After lights out, which did not come until nearly eleven o'clock in the relaxed Saturday night atmosphere, Ruth lay listening to the softly murmuring voices all around her, and thought of the emotionally see-sawing day she had endured since receiving her mail. The joy that had swept through her at hearing from Holger, the sickening plunge of spirits at learning of Bill's dangerous foolishness. She felt the wetness on her eyelids, and she fought to muffle the sound of her weeping.

★   ★   ★

'You're sure you won't mention any of this to your pals?' Michael Bates asked, unable to keep the trace of anxiety from his voice. 'I'm not going to start running an illegal mail service for POWs.'

194

Holger grinned wickedly. 'Perhaps they put you in here. One of us.' His expression became serious. 'I give my word.'

Bates could see how anxious he was to get his hands on the letter. The chaplain could not help glancing round quickly to see if they were observed before he slipped the folded paper across to him. Holger pushed it swiftly into his battledress blouse.

'I haven't read it,' Bates said simply. 'She said I could, though. There was a note to me in it. She said she wanted me to know there was nothing underhand or wrong in what she was doing. That's why she left it open. She seems like an eminently sensible young lady. I'd like to meet her some day.'

Holger nodded. 'I also. Again. Some day.' They stared out to the rise of heather-capped moorland beyond the wire, and, above that, the pale sky with its high billows of white cloud. The early June sun was at last warm enough to make overcoats redundant. Several hardy souls were in shirt-sleeves, and one dedicated group, in vests and shorts, was going through a strenuous routine of exercises under the direction of an officer.

The letter was like a magnet in his breast, almost pulling his hand towards it in his eagerness to read it, but he forced himself to continue walking with the padre, and to concentrate on the conversation.

'My comrades are afraid.' He smiled. 'They fear I am becoming — er, religious, you say?'

Michael Bates grinned back, his eyes screwed up in the strong sunlight. 'Wouldn't do you any harm!' The smile faded. 'You heard about the *Bismarck*? Bad business, eh? She put up quite a fight, I gather.'

'And the *Hood*,' Holger said, with belligerent loyalty. Bates checked his stride, looked as though he were about to say something, then shook his head instead. He continued to stroll.

'You must be keen to read your letter. I'll let you get off. I'll collect a reply from you next week, if you like.'

'Yes. Thank you very much, padre. You are very kind.' Holger stopped, held out his hand formally, and Bates gripped it tightly.

As he turned to go, Bates said laughingly, 'Does your girlfriend know? About your new British chum?'

'Of course!' Holger answered a shade defensively, and felt himself colouring. 'Thank you again, padre,' he said, and moved off towards his hut. Everyone was outside at this time of the morning, making the most of the fine weather, and Holger clambered up onto his bunk, anticipation knifing through him like a pain. For several seconds he stared at the unfamiliar script, savouring its neatness, the sense of clarity and purpose the bold roundness of the letters gave. There were two sheets: four pages closely filled with her words.

He lifted the paper to his nostrils, and sniffed. Then his conscience stabbed painfully, for this was what he always did with Heidi's letters, which she doused liberally with her perfume. Guiltily, he lowered the sheet of paper and began to read.

My dear Holger,

I can't tell you how wonderful it was to get your letter after all this time, and to know that you have been thinking about me, as I've been thinking of you, so much. And that's really true. I'm not just saying it. You've been in my thoughts such a lot. Every day. I pray for you every night, too.

It's wonderful of Captain Bates to do this for us, and to think that no one else will read our letters. That's if you want to keep writing to me. I hope you do, because I want very much to keep in touch. I don't know if you would ever have got a letter from me through official channels. I tried to find out where you are, but the army sent a very snotty (nasty) letter back saying no. Then I heard from someone that

Captain Bates's letter had been sent to the place where I worked before but they hadn't sent it on to me. I could have wept (in fact, I did!).

All's well that ends well, though. That's a saying in English, like a proverb. Shakespeare, I think. Your English is wonderful. As good as mine. Not that mine is good. Remember you laughed at the way I speak? My accent. You said it sounded like singing. We call it Geordie, the people where my home is are called Geordies. I hope you can understand my writing a little more easily.

How are you? You can tell me all about your life in the camp, how horrible it is, if you like. Nobody will ever see it except me. Tell me all about yourself. I want to know. What you would do if there was no war. What you and your Heidi plan to do when this is all over. (You see, I haven't forgotten anything you told me!). I remember her picture, how beautiful she is. Will she mind if we write to each other? I don't think she will, but tell me what you think — the truth! I'll try not to be too disappointed if you don't want me to keep on. Just write to me once more, to let me know you've got this.

I'm working in the forest now. Guess

where? Just a few miles from the hut — our hut, where we spent our time together. I went back to see it. I have also visited the grave of your friends, the rest of your bomber crew. They are in the churchyard at Kilbeck. It is very nice and well looked after. They were given a proper military funeral, with honours. It would be nice (sad but nice) if we could go there together some day.

I'd better go now. It is quite late. I live in a hut with fifteen other girls. I'm learning a lot, not all of it good! Sometimes the talk would make an airman blush! Take care of yourself, and please, please try not to be too miserable. I know it must be very hard for you, but try to keep busy and cheerful. It won't last for ever. And remember that I'll be thinking of you, and praying for you. Write soon. God bless.

All my love,
Ruth Palmer X X X

16

'Here! Bugger this for a lark! I've had enough of this!' Norah's face was almost purple. There were large dark patches of sweat under both the arms of the khaki shirt, and another between her shoulder blades. 'Come on girls!' She stood, and tore at the buckle of the belt around her waist and, while her companions watched in shocked and giggling incredulity, thrust the thick breeches down past her solid thighs. Then she sat and tugged off the woollen stockings, and kicked the clinging britches free of her feet. She lay back, waved her bare legs in the air with a fine sense of freedom.

'Damned right!' Irene laughed. She was the first to follow suit, but was swiftly copied by the others, until the whole group had exposed pale limbs and were larking about, their shirts flapping loose around their knees or mid-thighs. The surrounding bushes and piles of wood were festooned with the discarded garments, the heavy, dusty boots lined in friendly rows.

It was worth it, just to see the pop-eyed, outraged stares of the foresters when they came back from the slope where they had been felling.

'God! You'd think they'd never seen a pair of legs before!' Viv Heathcote, the most glamorous of the new batch of girls, said scornfully, and Norah chuckled.

'They haven't! Not like yours, any road!'

They were roused at 5.15 these days, and Harry Guy had them all paraded in the already warming sunlight of the August morning before they dispersed to their various work points.

'We're not running a striptease show!' he announced, ignoring the ironic cheers and staring hard at Norah's grinning, unrepentant squad.

'Too much for the old blood pressure, was it?' someone called out, to a burst of laughter.

'We'll have no more working in underwear, if you don't mind!' he continued sternly. 'I should've thought you lot had a bad enough reputation as it is! The weather's hot, I know, and likely to remain so. So I'm relaxing the rules as far as dress goes. You can wear what you want — as long as it's decent!' he added, loudly, over the yells of delight. 'Shorts are all right! And bare arms! Just don't come whingeing to me if you get cut and scratched all over with splinters and brambles and the like.' He gave them a steady look. 'Won't be the first time for some of you!' he concluded significantly.

The sense of freedom the relaxation of clothing rules gave the girls was worth the covert lechery and the mockery, for the heat in the woods was often stifling as August rolled by. Work, and backbreaking, wearying work at that, took up all the long day, but they were getting used to it. Muscles hardened, limbs tanned, the vigour of their outdoor life was reflected in their glowing health, though the job was not without its very real dangers. The sawmill was where most accidents took place, one or two extremely severe. One girl lost two fingers, another almost died after her forearm was nearly sliced in two by the whirring blade.

Then there were the crushed hands and feet from rolling logs, or the more common strains from the heaving which demanded so much of them. No longer shy of each other's bodies, they stood moaning with pleasure under the streaming showers, arms, necks and legs gleaming ever more ruddily, in contrast with the paler flesh which was not bared to the sunlight; or they waited, patiently or impatiently, buckets clutched vice-like in proprietorial hands, for the slumped figures to surrender the all too brief

202

moments of bliss in the zinc tubs filled with hot water.

Another increasingly important means of escape from the dreary harshness of working life for Ruth was the growing mass of letters she wrote and received from Holger Ficht-müller — one a week since they had first begun corresponding. She wished only to shut out the nightmare surrounding them; the nightmare that was forcing them apart and which dubbed them 'enemies'. An equally disturbing discomfort troubled her every time she took up her pen, or read his increasingly affectionate and intimate words to her. The image of the pretty, smiling girl in the photograph kept bobbing up in her mind.

★　★　★

Are you sure Heidi doesn't mind us writing to each other? she forced herself to write. *I could understand if she was upset about it. A lot of girls would be, I know. It's just that I was so worried about you, and felt — well, that we were close. Special friends, that's all.*

★　★　★

But the conflicting and turbulent emotions she endured as she wrote that last phrase made her feel deceitful, as though she were lying, even to herself.

* * *

I have told you before now, silly girl you are, Holger answered — and she could visualize that gently teasing smile — *that Heidi is not minding at all about our writing. She is very happy for it. She ask me many times to say thank you to you for your kindness and your help.*

* * *

'You're not writing to your Jerry again, Palmer!' Norah exclaimed exasperatedly, eyeing Ruth as she hurriedly began gathering her writing materials scattered over the counterpane.

'Don't be jealous!' Irene smiled sweetly. 'Our Ruthie can't help it if even the enemy fall under her spell, can she?'

'I'd have thought you'd be the one who was jealous!' Norah snapped back cattily, and though Ruth pinked a little, Irene continued to smile serenely.

'Seems a bleeding shame when there's so many of our own lads doing their bit who'd love to have a girl writing to them!' chipped

204

in Beryl Mills, quick to curry favour with the redoubtable Norah.

Ruth refused to rise to the bait, in spite of the anger which seized her chokingly. Again that phrase, 'doing your bit', stuck like a fish-bone in her throat. At once she relived all the unpleasantness of the previous weekend, when she had, at last, made the effort to get up home to Gateshead, with official permission for leave extended to forty-eight hours, which meant she did not have to be back at Allerton until lunch-time on the Monday. She was ashamed of the mixed emotions with which she began the tedious journey. She wanted to see them all again, of course she did. Especially her new niece. Angela was eight months old, Ruth calculated guiltily, and she had not seen her since the first few days of her little life.

But there was, undoubtedly, the less pleasant thought of the atmosphere surrounding Bill's departure — he had been gone more than a month, and was undergoing basic training down in Chatham. So her mother had told her, in one of her regular letters. Julia had not written again, though Ruth had penned a carefully worded answer to that single, outraged cry on paper. Ruth was worried that she would find it too difficult to hold in her own feelings about the matter, when the tirade started. And so it proved.

She did well at first. To be truthful, she was genuinely sorry for Julia. Her sister had not recovered her looks or her figure after Angela's birth, and Ruth was shocked at the extent to which she had 'let herself go'. The stringent diet, and sleepless nights had taken their toll — though the ferocity of the air-raids had died down a lot, there were still regular forays by German bombers, and, as the north-east was the most favoured spot for crossing the British coastline, the sirens wailed with wearying frequency, the all-clear generally not sounding until well into the early hours. The dark shadows about Julia's eyes added dramatically to the expression of bitterness and tragedy which she wrapped herself in.

She could not bring herself to be civil to Ruth, even after such a long separation.

'My God! Look what the wind's blew in!' she said sarcastically to Angela, who was gurgling and bouncing on her knee. As a greeting it did not bode well, and things got no better. Ruth could see that she was deeply hurt, even shocked, by Bill's leaving her. But she was so self-centred, even in her sadness. 'How could he do this to me?' she cried, and all the force of her rage and aggrievement was centred tellingly in that last syllable.

'She hasn't written to him. Not once!' Alice confided to Ruth privately. 'She's had about four from him!' The sense of smouldering resentment seemed to hang over the little house, affecting everyone. Her mother, too, was clearly deeply worried over what might happen to Willy, who had now completed his basic training, in the RAOC, and was in a camp in Wiltshire, working with tanks and waiting to be posted. Bearing all this in mind, Ruth was determined she would say nothing to aggravate the situation, but, sadly, this proved to be impossible.

She lasted out until the Sunday. Her father and Arnold were working as usual, so the traditional ceremonial Sunday dinner was postponed until teatime. They came off shift at four, to a strip-down wash in the scullery and a change into Sunday clothing of dark suits, white shirts — in Arnold's case with fiercely starched collar, and tie. George wrapped his white silk muffler cravat-style about his neck.

He sat magisterially at the head of the table, even though the pitifully small lump of meat before him was a far cry from the fat-sizzling joint of former times. With depressing predictability, the conversation drifted round to the exigencies of the war, and the way it had depleted the family.

'He had no right to desert wife and bairn like that!' Alice pronounced for the ump- teenth time, her tone long since moderated to one of judicious sorrow rather than anger.

'Daft young beggar!' George added, with an air of finality.

'Come off it, Mam!' Ruth was almost astonished herself at the way the words just popped out of her, with so much force.

Her mother sensed the tone of accusation at once. 'What d'you mean?' she bristled.

'Well, it was you lot that practically sent him on his way, wasn't it?' Ruth had a strangely helpless sense of listening to herself, to the quivering emotion which came pouring from her like a burst pipe. 'Making him feel guilty about not being called up like our Willy and the rest! Not doing his bit! I thought you'd have been delighted at him rushing to join up!'

Julia's voice rose with shrill ugliness. 'I thought you wouldn't be able to wait to get your two pennyworth in! You'll be saying it's my fault and all, I suppose for going and getting myself knocked up in the first place!'

'You said it, not me, but if the cap fits!' Ruth had a sudden hysterical urge to burst out laughing. How appropriate! She knew all about caps, now, and about all the other ways of avoiding 'getting knocked up', since she had lived with her colleagues at Allerton.

But Julia's face was suffused with her rage. She had half risen, was leaning over the table, her neck stretched. Ruth could see a tendon, vividly standing out at the side, a vein, swollen and throbbing.

'You smug little bitch! You think yourself so clever, don't you? You couldn't get over the fact that he picked me, could you? You'd've been dropping your drawers faster than that if he'd asked you!'

The rumbling protests from their father were unheeded by both girls. Ruth's face was pale, her nostrils quivering. She thrust forward, too, until their noses were all but touching.

'At least I would have waited until he *did* ask!' she hissed with controlled venom.

Julia gave a short, barking yelp of elemental fury. Her right hand came up to deliver a vicious, short-armed slap to the side of Ruth's face, while her left hand, fingers clawed, dug into Ruth's hair and twisted. Ruth had also reached out, seized hold of Julia's dark locks in both her hands, and they hung forward, arched over the laden table, wrestling and sobbing, until George rose like a referee, and, with a vigorous upward motion, used his own arms to knock them apart.

He pushed Ruth backwards into her seat. Julia's generous breasts hung dangerously near the vegetables as she leaned further, taloned fingers striving to claw at her sister's face, and all but succeeding until George caught her wrists and Arnold belatedly grabbed her about the hips. Between them, they forced her back, too, until she was sitting once more.

The imprint of the blow stood out like a brand. Ruth rubbed at the stinging flesh, the tears streaming.

'No wonder he left you!' she sobbed. 'The way you treated him! You never appreciated — '

'Shut up, you stuck up little cow! You always fancied yourself better than the rest of us! Full of jealousy, that's your trouble. That's why you left, wasn't it? Why you never come home any more! Because you can't stand to see us — me and Bill together. That, and the fact that you think yourself too good for us nowadays, don't you?' She gave a strident laugh, and appealed to the rest of the table. 'Listen to her! Even the way she talks, all posh now! Don't think we haven't noticed, madam!'

She stood, and leaned forward again. Ruth

tensed, and George moved to intervene, but Julia kept her knuckles resting on the cloth.

'Well, you can have him, your precious Bill!' she spat, her face livid. 'I've finished with him! You're welcome to him! You're two of a kind, the pair of you! Gormless, airy-fairy buggers, both of you!'

Ruth stood up, too, trying unsuccessfully to control her crying. She scraped back her chair noisily, squeezing out, ignoring her mother's plea to 'sit down, lass!' Julia's voice pursued her ringingly, with its stinging lash.

'Aye! That's right! Run off back to your toff friends and your cushy country life! You don't belong here no more!'

★   ★   ★

Bates handed over the hardbound copy of the thick novel.

'Dickens. That should keep you going for a few weeks.'

'Thank you.' Holger's hand looked red and raw as he took the book. He could see the pages of Ruth's letter sticking out a little.

'You are getting rid of these, still?' The chaplain asked worriedly. Quickly Holger passed over the folded sheets of his own missive, which Bates stuffed into the outside pocket of his greatcoat. Holger nodded. And

211

it was true now. He read each letter eagerly, as many times as he could, during the first few hours, held on to it overnight, going over its contents greedily again the following day, until he knew it almost by heart, before he steeled himself to consign it to swiftly flaring obliteration in the heavy square stove that stood now at the end of the hut.

At first, he had cheated. He did not want to part with them. Instead, though it pained him and made him feel doubly a treacherous swine, he had hidden them inside Heidi's letters, which were still in their envelopes, bundled on his shelf. But then, in one of the unannounced searches which took place now and then, some zealous soul had actually half pulled out the folded sheets from one of the envelopes carelessly tossed with the rest of his few possessions on the middle of his bunk. The German script on the opening page showed plainly. The guard had not bothered to pull out the letter entirely, or inspect it closely. Otherwise he would have found Ruth's letter inside.

That had caused him to act, nervous with relief, as soon as they were allowed back into the hut. Anyway, he told himself, and the thought made him uncomfortable as usual, if he had kept them, Ruth's letters would by now have greatly outnumbered those of his fiancée, for there was rarely a week when the padre did not have one to pass over to him, whereas Heidi's letters, coming through official channels, were limited to one per month.

And he had enough of those, he thought sourly, to remind him of the long time he had spent in captivity. His second Christmas at the camp was about to be celebrated. He smiled ironically at the word. They were rehearsing hard for the concert to be held on Boxing Night. He was deeply involved, as indeed were many of his fellow prisoners.

The severe weather — was there any other kind in this God-forsaken dump? they joked; even now, as he walked with the padre, the muddy slush of the trampled snow ground beneath their feet — had called a halt to the nefarious schemes set in motion by the escape committee, none of which had borne fruit in the past year. They had even started a tunnel under B-1's own hut. Holger had insisted on taking a turn at the digging, though they practically had to lift him out after a few hours, his knee agonizingly locked, and henceforth he had been relegated to the vital but unglamorous look-out duties. In any case, it lasted less than a week, thanks to some careless distribution of raw, outstandingly fresh earth in the very vicinity of the dig.

They came in and almost took the hut apart. They found the tunnel in less than an hour, but the inhabitants were kept outside for almost twenty-four, then inside for the next twenty-four, before life returned to 'normal'. Except for Wolfgang Deist, who was led off grinning to the cooler for a week, and who came back, with that same bared-teeth grimace flashing through his ragged beard.

The commandant, Major Waller, had taken great pleasure, Holger deduced, though his craggy poker-face remained impassive, in announcing the entry of the USA into the world conflict. Two mornings later, the prisoners had broken into a rousing chorus of 'Rule Britannia, Britannia rule the waves', under the bleak gaze of their captors, in order to let them know that the news of the sinking of *Repulse* and *Prince of Wales* by Japanese aircraft had not gone unnoticed, despite the official censorship. Even Holger had no idea where the clandestine radio-receiver was now, or who operated it.

Their own senior officer had been brashly defiant. 'It's good,' he told them, in his reaction to the news of America's entry into the war. 'They are not ready for it. They have no stomach for a fight. We would have had to take them on later. And they would have had more time to prepare themselves. Some of those fat Yankee Jews must be shitting themselves now, eh?'

The men laughed and cheered loyally, but a number were, like Holger, uneasy. The Russian campaign, which had gone so well throughout the summer months, appeared to have ground to a halt without succeeding in taking Moscow. One of the chaps had received news in a letter from home that hinted at terrible conditions on the eastern front, where he had a brother serving. They need us back home, Holger fretted, suffering badly from a despairing sense of helplessness. Then a letter from Ruth arrived, and was full of that special warmth, that sweetly exclusive world she was wonderfully able to create for them, and he felt guilty at his own sense of frustration.

It wasn't that she didn't let him see into the world that surrounded her. She did — that was the wonderful part. But she did it in such a private, intimate way, that it seemed to add to the closeness of the private bond between them. In this latest one she wrote:

The weather is awful here now. Snow and sleet and rain, then back to snow again. And it isn't even Christmas yet! All the taps were frozen the other day, we couldn't even get a shower or a wash. Not that baths are very popular just now. We must smell pretty awful, if you'll pardon my French, as they say. And you should see the get-ups we wear — underneath our uniforms I mean, to try to keep warm. Coms are all the rage — combinations is the proper name. They are like all in one — vest and long pants that come down to your ankles. They have buttons and flaps so — hark at me! I won't go on, I'm blushing even as I write! But they are very thick and make you itch all over. And very sweaty once you start work.

Aren't I awful going on about such things? I don't mean to be rude. But we certainly look some sights when we're getting ready, usually in the pitch black and freezing cold. I told you about Viv Heathcote — our new 'glamour puss'. She's gorgeous-looking, but even she doesn't shine too much now. Smothered in clothes, and with a cherry-red nose, always runny and sniffing just like the rest of us.

So there we are. Picture us sitting huddled round the stove in our hut last night, coughing and sneezing, and the guard rail hung with all kinds of strange garments that I shouldn't even mention and none of us would want to be seen dead in, by anyone! *All steaming away and adding to the pong of the cigarette smoke filling the room. I don't even smoke and I've got a hacking cough. I suppose it's just as well the place is so draughty or we'd all suffocate.*

We don't take clothes off any more to go to bed. We put them on. Socks, sweaters! I've even started wearing a scarf round my head! What a sight! Bet you're glad you can't see me!

So really, I'm probably not much different to you the way I live just now. I don't mean that of course. Just a silly joke. Don't be cross (angry) with me. I know how hard it must be for you, caged up all the time like that, ordered about from morn till night the whole time. I think about you every night, you know that don't you? Last thing, when I'm in bed. I say my prayers, then I try to imagine you, hope that you aren't too sad, that you have some real good friends, like I have here.

How is the family keeping — and Heidi of course? Send her my love. I hope things are not too bad for her. She must miss you so much. As you do — miss her, I mean.

Holger glanced up, felt the familiar guilt as he saw the bright grin on the photo. The hut was

217

crowded, the weather having driven everyone back inside. A group was gathered round the stove, which they were trying to relight with some illicit material, the ration of logs having been used up. Fresh supplies would not be brought until the afternoon, after the final roll-call. There was a fog of tobacco smoke, the smell of damp clothing, unwashed bodies. The windows letting in the grey light were steamy and beaded with moisture. It was impossible to see out of them. Heidi's grin beamed at him from another world, a world he felt he could scarcely recall.

★　★　★

Heidi first met Gerhard Waldeyer through Ingrid, a girl she had become very friendly with at work. Ingrid was a local girl, and from a similar, comfortable professional background. They began to visit and stay over at each other's houses at weekends. That was how Heidi came to be introduced to Gerhard, a darkly good-looking figure, whose emaciated look of strain and exhaustion only added to the mystique of his attractiveness. He was in his late twenties, and, in his presence, Heidi, who had always considered herself as something of a sophisticate in the limited circles in which she moved, felt little better than an untutored girl, despite her twenty-two years.

He was a cousin of Ingrid's.

'Very clever,' Ingrid assured Heidi, with a mixture of pride and awe. 'He works in Berlin. Something to do with the government. Gestapo, I think,' she whispered. 'He's on sick leave. Something to do with the pressure of his work, they say. He was away somewhere for several months. Somewhere on the eastern front, they reckon, but it's all very hush-hush.'

Heidi was intrigued, and both startled and flattered when he evinced an interest in her. He telephoned one day to invite her to a concert in Dusseldorf. Her mother was scandalized when she told her she had accepted his invitation.

'You can't!' Frau Krempel declared. 'You're engaged!'

'He knows that, Mama!' Heidi answered impatiently. 'It's only a concert we're going to. He hasn't asked me to spend a weekend with him! Do you think Holger would want me to spend my entire life living like a nun?'

'Will Ingrid be there?'

Heidi's cheeks pinked a little. 'Of course. I expect so.'

In her mind she heard that deep, persuasive tone again, as he said, *There's no need to say anything to Ingrid about this. I want you all to myself for a while. It will be our little secret. Are you good at keeping secrets, Heidi?*

She had laughed, trying to sound poised, in spite of her breathless excitement.

'Better than you would guess, Herr Waldeyer!'

'Oh, please! Not so formal. Gerhard will do fine!'

It was a concert of sacred music associated with the coming festival. 'Wear an evening gown' he had warned her. 'We'll go for a bite of supper afterwards.'

She wore the dark-blue dress she had worn for the engagement party. She remembered how smart she had thought it then. Now she stared at her reflection, and her eyes clouded with uncertainty.

'I look such a kid!' she pouted to her irritated mother. 'I want all this braid taken off the front.'

'You do that, my girl, and your bosom will be popping out of it. You look lovely.'

But Heidi took it secretly to Frau Langbein, the dressmaker the family had used for years. The elderly woman was busier than ever altering clothes in these hard times, but Heidi exerted all her persuasive charm.

'Please!' she begged. 'I'll pay something

extra, of course. Only I must have it for Saturday!'

Frau Langbein grumbled, but she did it, and charged Heidi over the odds for it.

When Heidi tried it on in the privacy of her room, she decided it had been well worth it. The bodice had been totally altered, so that it was now daringly low-cut, leaving a great deal of her shapely shoulders and pale breast on show. She would have to make sure she kept her wrap on. And it might be better if she could somehow prevent her parents from seeing it before Gerhard came to collect her, But she was happy that she no longer looked schoolgirlish.

The Krempels could not help but be impressed by the chauffeur-driven car, in these days of strict rationing. Nevertheless, at the first opportunity, Frau Krempel said, 'Heidi's fiancé is a POW, you know. He was a flier. Shot down in Britain in 'forty.'

Heidi was blushing, but Gerhard smiled, said easily, 'I know. She told me. She must be very proud. I am so glad he is safe. He's a very lucky young man.' He gestured smilingly towards Heidi. 'In more ways than one, eh?'

Heidi was anxious to get him away, but he gave the impression that he was in no hurry, that he was enjoying the chance to talk, to enjoy the family atmosphere. It worked, too.

Even Herr Krempel described him later as 'charming'.

'You are doing such vital work nowadays,' he told her father solemnly, standing before him and shaking hands formally. 'I salute you. You carry the torch for our young people.'

Sitting shivering slightly on the cold leather in the back of the car, Heidi felt a little awkward, and tense, after the strain of the last half-hour. 'You don't mind? I mean — you don't think it's wrong of me — being engaged — to be going out with you?'

'Do you?' he replied, probing teasingly. She was glad that in the chilly dimness he couldn't see her face clearly.

'No,' she said defensively. 'Holger wouldn't want — I mean I don't think I should cut myself off completely from everything going on around me. It doesn't do me any good. Or him!'

He took her hand in his, held on to it, patted it lightly. His hands felt smooth, and warm. She recognized how his touch aroused her, and she knew she was blushing even more. 'All I know is I'm very happy that you're here. That I'm sitting next to a beautiful girl. I can't believe it.'

She had difficulty in accepting the reality of events, too, when, afterwards, he took her to the most exclusive restaurant in the city, where he had reserved a table discreetly set in an alcove which assured almost complete privacy. Not that he behaved at all improperly, or even suggestively. Heidi's head swam, with the wine and the unaccustomed exotic food, and, most of all, with the captivating charm which the suave figure centred on her.

From that first evening alone in his company, she found herself fascinated with him. Her conscience pained her. After he had deposited her back at her door, after midnight, with nothing more than a decorous, brotherly peck on her cheek and a humble request to take her for a drive on the morrow, she went up to her room, avoiding, or at least postponing, a postmortem on the night with her mother, who called anxiously from the bedroom. The smiling photo of Holger, and the one of the two of them arm in arm, stared at her accusingly, and she began to cry quietly, angry with herself and her wretched guilt, and even, shamefully, angry with Holger for causing her such grief. I'll write and tell him all about it, she vowed before she tried to settle to sleep, but she did not keep her promise.

★　★　★

Heidi stared around the functional comfort of the room. She had known it would come to this, from the moment she had agreed to come up to the capital for a weekend. Appropriately enough, it was 1 April. And I'm a fool! she mocked herself, but she was helpless against the sweet pain of the excitement that gripped her at the thoughts of the coming tryst. There was a last-minute panic. Only a few nights before the rendezvous there was a bombing raid on Lübeck, a shockingly heavy attack, which did a great deal of damage.

Gerhard had rung her the next day.

'Will it be all right? Will I still be able to travel?' she asked anxiously.

'You have the pass I sent. Yes, it'll be fine. Even more important that we take this chance, my dear. I may be tied up for a while. Looks like the RAF are starting a terror campaign against us.'

He took her to what had been a quietly luxurious hotel on the outskirts of the city. Now it had been taken over for government officials only. Many of the staff appeared to be foreign workers, mostly French. 'They know all about service,' Gerhard grinned. She was almost relieved to note that he, too, was obviously a little tense, though he was better at hiding it than she was.

All at once, there in the explicit intimacy of this anonymous bedroom, she recovered something of her old poise. 'You know I find you very attractive,' she whispered. 'I think I'm in love with you.'

'I'm crazy about you!' he said hoarsely, and his voice shook with his passion. She moved over to him as he sat on the edge of the double bed, and slowly removed her jacket, unzipped her skirt, and let it fall about her ankles. She stepped out of it, eased off her fashionable shoes. She crossed her arms and pulled the silk slip over her head. She gazed down at him, her hands on his shoulders, and he buried his hot face against her perfumed skin, his lips sending shivers of desire throughout her frame.

17

'Listen,' Michael Bates said, a little awkwardly. 'There's a photograph in here. She's sent you her picture.' He tapped his side pocket, where the folded pieces of paper still lay. 'She put it with a note to me. Asking if it would be all right. If I could get it to you.' He saw Holger's face light up, the spark of eagerness. 'You didn't tell me what a looker she was! She's lovely!' He smiled. 'Only it's a bit of a problem, isn't it?'

'Why? What you mean?' Holger asked, looking at him sharply.

'Well. You won't want to destroy it, will you? It's something you'll want to hang on to. And where will you keep it?'

'Please — do not worry.' Holger tapped his own breast. 'I keep it with me always. With my identity. About me. No one finds it.'

'I hope so,' Bates answered significantly. 'We've got ourselves into quite a little conspiracy over these past months, eh?' They quickly effected the transfer of letters, taking care that nobody was observing them. He kept his gaze steadily on Holger as they moved slowly among the idling or walking figures in the sunshine.

'You think a lot of her, don't you?'

Holger looked away, crinkling his eyes against the strong light, watching the blue-green haze up on the distant hills. The summer of '42 had developed into a scorcher. So much space, and freedom, beyond the wire. The wire behind which he had been trapped for two long years.

He could feel himself colouring. 'She is very good. Very nice girl. Special for me.' At last he turned his face back towards the priest, met his look. 'Yes, I like her. Very much,' he said challengingly.

'More than you should?' suggested Bates gently.

'How is that possible? How can you like someone more than you should?' He echoed the chaplain's words even more provocatively.

'You're enemies,' Bates persisted doggedly. 'Your countries are at war. If you were not locked up here, you would be trying to kill her. You would bomb hundreds of people just like her.'

'But I am here!' Holger blazed suddenly, and Bates saw the passion there, felt a breath of the young man's helpless rage. Then his face closed down once more, his voice became sullen, almost like a boy's. 'It is different for us. For she — she is not like

— the war, for her — she does not believe in it.'

'She doesn't believe in your cause!' Bates fired back, more vigorously than he had intended, but Holger merely nodded, with a sad little smile.

'Of course.' His voice was soft. 'She does not believe in the killing. For anyone.'

'And what about your girlfriend? Your fiancée?' Bates pursued, again somewhat taken aback by his own harshness. Especially when he saw the naked pain which flashed for an instant across the young features.

The line of the jaw showed up as Holger clenched his teeth. He opened his mouth, as though searching desperately for words which he could not find. In the end, he subsided hopelessly again. He shook his head. 'Nein. It is — different. With Ruth . . . '

But he knew the priest had unerringly touched the sore of his conscience. Already he recognized the shaking of his fingers as he took out the letter as soon as the chaplain had left him, how his heart thumped as he fumbled between the folded sheets to extract the photograph. And there she was. Ruth. Smiling enigmatically, that exquisite hint of shyness, of vulnerability. He pulled himself up short, staring almost in awe at her picture.

The chaplain was right. She was a 'looker'.

This beautiful girl smiling out at him seemed almost like a stranger. Self-contained, mysterious. Apart. Not like the girl he had shared those precious hours with, in the hut in the forest.

Intrusively into his mind came the portrait of Heidi, her blondly sunny smile, her tempting figure in the flowered summer's dress, and it sickened him to compare their fair and dark beauty. But he could not help himself. Perhaps you could get the lads to vote. Which one would be the winner? Your fiancée? Or the little English piece?

He had received the monthly letter from Heidi a few days ago. He knew it more or less by heart already, even though he didn't have to toss it into the stove. He still even held the scented pages to his nostrils for a while, to savour their perfume.

I hope you won't mind, or be angry, or anything — he smarted with self-loathing at the pathetic aura of guilt which hung about her innocent confession — *but I've been up to Berlin again, to stay with those relations of Ingrid. The ones who have such high connections. I had a good time. We even went to the theatre, there are some wonderful plays on at the moment. And the food! It just shows what you can do if you're in the know!*

And now I feel so bad even telling you about it. There! There's a tear-stain, see it? I cry for you my darling, and for my own rotten weakness in even thinking I could enjoy myself without you beside me. Oh God! I wish we could be together. Sometimes I ache so fiercely for you, it's really like a torture to me. I miss you so much! I know I should be strong, and be trying to cheer you up. What a selfish bitch I am! When you come home, I swear I won't allow you out of my sight, not even to go to work.

There was more, in a much more physically intimate way which shamed him even as his body reacted excitedly to it. He must tell her the truth. And what was that? That he was in love with an English girl he had known for one night; whom he had once kissed and held, and in whose arms he had cried like a baby? And with whom he had done nothing more — except talk, and sleep beside, and feel closer to than any other person he had known. Closer than Heidi? Whose body he knew, so well, had made love to, in reality, and in his fevered imagination over so many long, weary, solitary nights since?

Holger headed for a spot near the first low

trip wire edging the compound, where he could be at least several yards from his nearest neighbours. He was looking forward keenly to his escape from his surroundings as he immersed himself in Ruth's latest letter. More and more, he had felt the urge lately to try and tell her at least of the depth of his emotions concerning her. Perhaps it would help him to clear it in his own mind if he did so. But still he held back, afraid that she would be deeply shocked and dismayed if he revealed how he felt. How could she possibly understand? They had spent scarcely more than a day together. He had created a beautiful fantasy, out of words on paper. And now a picture. He stared again at the hesitant, uncertain smile. He was shocked at himself and at the strength of feeling that stirred in him as he gazed at the picture.

★   ★   ★

Heidi watched Gerhard's reflection in the mirror as he came up behind her. She reached up, twisting her neck offeringly as he bent down and placed his lips on her fragrant skin. His fingers delicately slipped the thin straps of the cami-knickers off her shoulders, eased the lace-rimmed edging of the ice-blue silk down, helping her breasts out of the

231

confines of the garment. The small nipples blossomed to erection under his caress, and she shivered. She reached up her left arm, let it drape around his stooping shoulder.

'This is the only part of the evening I've been looking forward to.' She reached out with a pointed toe and kicked at the shining, ugly band of the corset she had just discarded, and the twin, snaking stockings, dropped in a small pile on the carpet. 'That thing was killing me!' she pouted. She let her hand fall between their bellies, stroked the bulge of his penis beneath the cloth of his trousers. 'You know what I want!' she whispered lewdly. 'What I've been waiting for all night long!'

He began to roll the folds of silk down, below her midriff to the slight swell of her hips.

'Wait!' she commanded urgently, and wriggled free, bending, not bothering to hide herself as she reached under her crotch and undid the three little buttons. 'There! Your turn, darling!' She stood, waiting in silence, while he tore off his clothing, waiting for him to gather her up, an arm behind her knees, another under her shoulders, to carry her the yard or so to the bed. 'Don't use anything — please!' she said fiercely, as he spread himself alongside her. 'No sheath! It'll be all right. I promise. I don't want anything — I just want to feel you inside me. Your love for me.'

'I don't care!' he declared hoarsely. 'It's only to protect you! I want you so much. Want you to be my wife. Want you to bear my children!

'You have to tell him, darling,' Gerhard told her gently as, later, they lay propped up on the pillows, their sated bodies covered with blankets. He flicked the ash from his cigarette into the ashtray, which lay across his stomach. 'And I'm going to speak to your folks. I can't wait any longer. We can be married next month.'

Her eyes, large and troubled, rested on his. 'I know,' she nodded ashamedly. 'But, it's just — I don't know what it'll do to him, poor boy. Wouldn't it be better to wait? I mean to tell him,' she added hastily. She reached over, pressed the stub of the cigarette into the tray, feeling it sink on the yielding softness of his body beneath the sheets. She kissed his shoulder gently. 'I want to go ahead. I'm just the same. I can't wait to be married to you.' She grinned impishly, looking very young suddenly, and patted her stomach. 'And be put up the spout by you!' Then the troubled expression resumed sway. 'But Holger doesn't have to know. Not right now. Even if we are

233

getting married. It'll break his heart, I just know it will!'

Gerhard shook his head, frowning. 'But it isn't right, is it, love? I'd hate the thought of us going ahead with him over there still thinking you belong to him. I'm sure he'd rather know than be deceived. And one day he's going to have to. Imagine how he'd feel then. 'Oh, by the way, I got married a while back. I have a lovely baby boy. I'm sorry'. I mean to say, it's just not on. Is it?'

'I suppose you're right,' she sighed. Suddenly, the world outside this comfortable room pressed in on her like shadows. The bombing was becoming truly frightening. Not even Berlin was safe. There were such shortages, so many things were difficult.

She felt guiltily uncomfortable when she thought what a vital difference her relationship with Gerhard had made to her life — and that of her family. Mummy and Daddy must know by now that her attachment to the government official was less than innocent — and more than simple friendship. But they said little. Accepted his gifts, his influence. Welcomed him warmly when he made his infrequent trips to Remscheid. He was right. It was time for them to act, to put their relationship on its proper footing.

And it wasn't as though she didn't love him. She was crazy about him, she was ready to admit it, to anybody. Except Holger, her wicked conscience goaded her. But tears came to her eyes every time she contemplated the hurt she would cause him. She felt she was not being melodramatic when she thought that it might even prove fatal. That he might be driven to do something desperate enough to put his life into mortal danger. Or maybe just let himself sink, lose the will to carry on the struggle to survive altogether. His letters sounded dispirited enough already, as though it were sometimes a real effort for him to put his mind to writing at all.

This damned war. Everybody pretending to be so cheerful, still. According to official reports, everything was going swimmingly. Marshal Rommel was still driving the British Eighth Army steadily back in North Africa; the Russian front had got moving again, with the passing of winter — the army had pushed as far as the River Don, having captured Sebastopol. But it was dragging on and on. No one could feel safe, not even here on German soil, in his, or her, own bed. You had to make the most of every opportunity, seize every moment.

The thought inspired her to reach out, under the bedclothes. He turned to her, grinning as they wriggled down once more. 'Careful, darling. Remember, I'm not a youngster like you! I'll be thirty next birthday. I can't — '

She turned towards him, lifting and wriggling, parting her legs to make herself available. 'You do believe, don't you? With Holger — we never — went all the way. No one's ever — made me feel . . . ' She sighed, thrust herself at him, letting the language of body and blood take over from the cloudiness of unsure words.

★   ★   ★

'That's shaken them! This could be the start of it now, eh?'

The girls were elated when they first heard the news that a landing had been made at Dieppe, and an attack carried out. 'Operation Jubilee' showed that we could carry the fight to the enemy, on territory he had claimed for his, and not only in the air. Announcement of the raid came almost at the same time as they learned of 'Winny's' visit to Moscow, for a meeting with 'Uncle Joe' Stalin. Although the girls were working practically all the daylight hours, and were awaiting any day the switch from forestry to the equally exhausting task of harvesting on the local farms for the next few weeks, their bellowed choruses of 'Run Rabbit' took on an additional heartiness.

It was several days before their optimism received a nasty dent as news of a different nature began to filter through, not all of it from official sources, or the press.

'Canadians took a right bashing,' Harry Guy told some of the girls soberly. 'Lost a lot of men. A lot taken prisoner, too. Over two thousand, they reckon.' As though to underline the sudden mood-swing, the next thing of note which they learned from the communal wireless set was the death of the Duke of Kent, on active service.

'We should chuck that bloody thing out!' Norah Graham grumbled. There was a distinct air of gloom as the girls settled down, most of them in their night clothes, for the last hour before lights out. 'What's up with you, you stupid cow?' She rounded on the dark-featured Beryl, who had just brought Norah her final mug of tea, and was sitting like a family pet at the foot of the blonde's bed, in her vast men's striped pyjamas, with sleeves and trouser-begs turned back in thick rolls. Beryl was sniffing loudly. 'Was he a mate of yours, or something?'

Ruth was already in bed. She had spent the last hour over in the rec hut with her writing-case, and she had Holger's latest offering in front of her now. It had both puzzled and disturbed her a great deal, and did so again, as she read it through for the umpteenth time. *Do not worry if I cannot write for some time. I expect to be busy. But remember, always I think of you and that you are very dear. My dearest friend.*

She blushed a little, ashamed of the deep-seated pleasure the emotive force of the words, their implied message of the depth of his feeling for her, gave to her. But then anxiety flooded back. Why could he not write? What was there in the dreariness of prison existence that could take up so much of his time that he could not write? A task that he enjoyed so much, he had told her often. His escape from the unending monotony of day after day with nothing worthwhile to do. Were they moving him? Was he being punished somehow?

She smiled across at her friend. She lifted the sheet of paper, shook it gently.

'I wish I could get to see him. Just once.' Her voice dropped slightly. It carried a hint of shy confession. 'I feel that close to him. We've been writing for over a year now, you know. Dozens of letters. And yet we've never met up. I'd love to.'

★ ★ ★

The tunnel was discovered in August. There was a collapse while two men were down there, and in the panic to get them out, the guards became suspicious at the activity around the ablutions hut. Despite the desperate efforts by Holger and the others planted around outside to delay them, the guards entered and found what was going on. It was just as well, some argued philosophically. The two diggers might well have suffocated before their comrades could have extricated them.

The cells of the punishment block were packed to capacity and beyond, but only for three days. It wasn't worthwhile, the commandant, Major Waller, decided. There were other ways to punish. He decided on a general shake-up, throughout the camp, which now contained over two hundred prisoners, for some naval personnel had been added to the Luftwaffe contingent. The huts were almost torn apart. Billets were rearranged, so that familiar room-mates no longer lived together. The veterans of Hut B-1 were scattered to the winds. Obstinately, they continued to stick together. They even conducted their own parade, after morning roll-call.

But the mood of dejection hung over everyone. The weather was wonderful now. In a couple of months or so, it would be foul once more, and would entrap them in this remote place far more effectively than all the wire and the guards which surrounded them. Holger felt more and more withdrawn, inward looking. One day, he actually got as far as writing to Heidi:

> *Look, I don't know how to do this without hurting you — there isn't any way — but I can't go on letting you believe that things are the same between us. Feelings change, and we've been apart so long. There's this English girl. I should have told you about her — properly, I mean. She's the one who helped me when I first landed here. We've been writing. For a whole year now. I feel close to her. I'm sorry, Heidi, but I can't go on calling myself your fiancé.*

He sat there, breathing heavily, as though he had been running. He read through the paragraph again, then, with a muffled cry of anger at his own weakness, he crumpled up the sheet savagely, crushing it in his fist. Jesus! I want to get out of here! He was shaken to feel how close to tears he was.

The next day, Ernst Schmidt sought him

240

out after the morning parade. Holger was surprised. Schmidt was a quiet, reflective fellow. A loner. His appearance was youthful, his frame slender and manner studious. His words startled Holger even more than his abrupt approach.

'I want to talk. I have my own plan. Nobody knows. But it'll work, I'm sure. I don't want to put it up to the committee. They'll only say no — or pinch it. We can get out. And soon. Will you listen?'

Holger grinned, masking his surprise, 'I've got no pressing appointments, as it happens. Let's stroll, shall we?'

The quiet voice went on, 'The ambulance truck brings supplies in to the sick bay. It always comes in the morning. About once a fortnight, but on different days. I don't know whether that's deliberate or not. But that doesn't matter. I've been assigned orderly duties over there because of my medic training. I can be around there a lot of the time without rousing suspicion. I've already had a good look at the truck. It's quite big. A three tonner. There's room for two of us to hide underneath. We'll have to hang on tight. But they don't do a really thorough search at the gate. Just a glance, that's all.'

'But it's no good if we don't know when the truck's going to be there,' Holger argued.

'It's always in the diary. In the sick bay office. I've seen it. They know a few days before. I can find out.'

'But even if we knew, how the hell could I get over there? We're not allowed anywhere near the sick bay.'

'What if you were already in there? As a patient? A trip to the bog — then, through the window and we're away!'

Holger felt his heart quicken. 'My God, yes!' he muttered softly, excitement dawning. 'My knee — I could make it worse — '

'We don't want you crippled!' Ernst protested. 'No. Stomach pains are best. Start complaining the day before we go. We should know at least a day in advance. Tell them you're puking blood. They daren't take a chance on your having an ulcer. They'll have you in the sick bay that night.'

'What about papers? And gear?' Holger asked.

'I think we should just take our chance!' Ernst said. 'We're right on the coast here. No more than a mile or two. We could find a boat, just shove off. See where we land up. Holland, maybe. Maybe a U-boat will find us!'

'I'm game!' Holger said tightly. He glanced at the thin face. 'Why me?' he asked, with real curiosity.

Schmidt coloured a little. 'I don't want to be mixed up with the committee and all that crap. You seem like someone who can keep his mouth shut.' He paused, went on with breathy embarrassment. 'I'm a bit nervous of going out alone. The two of us stand a better chance.'

★ ★ ★

They went at the end of the month. 'It's coming on Thursday!' Ernst said, his unsteady voice betraying his nervousness. 'Start complaining of stomach pains tonight. They'll have you in tomorrow morning at the latest. As long as you stick to your story. Puking blood and all that. I'll have some gear ready. Civvy clothes. I'll pass by the window when the truck's here. Try to time it as close as you can. It usually stays an hour or so. Go for a shit after half an hour. Your clothes'll be in the second cubicle. I'll try to make sure no one else goes in that one. I'll have unhooked the window. Be careful. It's tiny.

'Straight out, it's only five feet or so. Truck's parked round the side, you turn right. Remember — to the right of the fuel tank. Loop the belt round the tailpipe. Your feet'll fit into the metal struts. I'll follow, soon

243

as I can. You'll have to hold tight to me. Hold me on.'

Amazingly, though every fraught, heart-thumping second was a nightmare of tension, everything went as they planned, to the moment when, on the Thursday morning, Holger lay stretched out less than a foot above the wet grass, clinging on for dear life to the filth-encrusted underside of the medical truck, and suddenly Ernst was there, his body rolling frantically from the line of daylight into the dimness. Holger felt his shivering form fit with a lover's tightness into his. They tried to stop the thunder of their breathing. Minutes stretched out to an eternity

'Why don't they bloody go?' Holger breathed, his lips touching Ernst's ear.

Then there was real thunder, and choking fumes, the metal to which they clung shook and throbbed, and they closed their eyes, sick and disoriented as the ground flew past with increasing speed inches from their bodies. Another stop, interminable it seemed. They were at the gate! Holger held his breath, prayed and prayed. He was drenched in sweat.

They were off again, this time in a madly lurching, bucking ride that threatened at every jolt to dislodge them from their perch.

Mud and stones flung against them, as the truck laboured over the rough track that followed the course of the glen towards the high road. They had known all along that they would not be able to hang underneath the vehicle for any great length of time. All they needed was to put a safe distance between them and the camp.

Ernst had discovered in his innocent dealings with the English guards and the medical orderlies that the metalled road was three miles to the north of the camp. They had decided that they must release themselves from the lorry some time before it reached this road. When Holger felt it slow swayingly down as it negotiated both a bend and a slight incline, he furiously tore his wrists free of the knotted belt, and brought his knees up savagely into the backs of Ernst's thighs. They hit the rocky surface of the centre of the track, oblivious to the buffeting blow as they struck the ground, and immediately rolled, one to the left, the other to the right, to clear the track.

Holger lay gasping like a fish behind some spiky tussocks of grass, the white clouded sky spinning giddily over him. He felt a stinging pain, high on his wrist, and stared at it, seeing the long red mark, blistering slightly, utterly at a loss to explain it, until he suddenly remembered, vividly, the burn of the exhaust pipe as he had struggled to free himself of the belt. He lifted his head, saw the dark truck still battling along the narrow track, small with distance. 'Stay down!' he hissed.

Its motor faded. He scrambled up. 'Come on!' There was a steep natural gully. A stream, no more than a foot or two wide, flowed noisily through it, and they ran, stumbling, sobbing for breath, over the rough tussocks and boulders, following its course to where it veered sharply upwards, towards the brow of the high slope which reared over them. 'That's it!' Holger wheezed. 'We're all right. Take a breather!' Only now was he aware of the stabbing pain in his knee. What worried him, far more, was this breathlessness, the pain of his agonized lungs. Christ! I'm so unfit! he thought. Then he stared up at the vast sky all round them, the wild solitude of the landscape. Hysteria bubbled up, and he began to laugh and cry at the same time. For the first time in two long years he was free.

'We did it!' he screamed.

He looked at the slim form stretched out beside him. Ernst sat up. There were smears of soot and dirt across his features. Tears sparkled on his lashes, too. They both began to laugh together, the laughter shaking their bodies in great gusts, then they clasped each other tightly, hugging, and fell back, arms still locked, among the stones and the tall, rushy grass.

18

'What's this then? We got company, girls. Make sure you're decent!'

The girls straightened up, with an assortment of sighs and groans, glad of the excuse to stop, for whatever cause. Hands went to the small of the back, shoulders were flexed, others wiped the film of sweat and dust, which seemed to coat them in a thick mask during the backbreaking task. They were working on a farm on the far side of Skinnerdale from the Allerton Woods, high up the dale, near the road that linked the village with the coast road running to Whitby.

There was a black car parked by the gate, and a group of men were making their way across the field towards the clatter of the big thresher. Two were in khaki, one in civilian clothes. The other Ruth recognized as the village constable. Ruth felt her stomach give a lurch, then go hollow as if it had been sucked out of her. Her brain spun crazily. She had been here before. The constable had that same look of solemnity. He stepped forward, mouthing against the roar and rattle of the machinery, waving at her, and, jelly legged,

Ruth jumped down, followed him through the pale spikes of stubble away from the noise.

'Ruth Palmer?' the man in the civilian suit asked, with that impassive look of official-dom. 'We'd like you to come with us, if you would. Now, please'

She glanced round helplessly. Everyone had stopped work, several of the girls were already coming over to join them.

'What is it, Ruth? Everything all right?' Viv Heathcote came across. Even in her sinking dismay, Ruth noticed the fractional lifting of eyebrows, the quiver of response, that Viv's tall figure drew. Living up to their reputation, the girls had turned out for their work in the still warm September sun in a variety of gear, mostly of non-regulation origin and minimal concealment. Viv wore an almost sleeveless blouse of cheesecloth material, fine enough to give a misty hint of the brassiere beneath, whose admittedly plain top had in any case been peepingly on view until, tardily, she did up the blouse's top buttons with her grubby fingers. She had on a pair of brown shorts, and it was their brevity which caused the perceptive tremor to pass over her male audience. Their height on her thigh allowed an unencumbered display of her long, brown, scratched and dusty, yet undeniably magnificent legs.

Irene's shorter figure appeared. She pushed through to Ruth's side. 'What's up?' Nominally, she was in charge of the group, though she took an easy-going, thoroughly democratic attitude towards her responsibility.

'It's about Holger, isn't it?' Ruth said quietly.

The man in the suit held the impassive set of his features. 'We want to ask you some questions, Miss Palmer. If you wouldn't mind.'

Ruth glanced down helplessly at her own grimy form, the brown shorts, the dust-stained feet in sandals. 'But I'm — I need to change — '

'We'll go back to the camp,' the man said.

'Just a minute! You can't just take her away like this! Who are you? What's — '

'It's a Home Office matter, miss. I'm Detective Inspector Southam. Miss Palmer won't come to any harm. We won't interrupt your vital work any further. We may need to talk to you later,' he added significantly. Ruth had already begun to move away, painfully aware of all the curious stares directed at her.

It was just as bad at the camp. One of the two soldiers — the one with the two pips on his shoulders, a lieutenant — stood self-consciously outside the shower hut while she cleaned up, then on the veranda while she quickly changed into her best uniform. She could see his shadow falling in across the oblong of sunlight through the open doorway. He ostentatiously turned his back. She scrambled quickly into her clothes, too distracted and anxious to be really embarrassed.

She was sitting lacing her shoes when the inspector came in.

'Better pack a few things, miss. Change of underwear. Toothbrush, night things. Just in case.' In case of what? Ruth wondered. She'd done nothing wrong. Unless they'd decided that communicating at all with a German was a crime. Perhaps it was. It must be, for what else had she done? The worst thing was, they wouldn't tell her anything.

The camp was practically deserted, except for Mr Ross and his helpers in the kitchen. Ruth looked around at the familiar scene. From the sawmill came the buzz and whine of the machinery. Everything looked so normal, so everyday.

'Where are you taking me? Am I under arrest?'

The detective shook his head. 'No. You're being taken in for questioning. Under the Emergency Powers Act. Lieutenant Singleton's here because at the moment we're not sure whether this comes under military jurisdiction or not. We're taking you into Whitby. To start with. The station there.'

They had lost the village bobby on the way. Ruth sat in the back, wedged between the inspector and the lieutenant, while the other soldier, a sergeant, sat in front, beside the police driver.

'Please! Won't you tell me what this is about? Is it because of my letters? I've been writing to him, that's all. I didn't know that was wrong. I felt sorry for him.' She sniffled, dug down, and felt the policeman squirm accommodatingly as she fished for her handkerchief and extracted it from the pocket of her britches.

The lieutenant looked across at the inspector, raised his eyebrows, and Inspector Southam gave a little nod. He took a notebook from his suit.

'That's Holger Fichtmüller, is it?' He rattled off Holger's rank and service number. Ruth shrugged helplessly.

'I don't know about all that. But yes. That's him. I — '

'How'd you find him? How did you get letters to him?'

Ruth blushed. 'No — I . . . ' She paused, horribly conscious now of just how guilty and evasive she sounded. She thought of Michael

Bates, his kindness and concern. His friendship for Holger. 'It was — through a friend,' she stammered.

'So you didn't send them to the camp? Officially — through channels?' he probed.

She shook her head miserably. 'No. Through a friend,' she repeated hopelessly.

'This friend!' He gave the word heavy, condemnatory significance. 'And who might he be? How did he pass the letters on?'

She swallowed, sniffed. 'I'd rather — I don't want to cause any trouble. He was just — '

'Don't muck about!' Inspector Southam said, so sharply that she flinched. 'You've already caused enough trouble!' He echoed her words with biting sarcasm. 'You could find yourself on a very serious charge, young lady. We've already heard quite a bit about you. Thought you would have learned your lesson last time, helping that Jerry the way you did!' His voice was growing louder, harsher, all the time, flaying her. 'You were bloody lucky not to end up behind bars then! And now — lo and behold, we find you're up to your old tricks again! Love Nazis, do you? Like to see them over here, would you?'

'No!' she cried. Her head went down, and she began to cry in earnest, great sobs that sent her shoulders heaving. Then she stiffened in shock as she felt the lieutenant's hand fall heavily on her trousered thigh.

'Come on, Ruth!' the officer said encouragingly, his deep voice softer, avuncular. His hand was still on her thigh, transmitting a different message. 'I'm sure there's an innocent enough explanation. But the inspector's right. We have to know what's been going on. And we'll find out, too. It might take a bit longer, cause a bit more fuss, waste a few more precious man-hours. You don't want that, do you? You're a decent girl. You're doing your bit.' He let his hand slide up and down the corded breeches, patted her knee, to indicate her uniform, and what it stood for. She made a great effort, sat forward, blew her nose vigorously into her handkerchief. She made to cross her legs, knowing there wasn't really room for such a manoeuvre in the confines of the crowded car, but he got the message and let his hand fall away from her.

'We'll wait till we get to the station,' Inspector Southam declared portentously. 'Give you a chance to think things over. Reflect on your situation, like. All I'd say is the truth would be best, my girl. As the lieutenant says, it'll all come out, one way or the other.'

She could feel the heat bouncing from the tarred surface of the police yard. Already, she

254

felt hot and sticky in the thick clothing. As they mounted the steps, she could see away to the right the whole stretch of the river-mouth, the porcupine masts of the fishing fleet inside the twin piers, and, across the narrow estuary, the shimmering ruins of the abbey, and the solid church beside them. A pleasantly cool whisper of breeze ruffled her neck like a tender farewell before she stepped through the double doors into the dimness inside.

They left her briefly in a cell. She sat on the edge of the wooden bench fixed to the wall, and stared about her at the brick walls, painted a sickly pale yellow which changed halfway up to a bilious green. The lower surface around the shelf-type bed was scratched with a dozen or more sad little epigraphs, mostly just initials and dates, here and there a pathetically carved obscenity. A heavy black drape was pulled permanently across the small window high in the wall, making the harsh glare of the naked bulb overhead a necessity.

It was only later that it occurred to Ruth that they had left her in there deliberately, to frighten her. Then they returned, to question her in earnest, at great length. She finally gave them all the details of Captain Bates and his role in their communication, and handed over the thick bundle of Holger's letters, which she had wisely brought along with her. She had somewhat warmed towards the lieutenant, despite the repressed lechery she had sensed in his earlier touch in the car. His veneer of sympathy was preferable to the downright contempt and hostility of his civilian counterpart.

It was the lieutenant, who, finally, told her the reason behind the interrogation. 'Your Jerry friend did a bunk, my dear, that's what's wrong!' he said with a trace of good-humoured reproof in his deep voice. He stood over Ruth, who was sitting head bowed over the wooden table. He touched her again, this time letting his fingers grip and dig into her shoulder, in a gesture that, once more, could be interpreted as merely friendly. 'Oh, don't worry. He's been picked up again. And the pal that went with him. But we wondered, you know. If he had any outside help or something.' He chuckled. 'Especially when we found your pretty little picture in his wallet. And your love and kisses plastered all over the back of it.' He released his hold, moved away again.

Her head went down, on her folded arms, and she wept desolately. The inspector stared impassively, then pushed back his chair with a loud scrape.

'When you've finished blubbing, you can

write it all down. Everything you've told us, and anything you've left out. It's all right. We're all men of the world.' He laughed.

'And we all know what you land-girls are like! We'll have a look through these love-letters from your boyfriend. We'll be back in a while.'

Outside, he turned affably to the lieutenant, jerked his head back towards the closed door of the interview room. 'Reckon that's it,' he said decisively. 'Didn't think there was anything to it, I must admit.'

Singleton shook his head. 'We'll take her through to Catterick. Keep her there for the night. If that's all right with you, of course.' He paused. 'Pretty little thing, isn't she?'

Inspector Southam turned, raised a comic eyebrow. 'Fancy your chances there, do you? Well, she'll be keen to make amends, I daresay. And you know what Maxie Miller says about 'Mary from the Dairy'!'

★   ★   ★

Holger jerked awake, his heart thudding as the bright light pierced his eyes. In spite of the cold, and the ache of every muscle, exhaustion had driven him into a well of dreamless sleep. The reality of his surroundings descended smotheringly over him. The cold chink of the manacles at his wrists and feet smote into his consciousness.

'Come on, sunshine. Get your clothes on. You're going home, my son!'

One guard stood, his rifle pointing, while his companion unfastened the steel contraptions at wrists and ankles. Holger's clothes were stiff with dirt but he pulled them on with swift gratefulness. Home! The word rang with cruel mockery in his brain. He could see only too clearly how utterly naïve their initial optimism had been in those first heady hours of freedom.

'We've got to head eastward!' Holger had urged, as soon as they had put some distance between themselves and the track. But his knee slowed them down alarmingly, and, even in the splendid summer weather, the rugged nature of the rolling countryside made the going tougher. They knew that they were several miles north of the camp. 'We could probably steal a boat there,' Holger surmised. 'It's quite a big place.' On the other hand, it would be easier if they could come across some tiny fishing village. They could lie low until after dark, then sneak down and take something. The smaller and simpler the better, for neither of them could claim to be sailors of even average skill.

'All we have to do is get something that

doesn't sink!' Ernst argued positively. 'And we'll head away from this stinking island!'

It would be a race against time, Holger knew. 'It can't be long before they find out we've gone. Or at least I have,' he reasoned. 'Half an hour at the most. They'll have an alert out by now.'

'That's why we should be careful about Aberdeen,' Ernst said. 'They'll be looking out for us on the roads, and all the nearby towns.'

Holger gestured at the wild beauty surrounding them. 'Can't be many of those.'

They struck out across country, eastward, in what they hoped was a direct line for the coast. It was almost four o'clock before they were looking down from the bracken-covered slope above the tiny hamlet of Invercraig. There were four small fishermen's cottages, under the lee of the hill, where a stream opened out into the beach. Several small cobles were hauled up on the sand in front of them. Nets were draped around wooden posts, and a high pile of lobster-pots rose to one side. Two or three dogs were sleeping, some small children grubbing in the mud and dirt.

'Let's keep out of sight!' Holger said, again aware of a sensation of alarm sending his heart rate soaring. 'We'll wait till after dark.'

They retired back over the brow of the hill,

crouched in a nest of undergrowth, watching the sky fade to a delicately beautiful wash of colours as the sun sank over the land. Before it was dark, they heard the noise of a vehicle's engine, and distant shouts.

'Sounds like a lorry,' Holger hissed, keeping his voice low. 'It's not a car.'

'Perhaps they've come to collect the catch,' Ernst suggested. 'Should we take a look?'

Holger shook his head. 'Not worth it. Let's wait till it gets dark. All we want is a boat.' His stomach felt hollow, but it was not hunger. He tried a brave smile, reached out and lightly punched Ernst's arm. 'We're nearly there!'

★ ★ ★

They were caught at the very instant they stepped from the shadows on to the softness of the sand. Silent black shapes seemed to spring from the very ground all around them. Blows rained down, vicious jabs from rifle butts that made them yelp, then gasp for breath at the agonizing pain about their shoulders and backs as they curled into a ball, squirmed on the sand. They were manacled, flung into the back of a covered truck, forced to lie prone, huddled together on the bouncing floor for what seemed like a long journey over rough roads. They were bundled out, groaning and scarcely able to move, prodded into a brightly lit hut, in some sort of camp.

The figures around them were threatening enough, dehumanized by the black dirt smeared liberally over their faces. Two of them stayed with Holger. They put their guns aside and closed in on him, beating him severely about the body for a few, endless minutes, to leave him slumped, sobbing breathlessly, in a corner.

An officer came, and stood while his assailants stripped him of his clothes, then he was forced down onto a chair and questioned.

'Not too hard to find, were you, Fritz? You were seen by a local crossing the moors hours ago. Only place you could be heading for. Honestly! You might have given us a bit more of a game. Now then.'

One of the guards stood behind, and at his slightest hesitation, often because, in his pain and anxiety he could not properly understand the questions, this individual struck him hard across the back of the neck. The officer took his wallet, the false papers. He took out Ruth's photo, and his face registered considerable surprise. He flipped it over, read the inscription on the back.

'Who the fuck is this?' he asked softly.

19

'You're to report to Edinburgh. You'll be taken there under escort. There'll be an inquiry. Court Martial, I shouldn't wonder.' Major Waller stood himself, turned from his desk to look out through his office window at the roll of white hills. Michael Bates was still standing stiffly at the other side of the desk. He had not been invited to sit down. 'I must say I'm deeply disappointed in you, Padre. You must know how badly you've let the side down. I still can't believe you had anything to do with this business — '

'I knew nothing about it!' Bates declared emphatically. 'I had no idea he was planning an escape.'

'I hope not. Still — all this time. Passing messages back and forth. Between him and his little land-girl tart. Who knows what they could have concocted?'

'Both their letters were always left open for me to read.'

Major Waller grunted, his eyebrows gave a sardonic twitch. 'Huh! Enjoy playing Cupid, did you? Give you a bit of a thrill?'

Bates decided to ignore the innuendo. 'I

suppose it was a daft thing to do. But they'd been trying to get in touch with each other for months. It obviously meant a lot — to both of them. I should've known compassion would come way down on the list of human qualities at times like this,' he could not help adding bitterly.

The major grunted again. 'This is war, for God's sake! And that's exactly what I mean. Surely you don't need me to tell you just how evil Adolph and his thugs are? I dunno. Makes you wonder sometimes whose side you blasted clerics are on. This new archbishop — Temple. Sounds a bit of a bolshie. And as for this other feller — what's his name? This Bishop of Chichester — '

'George Bell.'

'That's it! Fine example he shows! Shooting his mouth off about the RAF raids. As though it's wrong to go and bomb Germany. After all we've been through!'

'If it was wrong for Hitler to bomb the cities, then surely it's wrong for us to do the same thing!'

'They've asked for it, haven't they? Besides, it's not true. We're going for military targets. More bloody fools us!'

'That's not what I've heard. It's blanket bombing. We can't be that accurate — '

'Well, you can argue the toss with HQ.'

Waller moved to the door, opened it. 'You'll leave at fourteen hundred.' He called out, 'Barnes! Escort Captain Bates back to his quarters!' He went on brutally, in front of the impassive features of the lance-corporal, 'You'd better pack your kit, Padre, Whatever happens, you won't be coming back here, I shouldn't think. Not if it's up to me, anyway. Stay in your room. Something will be sent across from the mess for lunch. Off you go. The lorry bringing your Jerry chum back should be here any minute. I don't think we'll have any tender reunions, thank you very much! Or tender farewells!'

★ ★ ★

They didn't keep Ruth hanging about this time. After one night at Catterick Camp, she was ordered to return to Allerton. The night in the detention centre was not much of an ordeal. She was given a room to herself, in the officers' accommodation, and ate in their mess. It was mid afternoon by the time she got back to camp, so that she had a long wait before the girls came back from their various work places. Her hut mates crowded round eagerly, full of questions, but, largely thanks to Irene's zeal, there was practically no animosity.

'You're a bloody idiot!' Norah Graham pronounced, without rancour, and most agreed. One or two of the other later arrivals at Allerton snubbed her, or were pointedly rude.

Far worse was the fact that she was packed off yet again the following day, despite their having been so short handed and working long hours on the harvesting.

'There's an inquiry up at regional office,' Harry Guy told her. 'Don't worry. I'll be sending in my report, telling them you may be daft but you're harmless. And that you're a good worker, and I don't want to do without you. Now blow your nose and get out of it. Make the most of it. You've got five days' leave.'

The thought did not particularly cheer her, for she could remember all too clearly the atmosphere when she returned home the first time. It was no better, but at least this time she felt more capable of sticking up for herself.

She decided to follow the adage of striking first. Julia had been working in one of the local factories for months now, leaving her mother to look after Angela. And making the most of any free time she had by going 'gadding about with a right fast crowd', as Alice had complained frequently in her letters to Ruth.

'I've done nothing to be ashamed of!' Ruth now insisted, against her mother's sad reprimands, and Julia's more aggressive attack. 'There's plenty of people done far worse than I have, and not many miles from here either!' And she looked at her sister so steadily and for so long that Julia coloured up. She in turn rounded on Alice with a sense of dramatic betrayal.

'Oh aye! And what's been said behind my back, then? At least I don't go trying to get off with Nazis! And I'm working bloody hard all week. It's not a crime to go out of a Saturday for a bit of enjoyment, is it?' Her voice had risen on the last few words to an unpleasant shriek.

'Methinks the lady doth protest too much!' Ruth smiled back nastily, using one of Irene's favourite quotations, and Julia swore again dismissively.

The regional director adopted a head-on approach. 'Poor show, my gel! What on earth possessed you to write letters to a blasted Hun, for goodness' sake? You know, you can thank your lucky stars you've got off so lightly. If the papers had got hold of it, they'd have given you a good roasting. And quite right too! You'd have had your head shaved and worse for collaborating, in the old days!'

Ruth was intimidated. But she was no longer prepared to let herself be browbeaten. 'I don't know about that, ma'am. I've got nothing to feel ashamed of, and I'd be quite willing to stand up and say so. To anybody. Holger Fichtmüller's just a young lad. A year or two older than me. Same age as my brother, Willy — he's in the army — Holger was all alone. He was scared, I know he was. I did nothing wrong when I helped him. And I've done nothing wrong since. Maybe the papers would be interested. But they might not think it was such a bad thing after all!'

Irene and Viv had said as much as Ruth was packing once again to travel up home for the inquiry, which was to take place in Newcastle. Certainly, Ruth's spirited words now seemed to have considerable effect on the bluff, matronly figure. A new and distinct note of conciliation came into being, suggestive of a brisk sweeping under the carpet.

'Well, let's just say no more about it, eh? Least said soonest mended.' And I've heard that before, Ruth thought. 'Your Forestry Officer, Mr Guy, obviously thinks a great deal of you. He's most insistent that he doesn't want to lose you. And you have given good service for — what? — over two years now.'

This time, however, Ruth was determined

not to go along with this philosophy. She had to get things into the open. Her friendship with Holger must be acknowledged. She knew, in any case, that she would not be able to continue using Captain Bates as a go-between. She was not really surprised when she returned, gladly, to Allerton, to find a letter from him.

Briefly, without any hint of recrimination, he explained that he was awaiting transfer, and that he had been officially reprimanded by the authorities. *A terrible blot on my service career*, he wrote and Ruth was greatly dismayed for a second until she carried on reading.

> *You've no idea how little distress that causes me! I look forward to the day when I can finally take off the uniform for good with as much enthusiasm as the unfortunate inmates of Glen Bankirk look forward to their day of freedom. Which surely, please God, must come some day?*

She scanned swiftly through the rest of his personal news, anxious to learn more about Holger.

> *I'm sorry I had no chance to see him after his recapture, but I was shipped out*

— they couldn't wait to get rid of me. But of course I don't blame him at all as far as my being involved goes. I mean of course in acting as personal postman for you two — I had no idea about the escape, as I'm sure you know. I would have tried desperately to stop him. Like you, I'm no traitor, and I'm well aware that Holger is still the enemy. And still honour-bound to carry on the fight in any way he can, according to his principles, which we must respect. I hope you feel that way too. He's a resilient young man, and doesn't appear to have suffered any adverse effects after his adventure. Which brings me to my next point. I've been sent on two weeks' leave, while the powers that be decide what to do with me. A pretty savage punishment, eh? I was wondering if you would care to meet me? Would Sunday next be convenient? I have some relatives in Robin Hood's Bay I should visit. Perhaps you could meet my train at Skinnerdale, or leave a message at the above number if you can't make it.

I hope very much you can. I'm looking forward so much to meeting you at last, and sharing the knowledge of our good mutual friend. And planning the next stage of our campaign to keep in touch, all three of us, I know how much that will mean to

Holger, and how much it would hurt him to lose you now.

Ruth saw the khaki-clad figure leaning out of the window as the train hissed to a steam-clouded halt. Although there were very few passengers waiting to catch the train to Whitby, the carriages were already quite full, from Middlesbrough and stations up the line, as people made the most of their precious Sunday leisure with a day out at the seaside. The September day was overcast, the swelling clouds dark with threatening rain, but it was still mild, the wind coming from almost due south.

Ruth was glad she had chosen not to wear uniform, but had made the effort to spruce herself up. She was wearing a light summer-dress of thin blue-and-white stripes and a loose but warm woollen cardigan. She had decided against stockings, thus avoiding the discomfort of a girdle and its attendant paraphernalia. Instead, she wore pristine white ankle-socks, and sandals.

The soldier waving at the window of the train had clearly recognized her. Ruth stepped forward, smiling shyly, as he stepped back, opened the carriage door for her. They had already spoken briefly, the previous evening, when Ruth had suggested she join the train at Skinnerdale and they could complete the journey to Whitby together. The old seaport was a much easier prospect for spending a day together, especially on the Sabbath.

'You're even prettier than your pictures,' Michael Bates declared gallantly as they shook hands. 'Shall we stay out here in the corridor? The train's quite crowded, and it's easier to talk out here.'

He was not as she had imagined. She had pictured a craggy, distinguished looking, silver-haired individual. In reality, the chaplain was of medium height, with a portly frame which did not look well in uniform. The drab battle-dress gave him a rather crumpled air, added to by the wispy untidiness of brown hair which was thinning rapidly at his brow. His face was round, pleasantly ordinary, but when he grinned it lit up with an enthusiastic warmth which stamped him with a look of engaging youthfulness. Ruth felt its effect immediately.

'So! You are the mystical Ruth!' he said, gently bantering, and she grinned back self-consciously.

Her smile faded. 'How is he?' she asked tremulously, then she gasped as though she was shocked. She put both hands on his sleeve. 'Oh, I'm so sorry, er — '

'Michael will do fine,' he encouraged, but she was looking at him, her dark eyes wide with eloquent dismay.

'I'm ever so sorry!' she continued, in a rush to get the words out. 'You must think I'm awful! I mean — getting you into so much trouble — mixed up in all of this. When all you were doing was — I can't tell you how much it meant when you wrote to me. Sent me that first letter from Holger. It was just wonderful!' She sighed helplessly, and he put his hand awkwardly over hers for a second, patting it.

'Glad to oblige. It made me happy, too. Especially when I saw how much your letters came to mean to him.'

'It didn't stop him from trying to escape though,' she blurted. 'How is he? Really?'

'I wasn't allowed to see him when they brought him back.' He sounded somewhat hesitant, almost reluctant, and Ruth's heart quickened with alarm. 'He'll have to spend some time in the cooler — that's the punishment cells. They put them on their own, away from the other POWs. He'll be all right though, he'll be out after a week or two'.

He quickly sketched in the kind of life prisoners faced at Glen Bankirk. 'It's not too bad,' he summarized. 'They organize games and shows and things. They have each other — there's a great spirit amongst them. Camaraderie, you know. They get their mail. Red Cross parcels sometimes. Some adapt to it pretty well. Holger was coping, I thought.' He paused delicately. 'Your letters really did mean an awful lot to him, you know. I could see. But come on. Tell me about yourself. There's a lot I want to know about you.'

As if they had made a pact, they switched to their own histories, and began to chat animatedly. He told her he was forty-four, 'a crusty old bachelor', he assured her hastily. 'Just haven't found a lady who could put up with my irritating ways. And vice versa.' Again, the twinkling schoolboy grin. 'And what about you? I can't believe there isn't some young man in the offing! Or a queue of swains pining away throughout the dales!'

She blushed and giggled. 'I should cocoa!' she answered, a little inadequately. She took him along the narrow street that ran alongside the harbour, past the Sunday quiet of the fish-dock. The herring boats were moored in a thick cluster, fenders rubbing as they bobbed gently. There were several dark-eyed individuals working on the nets and other gear, their heads enveloped in miniature clouds from their busy pipes. For the most part, they studiously ignored the stream of passers-by, who gazed down with interest from the quayside above.

The west pier was open, and they strolled out to the lighthouse, then on, along the arm of the final extension. They were both surprised by the force of the wind once they had left the shelter of the shore. It buffeted them, blew Ruth's dress against her body to reveal the contours of her legs, flung into disarray the careful hair-do Viv Heathcote had arranged for her last night.

Captain Bates linked her arm, saw her other hand surreptitiously pressing against her thigh to prevent the flapping hem of her dress from soaring. 'Should we turn back? You'll catch cold!'

'No! It's fine! Come on!'

They went down the slipway by the old battery on to the beach. Ruth clung onto him while she peeled off her socks and sandals, and linked the straps together for ease of carrying. She wriggled her toes in the sand.

'It's marvellous! You should try it!' He declined, watching, laughing, while she scampered into the breaking wavelets, then scuttled out again with a shriek of horrified delight. 'It's freezing!'

They would have liked to walk along the level beach as far as Sandsend, which they could see around the shallow curve of the coast a mile or two distant. But the ugly concrete emplacements, the barbed wire and the stark War Department warnings of the notices forbade them. Sobered by this reminder, they climbed onto West Cliff, then made their way slowly through the maze of narrow, cobbled streets and already smoking chimneys, back down the steep slope that led them to town again.

They found a cafe open in Station Square, but it was too crowded to talk at all intimately. Bates paid for their sandwiches and tea, and they were soon on the move again, this time heading over the swing-bridge onto the east side of the harbour, and along Church Street to the steps leading up to church and the ruined abbey on the towering headland.

'Gosh! I haven't been up here for years!' the padre told her. Half-way up, he stopped, his expression lugubrious. 'You go on if you like!' he puffed. 'You must be very fit or I'm terribly unfit!' His face was very red, and she waited penitently, then slowed her pace to suit his.

They got down to serious talk at last, settled on the cliff top, finding a relatively sheltered nook, and staring out over the expanse of grey sea spread below them.

'I've got to keep in touch with him,' Ruth

said simply. 'I wish they'd let me see him. Just once.'

'I've done some homework,' Bates told her. 'There's a Colonel Allnut. He's well up in the POW section. I've written his address for you. I'll write as well. I'll try and get to see him personally if I can. Sounds like he's not a bad sort. Then I think you should approach the Red Cross as well. I've given you a name and address there, too.'

'What about the man in charge at the camp? What's his name?'

Bates smiled gently, shook his head. 'He's one of your chief obstacles, I'd say. Major Waller plays by the book. I shouldn't think he'll be very sympathetic. Especially now — after the escape attempt.' Shyly, he patted her arm, 'Holger will come through all right, I'm sure.' He was rewarded by her grateful smile. 'But he will want you to keep in touch,' he went on delicately. 'You've come to mean so much to him. I'm not sure if either of you realize how much.'

There was another pause, during which Ruth felt herself reddening once more. His voice was even more cautious, feeling his way, over dangerous ground. 'I'm not prying, Ruth, believe me. But I — are you fond of him?'

Now her face crimsoned, and her head

swung towards him. 'I hardly know him.' She began speaking quickly, as though to rebut the implication in his question. 'We were only together for that — those few hours. But — ' She stopped abruptly, and gave a helpless little shrug. She leaned forward, her hands linked around her raised knees, on which she rested her chin, staring ahead. Her voice sank to a quiet murmur.

'Yes, I do feel close to him. Closer than anyone in some ways. Those letters. For two years, nearly. I know about his girlfriend. Heidi. His fiancée!' she corrected herself, striving to avoid bitterness, well aware of the official status the term gave to the pretty, smiling figure in the photograph, whom, she was forced to acknowledge, she looked on now as a rival.

'I'm sorry.' She smiled unsteadily. 'I can't think of him as an enemy at all. I'd like to see him. Get to know him. Properly. Is that bad?'

He laughed in turn, a sad little echo of her emotion. He put his hand briefly, again, on her forearm. 'You're a remarkable girl, Ruth. I knew you would be.' He glanced at his watch. 'I've already told Holger how lucky he is. Now — pull me up my dear! These old bones of mine are in a state of shock at all this unaccustomed exercise. We'd better head back to the station. I'll see you off. Now then — let's plan our strategy, eh? We'll have to keep in touch, too. Co-ordinate our efforts.'

She took hold of his arm, linked it through hers, squeezing affectionately. Their shoulders bumped as she grinned at him.

'I knew how you'd be. Really nice!'

★ ★ ★

It was a bright October day, of chill winds and high white clouds dragged out and flattened into ragged, swept edges, when Holger finally emerged from the cooler. He knew at once when they brought his clothes, for he had been kept stripped down to his underdrawers, even when they took him out for his thirty-minute exercise. It was the longest anyone had done in solitary. He could not help feeling proud of his record. Ernst Schmidt had been released days before, and had already been transferred, no one knew where. Holger was disappointed in some ways to learn that he was to be kept at Glen Bankirk, but there were compensations.

Although he fought hard not to show it, Holger was greatly relieved to be going back to the huts. They had refused him any reading material other than the Bible. The unheated cell had been so cold even in the autumn weather that he had been forced to spend most of the dreary hours of daylight huddled under the single blanket on the wooden bunk.

He was startled when the guards stopped him in the outer office of the punishment block, and produced a pair of leg-irons. 'What's this?' he asked disbelievingly. 'I have served my punishment.'

'Wouldn't want you to be different from your chums!' the guard grinned. 'Roll your pants up, Fritz!'

When Holger, shuffling self-consciously, passed through the wire door into the main compound, he realized the import of the guard's sniggering remarks. The whole of the POW contingent were similarly chained. It did not deter them from giving Holger a rousing reception. Their cheering caused the duty guard to turn out, with bayonets fixed. In spite of his protests, and in spite of the awkwardness of their irons, his fellow inmates lifted him, and carried him twice round the compound in a triumphal parade before they let him go.

'I was only out for a day!' Holger protested, embarrassed and also deeply moved, by their display.

'So what, man?' Wolfgang Deist roared. 'You got out! That's the important thing. You made it. It was worth it, even for five minutes!'

Holger indicated the degrading chains. 'What's all this in aid of?'

'It's because of that bloody Dieppe fiasco. They made such a cock-up of it, they got slaughtered. Some bastard said they'd seen newsreels of the prisoners afterwards. They'd been chained up. This is their reprisal!' Wolfgang broke off, and shuffled a few steps towards the wire. He did a foolish, capering dance, the short length of chain whipping up the dust at his feet. 'All right, Tommy?' he yelled at the nearest guard, who lifted his rifle threateningly. 'Careful!' Wolfgang mocked. 'Can you really afford a bullet? How's Marshal Rommel doing? Is he in Alexandria yet? Any day now, I think!'

Holger was the centre of attention, treated as a hero. It was all the more shocking when he received an urgent summons to report to the senior German officer's hut soon after lunch. The SGO now was a naval commander, none of the Luftwaffe contingent being of such elevated rank. Lieutenant Hoch and others of the escape committee were there also.

'I hope you're feeling pleased with yourself, Fichtmüller. You didn't clear your damned fool plan with anybody here, did you? Some of you types seem to think that because we are POWs you're not in the service any more.

Well, let me remind you, sonny, that you bloody well are! More than ever, we need to hold on to discipline. It's essential. Your conduct will be recorded. It will go down on your service sheet. You are reduced to corporal.'

Holger stared at him, his body quivering with the effort to keep his blazing anger within. The curt voice continued. 'Your stupid little scheme was ill-conceived and badly executed. You can thank your lucky stars you are in here right now. Otherwise you'd be in real trouble, my lad!'

20

As 1942 drew to a close, Ruth's private mood more than matched the optimism she could feel all around her. A couple of weeks after her meeting with Michael Bates, the bells had been rung to celebrate the Allied victory at El Alamein, since when Rommel's hitherto invincible Afrika Korps had been on the run. The importance of America's contribution to the progress of the war had been marked by the invasion of North Africa, where an American general, Eisenhower, had been placed in command of the combined forces.

The American presence was being felt, too, in Britain. Even in the dales! Some of the girls had gone to one of the Saturday night dances at Kilbeck, to find a party of US airmen in attendance. One or two of Ruth's colleagues were carrying on precarious alliances, contending with distance, the vagaries of telephone and postal services, and all too little time, as well as the greatest hazard of all, for most of the visitors were fliers. Their own pin-up, Viv, had been hotly pursued, and was now in regular passionate correspondence with one who bore the exotically martial title of Sergeant Waist-Gunner.

'It's them new utility knickers!' Norah taunted at every opportunity, repeating an already well worn joke in current usage which, nevertheless, usually raised a smutty giggle. 'One Yank and they're off!'

Churchill's stirring 'end of the beginning' speech was followed, a few days later, by the news that Tobruk had been recaptured by the Allies. Ruth prayed hard and gratefully, for she had at last received Holger's letter, a reply to hers, through the post. This time with official consent if not blessing. *Don't forget your mail will be censored. It will no doubt be very carefully scrutinized,* Michael Bates had warned her, in one of his own short, cheerful missives.

Taking heed of his caution, she had not referred directly to the escape at all. She knew how lucky she was that permission had been granted for her to write at all. She hoped that Holger would be able to read between the lines of her general expression of concern. *I hope all is well for you now and that you are keeping yourself fit and as happy as you can in your circumstances. Don't forget I still think about you and pray for you every single night.*

The official envelope containing his first

answering letter had the censor's stamp across it, but she forgot about the prying eyes of some stranger as she read on, and, with tearful happiness, absorbed the warmth of the powerful emotion she could sense in his words.

I cannot tell. I can only hope you will understand how much it means to me when I see the letter from you. I see the handwriting at once and I think my heart stopped! I could not believe it at first, then I open and there are your words to me. And your kisses. I keep them with me close always.

That's a love letter, her mind told her, with a sense of awe. He feels like you do — just the same. She wanted to smile and cry at the same time. Her stomach churned, she felt sick and empty. And wonderfully, dizzily, happy. It scared her, she could not make proper sense of it, her brain spun helplessly when she tried to think it out, see any kind of solution. But still there was this fragile, secret inner feeling, of being indissolubly linked to him, which would not leave her. It was how she had really felt for a long time, she acknowledged solemnly.

She was half listening to the wireless in the

crowded hut one night when Vera Lynn's song came on. Written that year, it had already been played countless times, she had heard it and hummed it unthinkingly over and over again, but now the plaintive words caught her with a power that truly over-whelmed. *We'll meet again, don't know where, don't know when.* She sprang up and rushed out, pushing through the blackout curtain, out into the chilly night, before anyone should spot the tears streaming down her cheeks.

★   ★   ★

The sirens' wailing brought Heidi, her heart racing madly, to abrupt wakefulness. She was stretched out on the couch in the living-room of the comfortable first-floor flat, and in those first seconds she blinked about her uncom-prehendingly. She had already changed into her night things and now swung her bare feet down to the floor, feeling the awkward bulk of her swollen belly, for she was in the seventh month of her pregnancy and felt huge.

She cursed vehemently. Gerhard was away, would not be back until tomorrow. She wished suddenly that she had taken his advice to move back to Remscheid, to stay with her parents. But she could not stand the thought of her mother's fussing, of both her parents' tight-lipped disapproval, which they had never expressed but which she was sure was there, nevertheless. She was also sure that her mother at least knew the reason for the somewhat hastily arranged marriage which had taken place in October, while the press was still trumpeting the triumph of the repulsion of an Allied invasion attempt at Dieppe.

'It's what I want more than anything in the world, my darling!' Gerhard assured her on their wedding-night, and she had sniffled, smiled tremulously through her tears.

'At least we don't have to worry any more,' she murmured, opening her arms, and her body, to him.

Tongues would wag soon enough, though, and brains click like busy adding-machines, as they worked out dates. 'You're showing quite a lot already,' her mother had said speculatively, during their last visit. 'It must be a boy.'

Gerhard had seemed far more concerned that she should inform poor Holger of her changed status and affections. So much so that she had, finally and reluctantly, lied to her new husband and told him she had written the dreaded letter. Painful though it was, lying was easier than actually breaking the news to her unfortunate ex-fiancé. Besides, she consoled herself, it would not be a lie for long.

One day soon she would find the necessary strength actually to tell Holger the news she knew would break his heart.

Only here she was, five months into her marriage, and seven months into her pregnancy, and the deed had still not been done. The letters in the blue envelopes continued to turn up every month at her parents' home.

'Just keep them for me,' Heidi told her mother uncomfortably. 'I told Holger he could continue to write to me for a while. But Gerhard might get a bit upset. I'll get them when I come down to see you.'

The building quivered slightly as the thumping bark of the AA batteries opened up. Fresh alarm seized her. The sirens had only just gone, yet the guns were firing already. The bombers must be overhead. Perhaps this was the start. People had been saying for months that Berlin would suffer one of the heavy raids the RAF were carrying out now. Cologne had signalled the beginning of these massive strikes, way back in June. Then, in the summer, had come daylight attacks on the Ruhr, perilously close to her home in Remscheid. They had heard the reverberations of the bombs, seen the pall of smoke to the north. She had found herself worrying over Holger's folks, wondering if they were all right in the city.

That was another disturbingly prickly problem. Frau Fichtmüller had telephoned Heidi's father in September, after not seeing or hearing from their son's fiancée for long weeks.

'I think you should speak to Heidi yourself,' Herr Krempel declared solemnly, and Heidi had briefly hated her father, before she was forced to recognize her own cowardice. She made the short journey to Dusseldorf the following weekend. It was at the time when she missed her first period and was convinced she was pregnant.

In the middle of the opening, awkward small talk, Heidi suddenly burst into tears. She was glad that Holger's mother was the only one present. She stammered out her tale, between her gulping sobs, in which Frau Fichtmüller soon joined, but with more restraint. She seemed more hurt than angry.

'Please don't tell Holger!' Heidi begged. 'There's no need to hurt him. Not yet. It will — being over there, like he is. I'll tell him myself. Soon. But we don't want to hurt him any more than — when there's no need.'

She was glad that the older woman had

agreed so readily. But that had been just before Heidi's wedding, a full five months ago. She had heard nothing from the Fichtmüllers since. She wondered tormentedly how they got round the problem of the engagement when they wrote to their son. The engagement he did not even know had been broken. Did not know that his sweetheart was now Frau Waldeyer. Part of her, a despicably cowardly part, half hoped that his mother would not have been able to keep secret the truth from her son, but Holger's short, falsely cheerful letters continued to arrive, did not change their tone of undemonstrative affection.

He had never been passionately expressive, she reflected, feeling ashamed that, even now, she would have been thrilled by an epistle throbbing with the intensity of his love for her. She found herself even more ashamedly recalling and comparing the painfully vigorous, frenetic nature of their lovemaking. It had not been the skilful, finely drawn-out performance she now enjoyed with Gerhard. Not that she had been an unwilling or disappointed participant in those early days. She had not known any better. She did now, though.

There was a deeper boom, and the shuttered windows trembled, the glasses in the drinks cabinet vibrated gently. A sense of panic seized her, and she fumbled her feet into the voluminous woollen pants of her suit, dragging the elastic waist up, stuffing in the silk hem of her nightgown, and her wrap, before she fought her head and arms through the heavy top. She did not stop to pull on the thick socks but thrust her feet into the felt slippers and hastened to the door. She must get down to the comparative safety of the basement.

She had just got in, panting with fear and relief, and the heavy steel doors were closed behind her again, when there was an almighty crash, which shook the whole building so violently she almost fell. Old Herr Brüner, ancient and bespectacled, grabbed at her, then they clutched each other in terror as the lights went out, plunging them into utter blackness, while the air was suddenly so thick with dust and smoke, and the stink of cordite that they began coughing and gasping.

She sank down, her knees drawn up, folded to the side, on the cold, mucky floor, her hands holding the swell of her belly. She whimpered; emitting short, smothered cries, holding herself against the stab of pains that truly frightened her. She felt Herr Brüner's clawlike, withered hands, with their ugly, long yellow nails, scratching and stroking at her dishevelled hair, and she buried her face gratefully, like a scared child, into his mustysmelling dressing-gown.

The chill was replaced by an increasingly stuffy warmth. There were about only a dozen people in the cellar, from the whole apartment block of nine flats. The beams of several torches revealed how dust-laden the polluted air was. They found the emergency lanterns, and tried to maintain some semblance of order.

'That was close!' they told one another, in hushed voices.

How close it had been they discovered when they found they could not open the doors from the basement, and that the rubbish-chute and air-vents appeared to be blocked, or partly blocked. There was, mercifully, some air still filtering through, though it brought with it the sharp smell of burning, and enough smoke to keep them coughing irritably. The pains in Heidi's stomach got worse, and she became truly terrified. She fought against the hysteria she could feel welling up.

'I don't feel well! I have to get out!' she cried, clutching at her stomach, clinging desperately to the distressed Herr Brüner.

The women took over, calming her a little. She went over to the corner where the buckets stood for emergency use, and squatted awkwardly, for her bladder was full. She blubbered, embarrassed at the amount of noise she made, until the women talked shrilly and cheerfully. They made up a bed on one of the benches, and made her lie down, wrapping her in blankets and coats. A handsome woman whose husband was on active service somewhere, sat and held her hand tightly, soothing her as though she were a sick child, and the pains faded.

But it was hours, well into the next morning, before rescuers removed the pile of rubble, shoring up the dangerous remnants of the building before they could excavate the trapped inhabitants. Heidi was taken straight to a Grade-A government clinic and put to bed, after a bath and change of clothing, and it was there a distracted Gerhard found her some time in the afternoon. She clung to him, sobbing fiercely, while he kissed her wet face over and over.

'I thought — the baby — ' she blubbered.

'It's all right,' he whispered, shushing her, rocking her back and forth. 'I'm taking you home — to your parents in the morning,' he murmured with gentle firmness. She no longer argued.

That night, sadly determined, she asked for pencil and paper, and began, at long last, a letter to Holger. She tried with all her heart to make it as gentle and loving as she could. It was very late by the time she had finished, and her cheeks were wet once more with tears. The knowledge of the despair he would feel lay like a cold stone in her breast, but at least it was done, and her sadness was overlaid with a feeling of huge relief.

★ ★ ★

Holger was in his hut — most of the prisoners were under cover, for an icy April shower was rattling down — when the Red Cross delegation arrived. They never stayed long, and the POWs weren't allowed anywhere near them, except for the SGO and one or two of the other officers. You were supposed to put in a request if you wished to speak with them for any reason. Hardly anyone bothered, no matter what domestic problems might be worrying him. Glen Bankirk was a very inward-looking place as far as the majority of its inmates were concerned. The reality of the world beyond the wire was as mistily vague as the heather-covered hills stretching emptily all around them.

'Fichtmüller!' The guard bawled his name from the open doorway. 'You're wanted over in the admin block. On the double!'

'Hey! Maybe they're sending you home!' some wag called. 'Swopping you for ten of theirs.'

'He's worth more than ten Englanders!'

Holger's heart quickened a little as he made his way across the wet compound, ducking against the driving rain. He could see the small civilian group, together with its escort, moving over by the kitchens. He was surprised to see Major Waller himself waiting on the wooden veranda outside his office. It must be bad news, he was convinced of it. His folks. Or Heidi. He knew that the RAF were carrying out heavy raids almost nightly on Germany now. Berlin. Essen, Stuttgart. And of course Düsseldorf would be a prime target too.

'There's a visitor for you,' Waller said, unable to disguise the hostility of his tone. 'Seems like part of your reward for making such a bloody nuisance of yourself. Letters from your inamorata! Visits! What next, I wonder!' His mouth curved in contempt. 'Through there. In the guardroom. In you go!'

It still didn't register. Holger thought it must be someone from the Red Cross committee. He knocked, entered the outer guardroom, where the seated figure of the duty NCO nodded silently towards the inner door. He went through into the smaller office. A slim girl was standing by the meshed window. He could see only her dark silhouette against the grey light. She was standing very straight, and very still. 'Holger!' She let out a sob, then his senses were filled with her fresh fragrance, her wonderful presence, as Ruth flung herself violently into his arms, and suddenly their mouths were open, pressed together.

'That'll do! Steady on!' The young lieutenant harrumphed with noisy, shocked embarrassment. 'Sit down please, miss!'

The embracing couple ignored him, were unaware of him, for further long seconds, until the need for breath finally tore them apart, and they collapsed, gasping. Ruth was clinging for dear life to his red, chapped hands, which she did not let go, even as she sank weakly onto the wooden chair across the small table.

Holger took the chair opposite, their hands joined still. His eyes were wide, devouring her as though he could not believe her reality. He said so, in a hushed voice, shaking his head slowly.

'I cannot believe. It is you! Ruth!'

She nodded, smiling, while the tears poured down her cheeks. 'Oh — my dear!'

she wept. 'I can hardly believe it myself. I've been waiting months! When they told me I could come — with the Red Cross delegation — I . . . ' Now it was her turn to shake her head as she tried to express her joy, the days of painfully sweet anticipation once she had learned of her visit. She lifted her hands, still joined to his. She pressed her lips against his red knuckles, he felt her mouth move against him, and it was one of the most wonderful sensations he had ever known.

'Oh, God! It's so good to see you, Holger! I've dreamt so much — thought about it, every night.' She stopped suddenly, her colour deepening, the vulnerable shyness sweeping into her features. He recognized it at once, felt the pang of it within his heart, how much it meant to him. Her eyes shone with her appeal as she fixed them on his.

He drew her hands towards him. Now he kissed her fingers, spoke against her touch. 'I also. I think of you. Always. Your letters are the most important to me. The most important!' He repeated it with passionate emphasis, so that she thought at once of Heidi, knew what he was meaning.

Her mouth was open, she looked very afraid. The words hung there between them, until she gave a little nod, and gripped his hands with quivering intensity. 'I feel the same.'

They sat there, holding onto each other, never letting go, through the whole hour. There were times of silence, when they simply looked, while the lieutenant, nursing his sense of outrage, turned his back, stared out of the window. Their voices at other times were low murmurs, which he tried not to listen to.

'I must write and tell Heidi,' Holger said.

Ruth nodded. 'I'm sorry,' she said helplessly, and meant it.

He shrugged. 'It has happened. It happened long time. I am so happy to tell you. There is no one for you?'

She shook her head. 'No one.' She smiled. 'Just you — for a long time.'

'Time up,' the officer announced bleakly, and stood waiting. He said nothing this time when the couple embraced, and Ruth hung sobbing in the German's arms. 'I'll be allowed another visit in three months, I think.' She pressed her face against his, and Holger tried to absorb into his pores the slender beauty, the fragrance of her, the tickling feel of the wisps of her hair against his nose.

They couldn't bear to part, and they had to. The lieutenant cleared his throat, noisily, several times, red and sweating, then stepped forward, reaching out gingerly to touch Ruth's shoulder.

'You'll have to go now, miss. Come along. Please!'

Finally, she couldn't look at Holger, couldn't see anything as somehow she tore herself away from his arms, her head turned down and sideways. 'Look after yourself!' she managed to gasp. 'One day we'll — it'll be all right.'

Holger stood still, empty, when she had gone, waiting for her to be out of sight, for suddenly he felt that he could not bear seeing her again, having to lose her again.

'I stay one minute,' he growled, scarcely finding his voice as the NCO came and stood there. The man nodded, turned away again, left him standing alone.

21

Ruth had learnt to be cautious, to try and hide the true nature of her feelings from the other girls, and from her family when she made her brief visits home. Except with Irene, of course. She had to share her secret with someone, was deeply grateful that she had one friend close enough to confide the truth to. Irene was more than sympathetic. 'At least he's safe where he is,' she told Ruth reassuringly.

Though Ruth had said nothing of how she truly felt to Ernie Long, she was more than half-convinced that he knew anyway. He had been aware of her long correspondence with the German, and, typically, refused to condemn it, or to criticize. It was he who, with his typical unfussiness, came up with the idea which brought Ruth such new and unexpected hope. She was telling him about the difficulties in both the bureaucracy and the physical obstacles of distance and transport involved in her visit to the POW camp.

He removed his pipe from between his teeth, and pointed it judiciously in her direction. 'You should tell him he should get himself transferred. A bit nearer, like.'

She stared at him in amazement. 'Transfer? How? What — '

'It's the latest idea. Sir George were telling me the other day. They're going to start using gangs of Eyetie prisoners to work on the land. Reckon we could be getting some up our way soon. There's a big camp over towards Pickering way. Mebbes your Jerry could get himself on one of these here gangs.' He chuckled. 'Funny if he ended up back here, eh?'

He stood back, dusted off his gritty hands on the sides of his grey flannels, from force of habit. He was unaware of the storm of emotion he had raised in Ruth, nor of the rapid patter of her heart as she contemplated the too-good-to-be-true possibility his words had conjured up in her racing brain.

★ ★ ★

'I'm very sorry, Fichtmüller,' the senior German officer said stiffly. 'Major Waller gave me the news just minutes ago. I thought it best to tell you myself.'

Holger had been prepared for yet another confrontational meeting. Ever since his escape attempt a year ago, he had been considered something of a rebel. He had picked the sergeant's stripes from his sleeves, refused to replace them with the twin corporal's stripes.

'It's fine. I'd rather be a bloody airman!' He refused to acknowledge his officially reduced rank.

In all these months he had not been involved in any of the approved escape plans. 'Bolshie bastard!' Wolfgang Diest had humorously dubbed him, but most of the other ranks supported his stand. To them, he was the only one who had got over the wire, with official blessing or not.

He took his time when he was ordered to report to the SGO. He had a reputation to live up to. He was sure that was why he was being sent for. To be given a reprimand, a verbal boot up the backside, though in truth most of his contemporaries merited it no less than he did. Morale was at an all-time low. Sicily was about to fall, the Italians surrendering in their thousands to this American general, Patton, and *Il Duce* was about to have command of the forces taken from him by his own people. And, just two days ago, had come word of a massive raid on Hamburg, with reports of the resultant fires being visible from a distance of two hundred miles. In view of such news, Holger should have been more prepared for the SGO's solemnly formal announcement. But he was metaphorically bowled over by it, he felt as though the air had been sucked from his lungs.

'I regret to have to inform you, your father has died. He was killed in a bombing raid, last Sunday night.'

It wasn't until the end of the month that Holger got a letter from his mother, giving him more detail. It came the day after Hamburg suffered its seventh raid in as many days, and the badly stretched authorities were forced to organize a mass evacuation of civilians from the stricken city, where almost two hundred thousand were homeless.

In the monthly batch of mail, Holger also saw Ruth's handwriting. For five days, since he had been told of his father's death, Holger had found himself unable to write a single word to her, though he had tried, sitting there with pencil and paper before him, his mind a whirring conflict of emotions. It was a long while now since he'd received Heidi's tender, conscience-stricken message of the end of their engagement. He had laughed almost hysterically at the timeliness of its arrival, when he had been struggling for so long with the painful difficulty of doing exactly the same thing to her. When he had passed on this news to Ruth, he had fondly believed that the one huge obstacle between them had been magically lifted, that nothing now stood between their closeness. With the force of a sickening and sudden blow, came a realization that they were enemies. That blood lay between them. He felt that powerful, choking sensation now, and put her letter aside while he opened that from his mother.

There had been raids on Essen, and Düsseldorf — it must have been before the Hamburg raid, Holger calculated. His dad had been on day-shift at the factory, and so was on the roster for the nightly civil-defence duties. He was working with a rescue team, in the rubble of a building whose ruin had collapsed on a group of them. They had managed to dig themselves out, but Herr Fichtmüller had suffered a severe heart-attack, and had died within an hour or two, at a makeshift casualty station, before they could get him to hospital, because of the disruptions caused by the raid.

He could feel the pangs of his mother's grief through every one of her starkly simple words. He could see her, newly alone, in the spacious, old-fashioned flat, fiercely determined to preserve her dignity, her pride, accepting the condolences and sympathy of her neighbours with her somewhat distant graciousness. Holger was her only surviving child. He had had a brother, born when Holger was three. The birth was difficult and dangerous, the infant lasted no more than two months. His mother could have no more children.

Though it hurt, Holger could not help recalling a lengthy period, starting when he was about ten, when his father had scarcely been at home, seeming to disappear for days on end, drinking quite heavily when he was around. It was much later that Holger found out how serious the breach between his parents had been. His father had taken up with another woman, a mistress, or 'fancy woman' as his mother had tearfully referred to her. Herr Fichtmüller had eventually returned to the marital fold. Wife and husband treated each other with a careful mutual respect, Frau Fichtmüller proud to be considered a model wife in the eyes of the world. In the eyes of her husband and son, too. But as he passed through his teens, Holger had been aware of something, a kind of indefinable reserve between them. But he knew now his mother would be weeping no less for that.

Holger walked, round and round the bare earth of the compound. He repelled any friendly advances, and they soon left him alone. They were used to one another's moods in the camp; the black despair that could seize an individual, stamp itself over his features and his whole stance, and which could lock him as securely as any closed door in his private world of misery.

Ruth's letter was in his pocket, still unopened. He thought of the interminable hours stretching ahead. The final meal, the roll-call, and the lock-up before sunset.

The crowdedness and fug and endless chatter of the hut. He stared up at the wooden guard towers, the low tripwire, and the sacrosanct stretch of grass which led to the tall, angled barbedwire fence that marked the outer limits. He had a sudden almost irresistible urge to run straight through the still open wire door of the cage separating the compound from the rest of the camp, to sprint down the tarmac roadway, past the admin block, head straight for the gate and its lowered barrier, just keep on running, blindly, until they were forced to let him go, or cut him down.

They would be so astonished they might well let him set foot once more on free ground before they reacted. Would they shoot? Why not find out? A quick, savage burst, ripping him in two. Would he even feel it, hear it? Hi, Dad. Mind if I join you?

He saw the duty cooks moving over to the kitchens, to draw the meal. The sun was already well down towards the dark line of the hills. He took out the envelope, gazed at his own name, his number, then turned it over. *Miss R. Palmer.* Still he felt that reluctance to take the folded sheets out. It was odd to think that the British censor, perhaps even sour-faced Major Waller himself, had already read Ruth's unfailingly cheerful, loving words.

He stuffed the envelope back in his pocket, instead pulled out his pay-book, turned to its inside cover, to stare at the photograph Ruth had sent him, to replace the one that had been taken from him after his recapture. The picture was very similar. Again taken in a studio, the same one, he guessed, the same uniform, the same rather shy, restrained smile. A beautiful girl. Not in the same, immediately striking, blonde beauty of Heidi. Ruth's figure was slimmer, slighter altogether, her breasts undoubtedly smaller . . .

The smile blurred and dissolved under his gaze, he shuddered, and moved off again, faster, savouring the increasing sharpness of the pain in his knee. This girl was English. Thousands of his countrymen had been killed, in less than one week. His own father, for God's sake! How could he love this girl? If he had not been captured, Heidi would have been bearing *his* child, not dropping the issue of some chinless wonder of a civil servant.

This girl was English. How could he say he loved her? He was a traitor even to think it. If only he could get out of here, get back home. He would be up there, flying again, plastering this whole damned country with high explosive. The bastards! All of them!

He realized all at once that the compound had been deserted for some time. People were now spilling out of the huts again, assembling for the final roll-call. He made a huge effort to swallow all the hopeless rage and despair wrapped around him, and moved to the ragged line forming in front of his own hut.

★　　★　　★

Ruth should have taken a weekend leave to go home, but she was waiting anxiously for permission to visit Holger, for which she would need at least three days' leave, she reckoned. She could only hope that Harry Guy would prove sympathetic to her request when the time came, for it might well fall again in mid-week. She couldn't help being a little envious as she watched Irene packing an overnight bag for her own trip home on the Friday night.

'Off for a dirty weekend, are we?' Norah Graham observed when she came into the hut.

'I hope so,' Irene answered perkily, and the blonde grimaced sardonically.

'You two wouldn't know what to do with one if it bit you on the bum!' Norah retorted, including Ruth in her scornful assessment. 'Anyway, lads round here are on the wrong side for Palmer, isn't that right?'

Ruth made no answer. The prospect of two days without Irene's company, and one of those a leisurely Sunday, did not appeal to Ruth. Even the underlying tensions of Roper Terrace, and the uneasy truce between her and Julia would have been preferable to the dreariness of the camp.

A day later, her spirits soared at the familiar sight of the envelope on the mess table. Once more, she rigorously asserted self-discipline, and restrained herself from opening it until she could find some private moments alone. When she did, she sat staring at it through blurring tears.

My father is dead, from the bombing. They say in Hamburg there is more dead in one week than in the entire Britain in four years of war. Why had the censor allowed that to pass? Ruth's spinning mind wondered. Did he regard it as something to be proud of, to gloat over? *I am sorry to say this to you. How can we go on to write, to say we love? It is impossible. I do not forget you. Your friend, Holger.*

She got out of the hut as swiftly as she could. She walked, up through the largely cleared landscape, and the rows of young trees which they had planted, heading uphill always, to the brow which led to the open moor of the Tops. She cried out her despair, while she sat and watched the expanse of the moor grow dark, and hazy. Then she felt a new resolution stir, a fierce determination to fight, not to be beaten. She would write again. Yes, but she would also get on to the War Office. They still had not given her permission to pay another visit to Glen Bankirk. They must.

She had to see him face to face. She could not give him up. Nothing would come between them, not even the dead father whom she would never meet.

As she came in through the wire and the open wooden gate, she saw a dim light showing through the doorway of the rec hut. Voices were raised, she saw a huddled group. Someone was crying, rawly, noisily. She recognized the yellow hair of Norah, who stared bleakly at her.

'What's wrong?' Ruth asked apprehensively.

'It's Frank Perry. Viv's Yank. She's been waiting since yesterday for a phone call. He's had it. They lost half the bloody squadron in the raid on Sunday. Some bloody oil fields somewhere. Seems like your Nazi friends still have a few teeth left yet, sod 'em!'

The following night, Ruth set her heart out on the thin sheets of paper. The news from the outside world was full of Allied successes. The Russians were pushing forward, retaking the vast areas of ground from the German forces. The British Eighth Army was advancing towards Messina, in the north of Sicily, and the Germans were preparing a massive evacuation of their troops from the island, which must surely fall soon. In contrast, an air of gloom seemed to have settled over the camp. Quite a number of girls had made liaisons with the American airmen, some casual, some not, from the same squadron of B-24s as Frank Perry's, and several of Ruth's workmates besides Viv mourned the abrupt ending of these friendships, for fifty-four bombers had been lost on the long flight to the Rumanian oil fields.

For once, Norah's gibes at Ruth held real

venom, and were echoed by others. She had never before felt so isolated. Once again, it was Irene who, with impetuous loyalty, blurted out the reason for Ruth's own private sorrow.

'That *Jerry*,' She gave the word savage emphasis, 'has just lost his own father in an air-raid!'

One or two had the grace to look a little sheepish, but there was a cruel answer of, 'Serve him bloody well right!' from someone in the background.

There was an ugly scene in the crowded wash-place that same evening, when Ruth again found herself challenged by a ring of angry faces, this time egged on by the diminutive, vicious, Beryl Mills. Ruth was trapped by the threatening assailants, afraid that they might actually assault her physically. That might well have happened, but for the intervention of Viv herself. The tall, normally diffident figure thrust herself bodily through their ranks.

'For God's sake!' the blonde girl cried passionately, her gentle, tearful eyes blazing. 'Pack it in! What the hell are we fighting for? There's enough of that going on, isn't there?'

She turned to Ruth, put her arms round her, and began to weep, the sobs shaking her whole body. Ruth's arms came up to enfold her, she pulled the golden head down to her.

'I'm so sorry, love,' she wept in turn, and Viv nodded.

After that, they left her alone, and in a day or two Norah's taunts lost their sting. It did not help Ruth's feelings of sadness, however, and she poured them out into the words on the paper, in the comparative quiet of the corner of the rec hut, apart from the mirthful shrieks and squabbles from the far end, and the gentle, woodpecker rapping of the ping-pong ball.

★ ★ ★

I've cried deeply and bitterly for your father, Ruth wrote, *and for the awful sadness it has caused you. If things had worked out different, if your plane had not been shot down that night, you might have killed my dad yourself, or hundreds of other dads, and mothers, and sons, and daughters, husbands and wives. It's all part of this crazy tragedy we're caught up in, and maybe we are actually somehow to blame for it, I don't know.*

But I do know that I love you, and that hurts too. You say we don't know each other, that we've never even been together. I can't argue with that. But all our letters — a week on Sunday it will be three years to the day since we met, do you realize that? — it was a day I'll never forget, the most important of my life.

I've never felt for anyone the way I feel for you. And it's there between us — I know you felt it too. Has it really gone? Please tell me the truth. And the truth is, I didn't kill your father, and you didn't kill mine. My brother is in Sicily fighting now, and I pray for him every night, but if anything happens to him, it won't be your fault, and I won't stop loving you.

★ ★ ★

She had the room to herself eventually. She had to rush, and even then she had to finish undressing in the dark, after lights out, but, though she had wept again as she sealed the envelope, she felt a lot better for it.

★ ★ ★

The arrival of the Italian prisoners in the dale, in time to give much needed help with the bumper harvest, caused tremors of excitement, not only among the girls of the Corps, who had once again been seconded

313

from their normal task, but among the entire community. At first, they were viewed with wary, and in some cases, downright hostile, curiosity. But the figures, in the shabby battle-dress with the black diamond patches sewn on sleeve or between shoulders, were so courteous and polite, and, far from having an air of sullenness or resentment, were so unfailingly cheerful, with flashing grins and dancing, dark eyes, that even the dour farmers' wives softened to them. As for the Land-Girls, they were soon flirting outrageously, and, in several cases, giving cause for some heftily scandalous rumours to go flying about.

The English that the prisoners spoke — and most of them had a surprisingly good command of the language — was effusively gallant, bold, like their looks, but always polite. None of the girls was immune to it. Not even Ruth, but this exotic contact only served to turn her thoughts more and more towards Holger.

He had written, in answer to her impassioned plea. She had felt weak-kneed with relief at the sight of the envelope, even though she was afraid of what its contents might be. There was something almost painful in his confession of his continuing love for her, as though it hurt him to admit it.

314

And there was a note of fatalistic sadness, too, which disturbed her deeply. He did not refer to the future at all. The awful thought smote her that perhaps he did not see one for them.

And still her application to visit again had been delayed. The influx of Italian prisoners, the expectation of far more, including Germans in the near future — all these, despite the official tone of the correspondence, smacked to her of excuses. She wrote of her growing desperation to Michael Bates, who was now down on the south coast in a large military training-camp somewhere. No doubt something to do with this second front which everyone was talking about, as more and more American forces continued to arrive in Britain.

She told him of Herr Fichtmüller's death and Holger's reaction to it. *I really need to see him,* she wrote. *I know you're busy, probably worked to death, but please, is there anything you can do to help me get up there again?*

He promised to try. He was as good as his word. She received the permit on the last day of September, the day the Allies announced the capture of Pompeii. Air-raid casualties for the month were declared triumphantly to be the lowest since May, 1940, with only five deaths, and eleven people put in hospital. The Air Ministry added, with grim self-righteousness, that Hamburg had suffered 'probably the most complete blotting out of a city that ever happened'.

22

Heidi was almost pleased when Gerhard told her that he was going to be posted abroad, to Denmark, on important government work. The air raids on Berlin had worsened throughout the summer. After the attack on the last night of August, Gerhard said, more than 5,000 had been killed. 'For God's sake, don't spread it around!' he urged her, unnecessarily, for the official figures were much lower.

He had always been thin. Now, he looked positively gaunt, there were deep vertical lines etched down his face, along the jawbone, the eyes gazed out wearily from the dark shadows which ringed them.

He did not volunteer much about his work, and Heidi was content not to ask him. It was important, and highly confidential, she knew that much. The undercurrents of rumour about the Gestapo made her uncomfortable. He was not able to be present at the nursing home in Remscheid when Inge was born, on 7 May — the day Tunis had fallen to the Allies — and Heidi was gladder than ever of her parents' support. The baby was more than a week old before Gerhard managed to snatch time off for a brief visit, which was only of one night's duration.

'I'll be able to get some proper leave soon,' he promised her tenderly. It was more than a month before he could make good his promise, and it coincided with a pronouncement from Goebbels that Berlin had finally been cleared of Jews.

Because of the air attacks, the capital was partially evacuated. Though their rest was disturbed every night at Remscheid, necessitating a move to the shelter at sunset, where they spent the night listening to the distant crump of the bombs and the answering bark of the AA guns, they were sufficiently distanced from Düsseldorf, and the industrial cities of the Ruhr, to be rarely at threat, except for the occasional stray.

In fact, Heidi's father and his neighbours often spent much of the time outside, watching the far-off glow of fires, and the arcing searchlights. With increasing frequency, they were patriotically stirred by a flashing explosion in the sky, or the starry trail of a stricken enemy plane falling, as the techniques of their own fighters steadily improved.

Gerhard came on his brief leave before his posting to Denmark on the day that Italy's

318

surrender to the Allies was announced, though it had in fact been signed in secret days earlier. The occupied territory of the Danes had been in the news the previous week. A campaign of sabotage had flared up, and martial law had been declared. The Royal Family was virtually under arrest and heavily guarded.

'Please — be careful!' Heidi said tearfully. She wished, not for the first time, that he could be in uniform. It would give his status recognition, protect him even. And take away some of the sinister mystery and clandestine nature of his work. He would also look rather good in the handsome uniforms the German officers wore.

He was still very much in love with her, and that brought her a great deal of comfort. She had taken a lot of care with her appearance, working hard on a series of painfully strenuous exercises to get her figure back after Inge's birth, ignoring her mother's irritating criticism of her efforts. 'You're a married woman now. A mother.' As though that was sufficient excuse to let herself go, that looks and smartness no longer mattered. They were more important than ever, Heidi considered.

It was the same when she weaned the baby from the breast, and put her on the powdered-milk formula. Her mother had behaved as though she had done something wicked.

'I fed you until you were almost a year,' Frau Krempel observed tartly.

'My milk's not good enough for her!' Heidi had been forced to lie. 'She'll be better off on the bottle.' She was deeply soothed by the hungrily appreciative gaze of her husband when she changed her clothes in the privacy of their room the day he arrived. She was blushing a little as she told her parents at the dining-table that evening, 'Gerhard and I aren't going to bother going to the shelter tonight. He needs a good night's sleep, poor thing!'

Mutual embarrassment hung in the air over all four of them. 'I think we should take Inge with us,' Frau Krempel said stiffly. 'I'd never forgive myself . . . '

Heidi agreed fervently, even as the sentence lingered with unfinished eloquence.

'I miss you so much!' he said confessionally, as they lay sweating in the rumbling darkness, after making love.

She turned, wrapped her body again tightly about his. 'Take care, my darling! I couldn't bear it — couldn't go on without you!'

Grey dawn was seeping through the edges of the heavy blackout curtains when she woke, still entangled in his arms. She moved, slowly, on top of him, heard his waking grunt, his gasp of shocked delight. She reached down, fumbled in the heat between their bellies, felt him harden, and guided him to her, lifting herself joyously, her blood clamouring for him. 'But what about — ' Her lips sealed his automatic protest, and seconds passed. She broke the kiss.

'I just want you — inside me!' she panted. 'Nothing else!'

★ ★ ★

Rain was spattering on the windows. Ruth turned from the bleak scene outside as Holger came into the office. He stopped just inside the room.

'I knew it was you,' he said. She moved forward, round the table, forgetting the officer in the background, forgetting everything except her need to be in his arms. She felt his resistance as she flung herself against him, almost roughly flung her arms about his neck, pulling him into her, blatantly pressed her body against him, her thighs and knees. She felt his mouth open, belatedly, and he began to return her kiss with savage intensity.

'I say! You shouldn't do that!' The lieutenant was elderly this time, a jolly, rotund figure, whose visage was red now with embarrassment or anger.

Ruth was crying. She jerked her head round, still clinging convulsively to Holger. 'You don't have to watch!' she snarled, and turned back, once more thrust herself against Holger, sought out his mouth again. Eventually they broke, and she led him by the hand to the table, where there were two chairs opposite each other. She looked up at the dark shape of the officer against the light, and wiped away the tears from her cheek unconsciously.

'I'm sorry,' she said penitently. 'I didn't mean to be so rude. But it's so difficult! Please! We need to be alone. I swear — we're not planning anything, there's no secrets. We just — can't you give us a little time?'

She stared up at him, her face naked with her need, and the lieutenant looked even more embarrassed. There was a distinct pause, then he said curtly, 'I'll be in the outer office. You've an hour.' He was gone before she could thank him.

'I can't beheve it!' she murmured, holding onto Holger with both hands. They did not kiss again, but sat as before at the table. 'I've been waiting so long for this. To see you again.' She raised his hand to her cheek, held it there, against her smooth skin, rubbed herself gently against his fingers. 'I miss you so much.' He stared at her, said nothing. His blue eyes reflected his pain. She smiled. 'I'll be twenty-four next week. I was twenty when we first met. Remember?' He nodded slowly, his eyes still on hers. 'It seems so long ago now, doesn't it? It is. More than three years. That's how long we've known one another.'

There was something challenging in her tone. He pulled his hands free of her, stood suddenly, and moved over to the window, kept his back to her for a second or two, while he stared at the rain pocked hills.

'Three years I am prisoner.' He turned back to her. 'What we can do?' he said hopelessly. 'I think we will lose the war. Germany. Or we are forced to make peace soon. I cannot stay. You cannot go.'

'Have you heard from your mother?' she interrupted, almost harshly, again on the note of challenge, as though she were flinging the issue of his father's death down there on the table before them. She hadn't moved, and he came and sat down again.

'Yes. I have one letter. She is — how you say — doing good. She is brave.'

Ruth reached out, kept her hands outstretched, palms uppermost, supplicating, until, after a perceptible pause, he reached forward and took them in his. At once, he felt her fingers curve, dig into his in a fierce grip. 'I love you. Do you love me? Tell me.'

He shrugged, he even glanced away, then his gaze came back again to her, helplessly. 'You make me say? Yes. I think so.' Again, his shoulders jerked upward. 'But is no good, *ja*? There is nothing to do — '

'We love each other!' she said, her voice low, vibrant with emotion. The fingers dug into him again, her hands leapt on the table. 'That's all that matters, really. That's what we must always remember. It doesn't matter what happens, that's what counts!'

He looked at her then with such tormented sadness that her heart seemed to stop. Then his whole body wilted, his unkempt, fair head lowered until his face was hidden from her, and she saw his frame shiver. With a low cry, she wrested her hands free, moved rapidly round the table, and gathered him to her. Her fingers curled around his head, his hair, and she held him, felt his face, his warm breath, press into the softness of her body as she stood over him, holding him to her, rocking gently, stroking and caressing him while he convulsed in weeping that tore cathartically through him.

★   ★   ★

On Ruth's birthday, a hospital ship docked in Liverpool carrying almost eight hundred wounded Allied prisoners who had been repatriated from Germany. A month later, in the midst of the RAF's 'Battle of Berlin', when the capital had been described in official bulletins as 'a sea of flames', Holger stood in front of the commandant in his office. A pile of official-looking papers, all paper-clipped together, lay on his desk.

'Your girlfriend hasn't been wasting her time,' Major Waller said gruffly. He tapped the documents in front of him. 'Did you know about all this?'

'About the transfer? Yes. She wrote to me about it,' Holger answered. 'That is possible to move. To be given work on farms.' He felt his heart thump rapidly, his stomach hollow. He forced himself to silence, to keep his expression as stolid as he could.

'Looks like she's got some powerful friends,' the major grunted. 'And your friend the padre's been sticking his neck out for you. You're a lucky lad!' He grinned sardonically. He turned over the topmost sheets. 'You've even got some country squire offering to stand as guarantor. Sir George Whiteley.' He read slowly. 'Skinnerdale Hall. Impressive, eh? There's a posting to his estate. Some market-garden concern.' He looked up at

Holger, bared his teeth in a grin. 'What do you reckon?'

Holger looked puzzled, then said uncertainly, 'There is choice? I have choice?'

'You're not going to say no, surely? Chance to get out of here — practically next door to your girl.'

Holger still felt dreamlike. He nodded, fought to keep his voice, his demeanour steady. 'I say yes.'

''Course you do! Be a bloody fool not to, eh? Can't say I'll be sorry to let you go. You've always made me a bit uneasy, as you well know.'

Was that it? As simple as that, after all this time? Holger fought hard to stop himself from shaking. He stood there, the silence lengthening. Waller stared abstractedly at the papers, his fingers caressing the thin sandy line of his moustache. He glanced up again, gave a keenly appraising look.

'There is just one snag. Well, not really a snag,' he amended, still in that slow, thoughtful tone. 'You'll be on parole. You'll have to sign something. A written declaration. Giving your word, your promise — that you won't try to escape. Or indulge in any warlike acts.'

Holger felt the hot colour mount up his face, was acutely conscious of the major's steady stare. The Englishman knew how hard this had hit him.

'Is that a problem?' the major asked, with that same smile, broadening as Holger didn't answer. 'No skin off my nose,' Waller continued casually. 'Stay or go. Makes no difference to me. We'll have camps all over the country soon. Thousands of your types to work the land once Italy goes. Any day now.'

Holger felt a burning, white-hot rage gnawing like indigestion in his chest. He damped down the anger and his disgust at this coldly taunting figure sitting before him. He closed his eyes briefly. With a great effort of will, he summoned the vision of Ruth, her tear-stained face when she had left him last month, the powerful simplicity of the loving words she had written to him. The feel of her trembling, warm body and mouth on him. He drew a deep breath. Nodded.

'I sign,' he said.

★   ★   ★

He hardly slept the last night. He was up in the freezing dark of the early morning. He had been given some new underclothes. Shaving kit, towels, socks. Even two grey shirts and a new thick pullover. Everything was packed in the small kitbag he had also

327

been issued with. It had an English name and number stencilled in white on it. Perhaps the poor bastard had been shot, or wounded. Maybe he was a POW, Holger thought, with somewhat grim humour. But he was too keyed up to worry about some unknown's fate.

It seemed as though nine o'clock would never come. After a feeble attempt to eat the thin gruel and the bread they were given for breakfast, Holger made a tour of the huts, searching out his original companions of B-1, to make his final farewells. It was an emotional few moments, even though, for months now, Holger had rather cut himself off from any close association with them.

He was uncomfortable about Wolfgang Deist, knew damned well that the charismatic blond figure had been avoiding him over the past weeks. Wolfgang was in his hut, the place was crowded because of the severe weather.

'I'm off,' Holger said, a little stiffly, reddening a little.

Wolfgang stared at him piercingly, a mocking little smile playing about his mouth. After a pause, he said brightly, 'Of course you are!' He turned to the others crowding about with their good wishes. 'Our little Englander! Off to the arms of his beloved Land-Girl! Give her one for us, won't you?'

'Cut it out!' Holger said tautly. 'You're a sad bastard!' he said, so softly it was almost a whisper. He swung away, felt his arm grabbed as Wolfgang pulled him round again.

'Take a good look, chaps! Not often you get the chance to see a full-blown traitor!' There were several loud protests, embarrassed mutters. Holger faced him, their eyes locked.

Wolfgang suddenly drew himself up rigidly, and gave a heel-clicking, exemplary military salute. 'Heil Hitler!' The arm snapped down and Holger flinched as the gobbet of spittle struck him full on the cheek.

★　★　★

On Monday 3 January, 1944, there was a crowd of the girls at Middlesborough, waiting for the train through to Skinnerdale and the coast, and they held a noisily shrieking reunion in the middle of the platform, which caused passengers to turn their heads in curiosity.

'God! You'd think it had been a year, not a week, since we'd seen each other!'

They were delighted to find the camp lorry waiting in the station yard at Skinnerdale, particularly as the first small flakes of snow were beginning to fall from the laden sky. As soon as they got back to the camp, Ruth eagerly scanned the table where the mail had been spread out, and felt a deep disappointment at failing to find a letter from Holger.

'No news?' Irene asked sympathetically. She had arrived well after most of the others, by taxi, and loaded with extra goodies to be shared with her room mates.

Ruth smiled, tried to be philosophical. 'You know what it's like. All that red tape. It'll probably take ages.'

There was a thick layer of snow when they woke in the gloom of early morning.

'We won't be working today, surely?' they protested with faint hope, and groaned when Harry Guy appeared in the doorway, grinning at the mock screams and scuttling figures.

'I dunno what you're acting so shy for. Most of you wear more in bed than I've got on now, and I'm well wrapped up! On the job in half an hour, ladies!'

'We should be so lucky!' someone muttered feelingly at his departing back, and there was a burst of laughter.

Swathed so thickly in gear that they could hardly move, they assembled after breakfast and were quickly detailed off into their working squads.

'Palmer!' Harry Guy called. 'I need a volunteer to go down into Skinnerdale this morning. Some paperwork for the estate office. It's urgent. You'll do nicely! Come into my office.'

There were whistles and catcalls aplenty. 'Aye aye! What you been doing for the boss, eh?'

'You jammy tart, Ruthie!'

She waited while he sorted out some documents and slipped them in a manila folder.

'Don't let them get wet. Tuck them up your jumper or something! Can't give you a lift, I'm afraid. The truck's out. And the van. Still, you'll enjoy the walk, won't you?' He grinned. 'Take your time. As long as you're back for this afternoon. Be a chance for you to find out what's happening with that boyfriend of yours!'

She blushed slightly and nodded, grateful that he had picked her for what was a pleasant break from routine. He was right. She *would* enjoy the long walk down into the village. The dale was like a picture postcard in the new snowfall. She would even have time to pop in and see Ernie, and maybe Maggie. Share a welcome and leisurely cup of tea with them.

When she arrived, sweating inside the layers of clothing and glowing healthily, one of Ernie's Land-Girls was waiting for her outside the office.

'Oh, I'm glad I caught you. Mr Long says you're to go over to the house. Quick as you can. The squire wants to see you. Something to do with that Jerry that was supposed to come here.'

The 'was' smote Ruth like a knife in the ribs. Her eyes widened.

'Why? Nothing wrong, is there?'

The girl shrugged, maintained a carefully neutral face. 'Dunno. Best get over there.'

Ruth ran, slipping and sliding, along the frozen pathway, cursing the clumsy heaviness of the gumboots. It was like wading through deep water! She found herself praying, and fighting back threatening tears. Oh no! Please, God, let there be nothing wrong! Not now! Was it Holger? Had he changed his mind? It suddenly seemed a terrible possibility. She had been afraid all along about the parole paper he had to sign. How he would feel about it.

She was panting, and sick with dread by the time she reached the door in the stable yard, which led into the house. Ernie was standing just inside, talking to May Wynn. Ruth's heart lurched when she saw his lugubrious face.

'What is it?' she gasped.

He nodded over her shoulder, back across the yard. 'Squire's in the stable there, lass.

He'd best tell you himself.' He made a clicking noise and shook his head solemnly.

She swallowed hard, spun round in panic. The wide doors at the far end were open. This was the room they had fitted out to house the prisoners. The three Italians were already in residence here, she knew.

The grey light spilled in, showing the whitewashed stone walls, the stark simplicity of the four iron bedsteads, the small lockers beside them. The room was empty. Bewildered, she turned to go out again, and then gave a small cry of shock as a dark figure stepped from the shadowy angle of the door and the wall. It was wearing a khaki greatcoat that hung to its booted ankles. She could see only the black silhouette.

'Ruth. Liebchen!'

She felt the strength drain from her, as he came quickly forward and took her in his arms. She pressed her face against the roughness of the coat, her body racked with huge, convulsing sobs of shock and rehef.

'Oh — darling!' she blubbered. She shook her head. 'The blighters!' Far more profane words, words she would not have known four years ago, sprang to mind. 'I had no idea — they never said — '

The rest of her protests were cut off with

devastating effect by his sealing mouth. It closed over hers, possessed her, and nothing in the world mattered any more, only the touch and taste and feel of him, his enveloping and solidly real presence.

23

Holger sensed the cold hostility at once, could see it in Maggie Long's flushed face, its blank expression and the thin set of the mouth. Her hand was shaking slightly as she handed him the mug of tea, and the sudden thought came to Holger that, if she had her way, she would never use the vessel again, but would fling it out as soon as he had left.

Ernie tried to battle on bravely, loudly, against the wall of enmity from his wife, while Holger reflected bitterly that almost all his dealings with the English were like this. Even the most innocent conversations were full of pitfalls, not that many had bothered to socialize with him. Mostly he encountered bristling hostility or, at best, drop-jawed, gaping curiosity, as though he had fallen from another planet.

He could understand it, of course. The reality of the war was inescapable, as palpable as the black patch they had made him sew on his clothing. This woman, Frau Long, he knew had a son at sea, braving the dangers of the convoys to Russia. And here was the enemy, sitting in her kitchen, hale and hearty, drinking her tea. And they were enemies, no doubt of it. These people were his captors, all of them.

It was no less painful, for all his understanding of it. He had never felt so lonely, so isolated. Even with his fellow prisoners, it was the differences which marked his relationship with them. Marco, Tony, and Rico, the three Italians, had a different attitude and were treated differently, too, by the English. The three of them were always relaxed, laughing, ready to chat. He resented that they were accepted in a way that he wasn't. Of course, he knew that officially they were no longer even prisoners of war, that Britain and Italy were now allies — that they were in fact yet another on the long list of his 'enemies', for it was his fellow countrymen who were fighting and dying in grim defence of the Italian mainland. That touched him in a close and personal way, too. Ruth's brother had just been repatriated to a military hospital on the south coast of England after taking part in the campaign.

Ruth. If it hadn't been for the fact that she was so near now, only a few miles distant, he would have been desperately unhappy at times. He recognized too well the irony of his sometimes nostalgic longing for the enveloping closeness of the bonds forged at Glen

Bankirk. In some ways, the intrusiveness of Sir George's supervision, and his lackeys in the Home Guard unit, and the regular trips of the village policeman on his creaking bicycle, were as irksome as the roll-calls of Major Waller and his merry men. They were still locked into their stable room every night, though George, the lad who usually performed this ceremony, made something of a joke of it, at least with the three Italians, and very often it was the housekeeper from the Hall, May, who let them out in the morning.

He clung to the knowledge of Ruth's nearness. Even that, precious as it was, had its pain. They could only meet at weekends — he had seen her twice only so far, on both the Sundays since she had come back from her leave. And there was nowhere for them to go. They couldn't go into the village — Sir George had told him in that bluff way of his that he should stay within the grounds of the Hall — 'better all round if you lie low for a while, what!' — and he couldn't very well take her into his room, with those three grinning Latins waiting like vultures.

Instead, they had walked arm in arm around the gardens. Oh, there were sheltered spots, hidden away discreetly enough, so that they could cling together and kiss, until they were breathless and hot, despite the freezing weather, but January in this climate was no month for outdoor courting. And how he longed — his whole body ached — to be able to make love to Ruth properly, to show her just how much he *did* love her, everything about her. It scared him when he thought about the depth of his feeling for her, and hers for him, he was sure. It made his heart race with fear, for he could see no way ahead for them. All the more reason, therefore, to take all the sweetness they could from it now, when they had, against all odds, been brought together again.

So near — and yet so tantalizingly far. It galled him even more to see how one of his fellow prisoners, Marco, had struck up such an intimate relationship with one of the Land-Girls. And how convenient and success-ful. Gillian Taylor was one of the girls living literally over their heads, in the flat above the stables, which Ruth told him she once occupied herself. She was a pretty girl, rather Mediterranean-looking herself, with her raven-black hair, cut short, and her dark eyes. Eyes which always seemed to be laughing, and flashing a message unmistakable in its inviting candour, an invitation Marco had been quick to take up.

It was as well they were locked in for the night, or Marco would not be spending his nights in his own bed, Holger was certain. Not that he didn't make the most of other ample opportunities. He was often missing in the early evening, and his two compatriots would grin and nod eloquently towards the ceiling. One afternoon, Holger had been working on one of the compost pits, and Ernie sent him off early to get cleaned up. As Holger pushed open the heavy door of their quarters, he heard a gasp, and Marco's voice hissed urgently, 'Please! You wait, huh? Five minutes, yeah?'

Holger saw the dim hump of figures on the bed before he turned swiftly away. From where he waited outside, he could hear the low but furious gabble of voices, then, considerably sooner than the five minutes negotiated, Gillian Taylor came out, red-faced and decidedly ruffled. She did not look at him as she muttered something smothered by her breathless giggle. As she walked away, her fingers busy in her tangled hair, Holger noted that below her jersey, the tell-tale flap of her shirt tail hung down outside her slacks.

'We'll have a walk up to Kilbeck,' Ruth said, when they met the following Sunday. 'I can show you the camp on the way.'

'Sir George tell me — ', Holger began, but Ruth brushed aside his reservations. 'We won't go through the village. We won't come to any harm. It's up through the woods. We'll be all right. There's something I want to show you.'

He knew from her voice that it was important to her, and he reached for his battledress jacket. He thought it was the hut she was going to take him to. He gazed about him, drinking in the sharp, wintry solitude of the woodland, dizzy almost with the sense of freedom he had not known for so long, and, most precious of all, her presence at his side. 'It is like dream,' he said simply, and she nodded. But when he asked her if it was their hut she was leading him to, she smiled with tender regret, and shook her head.

'There'll probably be people up there now. It's Sunday. The Home Guard use it for drills and things. They'll be there now, I expect.'

Holger was blowing hard by the time they cleared the edge of the forest and found themselves with dramatic suddenness up on the open moor and the curve of narrow road that led to the village of Kilbeck. Clouds had gathered, and already the waning daylight was damp and chill, but she clung tightly to his arm with both her hands. When he saw the dark grey tower of the church, he knew. He felt a strange reluctance to go on, but he knew it meant a great deal to her. And to him, of course, he added hastily in his mind.

340

'Remember I said once how nice it would be if we could be here together?' He nodded.

And it was, powerfully so, as he stood a moment later in the wet grass and stared down at the stone slab, read the names of his comrades. She made to detach herself from his arm, to move away, and he turned, caught at her fiercely.

'No!' he said urgently. 'I want you with me!' He could hardly speak, his throat was clogged, and he slipped his arm around her waist, pulled her in tightly to him, feeling the tears well up, the names in black dancing before him. He conjured up their faces one by one. Goodbye, chaps. Sleep well.

He was overwhelmed by a profound sense of gratitude. A 'free-thinker', he had described himself, since the days of his teens in the Youth Movement. He recalled the many good-natured arguments he had had with Michael Bates as they strolled round the bleak compound of Glen Bankirk. Now, all at once, he was swamped by his emotion of love, his powerful need to believe in some divine providence. He pulled Ruth into him, sought out her lips desperately.

'We go inside,' he murmured, when they broke. 'I say prayer.' He caught at her hand again as she made to return across the grass. 'I want to believe. As you do.'

'Oh, Holger! I love you! So much!' She returned his kiss, pulled him after her. 'I'm a chapel, really,' she smiled over her shoulder at him. 'But I don't suppose God will mind very much, this once.'

She had expected to find the church empty at this time of the afternoon, but there was a Sunday school class going on, at the back of the church, just inside the porch. The children, all youngsters, were grouped in a semicircle, sitting on tiny wooden chairs whose legs were no more than a foot long. Facing them was their teacher, a handsome, middle-aged woman, in a smart blue hat with a little veil caught at its brim, and a wide-shouldered winter coat whose high collar was turned up. The children turned in whispering curiosity, and their teacher smiled at the newcomers, ordering her charges not to stare.

Rather self-consciously, Ruth and Holger walked down the aisle, towards the altar, aware of the echoing of their footsteps. They knelt on the faded hassocks of the font pew, their shoulders touching, and clasped their hands on the wood in front of them. Holger closed his eyes, tried to focus his wandering thoughts to form a coherent prayer, could not do so. He guessed that there must have been a service in here, with the coffins placed out front, yet somehow he found it hard to associate the grave outside, the deep sadness of his comrades' deaths, with the remote, mystical dimness inside the church. He had felt much closer to them standing out at their graveside.

He heard the soft scufflings, and hushed voices as the Sunday school class dispersed. He peeped sideways at Ruth. Her eyes were closed, her face relaxed, and her lips were very softly moving as she prayed. Again he felt that wave of tenderness, sweetly painful. Oh God! I love her, he thought. That was something he was sure of, at least. And that was as near as he could come to a prayer,

He pushed himself up, and sat on the polished, cold pew. After a moment, Ruth raised herself to sit beside him. She turned to him, smiling, and put her hand in his, then they just sat there, together, in the peaceful silence. Holger was half-lost in drifting thought when he heard the quick, striding steps behind him, then almost immediately, a hand struck him on the shoulder, like a blow. They both turned, to see the Sunday-school teacher standing loomingly over them. Her carefully made-up face was flushed, and alive with a hatred that was shocking. Her tones were even more shocking, ringing loudly with accusation.

'You've come in here to beg forgiveness, have you? God will not forgive you for what you've done, believe me!' They sat horrified, trapped by her fury. Holger saw her teeth, big, white, even, bared at him. 'Yesterday your people dropped a bomb, on a cinema in Croydon. Killed seven, it did!' She gestured wildly at the white cloth of the altar, raised on the blue-carpeted floor a few yards in front of them. 'A miracle, they said it was. More than a thousand in there. But there's seven families grieving now. It's no miracle for them, is it?'

She drew herself up, the hate transforming the handsome face into ugliness. 'There's no place for your kind here!' she said thickly. 'God doesn't forgive everything!'

'That's not fair!' Ruth cried out passionately, but the woman had already turned, was stomping back up the aisle. What about Hamburg? Ruth wanted to yell. What about Berlin? But the ringing footsteps faded, the church door clashed like thunder on their helplessness, and Ruth reached blindly for Holger's hand. He was sitting absolutely motionless, staring straight ahead at the ghostly white cloth, the tarnished silver and the dark wooden cross.

*   *   *

'Why you wear trousers?'

The aggressive bluntness of Holger's question was like a slap. She stared at him, coloured up immediately, for she knew exactly what he meant by it.

'Well, it's still cold, even if it *is* April,' she answered with quick defensiveness. 'And for walking it's much easier. You know — than a skirt, and stockings and all that.'

'I never see you in dress.' His hand waved exasperatedly in the air. 'All the girls. All the time. In trousers. Those breeches! Gillian was in a dress last evening, I see legs, in stockings, I say, 'What is this?' I am forgetting what a girl's legs look like!'

'She shows *hers* off plenty from what *I've* heard!' Ruth caught at Holger's hand. Her eyes were wide, pleading. 'Don't be mean to me! I just want to be with you. I didn't think . . . '

He gave a smothered groan, then reached for her, pulled her down beside him, pressed his body on hers as he kissed her hard on the mouth. She did not resist. Her arms came round him, she could feel herself trembling against him. His lips moved against her cheek as he spoke.

'I want to love you — to be alone with you. To touch, to see you — to be normal!' His voice shook, caught in his throat, and he kissed her again, until she was gulping dizzily for breath when he finally pulled away his mouth. He did not let her go. His knee was pressing between hers, he turned her so that he was lying half on top of her.

'I want that, too. I love you — you know that. But — but, I want it to be right for us. Please . . . '

They kissed again, his tongue driving into her mouth, his body thrusting against her, and there was that giddy sensation of desire, and of fear. His hand scrabbled at the hem of her jersey, burrowed up over the smoothness of her blouse, the fingers pressing against the contours of her breasts, and she wondered briefly whether she wanted him to stop, or to go on. She tried to stop the tears, swallowed hard, felt them brimming, filling her eyes, seeping to her cheeks as she buried her chin in his shoulder, and his rough, hard, alien fingers clawed like some frantic animal at the buttons of the blouse, dug into her warm flesh, touched the cotton of her brassiére, dragged the cup until it caught, digging into the softness of her right breast at the very point of her nipple. Then it was gone, her breast was free, and his fingers were plucking, touching at the hard little teat. She shivered, clung to him, her body swept by this feeling of invasion, of melting, soft need, and her wish to hide herself against him.

The caressing hand was pulled roughly away, leaving her clothing beneath the concealing jumper in disarray. He rolled fully on top of her, his hands came up to pin her by the shoulders, pressing her down into the dampness of the earth, then, shockingly, she felt his loins and belly jerk madly against hers in the quick rhythms of coition, with such force that they were both grunting. The thick layers of the clothing separating their heaving bodies made it all the more shockingly obscene.

The tears were flowing down the sides of her temples. Through them, she saw his face, lifted blindly, screwed in agony, until, all at once, a convulsive shudder passed right through him and he rolled off her with a despairing moan, and lay untouching on his stomach, his face hidden in his folded arms.

She lay awhile, recovering from the shock, and the fear of those wild moments. She felt as though she had been crushed, driven into the earth. The violence of it brought the fear bubbling up again. What must it be like to make love?

She heard him move. He stood up, brushing the leaves from him, shaking her crumpled mackintosh. She was busy with her handkerchief, with her disarranged clothing, crouched, half-turned away, then she faced him. She moved to him, smiled humbly. 'I'm sorry.'

For a second, he stared at her almost coldly, she thought, then she saw the sadness that made her want to weep again, for both of them.

'No, no! It is I who should apologize. Ask your forgiveness. I cannot help myself. Come. Let us walk.'

'Holger!' She cried his name, pulled fiercely at his arm, swinging him round with her strength. She reached up, blatantly offered her mouth, waiting, until he was forced to bend, kiss her on the lips. 'I *do* want you,' she whispered. 'I want to go to bed with you. I want to do everything with you. You *do* believe that, don't you?'

'Let us walk.' He smiled, and its sadness hurt her almost as much as the fact that he didn't answer her question.

★   ★   ★

'Come on, ladies! Tough as leather, hard as steel!'

Heidi drew in a deep breath to emphasize the full swell of her breasts straining beneath her dark uniform. She felt the leather belt cutting painfully at her waist. She had drawn

348

it in as tightly as she could bear it, knowing that it highlighted the voluptuous quality of her figure. She felt a fleeting pity for the groaning, scurrying figures at the long rows of metal washbasins. With very few exceptions, they looked so thin, their skinniness evident in the white vests and black knickers they all wore. The shoulder-bones, the knobs of their spines, jutted even more noticeably because of their crouched stance over the basins. These girls were all fourteen-and fifteen-year-olds, yet many of them had not even started menstruating yet, and there was scarcely a discernible bosom among them.

It was all down to the miserable diet, Heidi knew, and felt a discomfiting prick of guilt as she thought of how well she herself lived. And her parents, and little Inge, thank God. When Heidi quoted the Youth Movement motto at her charges, she was not surprised or dismayed at the subdued rebellion she could hear in the mutterings which followed. It was necessary for her to toe the party line, more important than ever that she should strive to lift morale at a time when, everywhere, there were so many alarming signs of bitter disillusionment.

Not only food but almost everything else was scarce, while the dreadful air-raids went on and on, day and night, unceasingly. The

349

papers were full of the vast numbers of Allied planes destroyed, and Gerhard had told her it was true, the night fighters were having a high rate of success in their efforts, but the Allies seemed to have an inexhaustible supply of bombers. There were dark rumours, mutterings on all sides. The phrase 'the enemy within' had taken on a newly sinister meaning.

She knew Gerhard was deeply involved in that side of things, though he talked very little of his work, telling her it was far better for her not to know too much of what went on. Although he had come back from Denmark early in the new year, to announce proudly his promotion to full colonel as a reward for the work he had done there, he still spent the vast majority of his time away from home, travelling all over Germany, away for days at a time. Since the announcement had been made that Goebbels had taken overall charge of the capital last month, Gerhard had been busier than ever. She worried constantly about him.

★ ★ ★

Gerhard Waldeyer nodded to his subordinates, and the three of them climbed from the black car as the canvas-covered lorry came into sight. It pulled up on the track a few yards from them. The light machine-guns had already been set up on their tripods, facing the steep slope of the meadow which reared up from the side of the track. A line of fir trees stood out, dark and high above them, on the skyline. On the other side of the track, a high hedge hid the surrounding farmland from their view.

It was a beautiful late spring day. The grassy margins at the edge of the track were a mass of stirring colours and softly buzzing insects: white clover, nodding field-poppies, the blaring yellow of dandelions below, blue spots of harebells. White fleeced clouds moved far above. Gerhard walked over to the two couples kneeling by the weapons. The trail of bullets gleamed in the sunshine. He nodded at them, saw their strained, pale faces stare up at him. An Adam's apple bobbed in a freckled throat.

The uniformed guards had already dismounted from the truck. They had bayonets fixed to their rifles. Gerhard walked round to the tailboard of the lorry, where a young lieutenant was standing, his revolver drawn. He had buttoned his tunic correctly, the SS flash at his neckband showing prominently.

Gerhard nodded again, and the canvas covers were pulled back.

'Out, please, gentlemen,' Gerhard called smoothly, in English. They were blinking against the light as they dropped down stiffly from the back of the lorry. They all looked pale, exhausted, most of them shadowy with a growth of whiskers. They were dressed in their attempts at civvy clothing, which they had worn for their escape bids. Several had been injured during their recapture. One, with a pale and unimpressive line of moustache, which somehow seemed only to add to his air of extreme youthfulness, had a large, very dirty bandage tied round his head. The brow was darkly stained where the blood had seeped through. One of his companions helped him down, supported him as he stood.

They were completely silent. The young lieutenant shouted orders in German, the guards herded them with their rifles crossed over their chests.

'A change in the schedule, gentlemen!' Gerhard called out, in a reassuring voice. 'We have to change transport here. For your own safety. Line up, please.'

They formed a ragged line, staring, apathetic, then the fear dawned in their faces as they saw the twin machine-guns directly opposite.

'Fire!' Gerhard yelled, and the fourteen bodies were cut down as they stood. Only two managed to turn and take a last agonising step. Another fell weeping to his knees before he was whipped over on to his lifeless back by the force of the streaming bullets.

The silence was shocking when the guns stopped. A faint blue cloud drifted swiftly away on the sunlight, the sharp smell of the cordite lingered. There was a groan, obscenely clear, from the careless tumble of bodies. The lieutenant was grey as his uniform, staring wide-eyed. Gerhard knew he had to act. He took the service revolver from the man's limp grasp. The butt was unpleasantly damp with his sweat.

Gerhard walked among the bodies, signalling for his own men to join him. They already had their revolvers out. They examined each body, bent and fired dispatching shots at one or two. The bandaged youth was alive still. His eyes were open, they were swimming with tears. He had long, fine lashes, they were pale in the sun. Beautiful, like a girl's. A picture of Heidi flashed into Gerhard's mind, her rosily replete gaze after they had made love. The RAF flier's eyes stared up at him, beseeching, then closed, and Gerhard saw the teardrops form at those lashes. He bent, held the barrel of the gun at the temple and pulled the trigger.

24

Ruth was at work, on the Tuesday, when the news broke. They were miles away from the camp, well down the dale, on land that belonged to one of the other wealthy owners. It was almost lunchtime when Harry Guy himself appeared, in the estate car. Ruth and Irene were operating one of the heavy two-man saws, stripping the branches from the felled trunks. They were sweating in spite of the chilliness of the overcast day and were glad of the excuse to stop for a breather.

They knew at once from the wild shrieks of the girls nearest to the head forester. Couples embraced, danced round madly, clinging on to one another. Ruth and Irene hugged, then the shorter, dark-haired girl drew back a little, gazed at Ruth, who pinked a little. She understood the concern behind the look.

'I'm glad,' Ruth murmured. 'I really am. I just hope we can get this madness over with once and for all!'

But in the days that followed, she had cause to doubt her own emotions at times. She said the same thing, more urgently, over and over to Holger, but still she felt the awful weight of the misery and conflict she could see all too well in his face. The world pressed inescapably in upon them. Talk was of nothing else. After the initial euphoria came the anxiety of the difficulties facing the Allied forces as they tried to break out from Normandy. The name Caen sprang into unwelcome prominence. Pessimists began to wonder if we might after all be driven back to the sea; and the nightmare of the Dieppe tragedy was remembered.

And then, only a week after the landings, a new terror came to light, in the form of a German bomb — a pilotless bomb, with its own engine, so that no plane was needed to deliver it. This new scourge, known as the V-1, could be directed day or night at Britain's cities. It was rumoured that Hitler had hundreds ready, that this was the secret weapon which he had predicted would change the course of the war. At the moment they were all aimed at London, but who knew when the 'flying bombs' would start hitting other cities?

There was something inhuman about this kind of warfare, about missiles sent to fall indiscriminately over a city. People felt helpless, there was a kind of superstitious dread of this terrifying menace. Stories abounded. You could hear the motors throbbing away, then, worst of all, you could hear them stop and you knew the missile was falling, somewhere near. Yet another evacuation of the children from the capital was set in motion. Victory, which had seemed so near, moved agonizingly away again, and it was hard to summon up the spirit of the blitz, which had seen people through, four long years ago.

In the midst of all this, Ruth and Holger clung to their relationship with a desperation that came perilously close to despair. They were afraid to be seen out in public together. Sir George insisted once more that Holger confine himself to the environs of the Hall, whereas his three Italian counterparts were allowed to roam at will, throughout the village and the surrounding countryside. They even went for excursions into Whitby on Sundays.

'What is there for us?' Holger asked wretchedly, as they walked hand in hand through the plantation edging Barker's Farm, along the path where they recognized every bush and tree. It was a mid-July Sunday, and Ruth had put on her prettiest frock, and the white ankle-socks which showed off the pale-honey colour of her limbs.

At his question, she stopped. 'The war's not going to last for ever. It's got — '

'They will never allow us to marry! You know this! For many years!'

His words hung sickeningly, on the air, burned themselves into her mind.

'We can make them! We'll ask permission — let everyone know. We love each other.' But already he was moving again, along the narrow pathway, in front of her, his hands pushed into the pockets of his shabby trousers. His shoulders were bent. Between them she could see the large, roughly sewn diamond of the black patch. 'Just like they made the Jews wear?' one of the girls had said when someone had remarked on the distinctive mark the Italian POWs wore.

Ruth had come to a momentous decision. However hopeless it might appear, the one rock-certain fact in her life was that she loved Holger, and that he loved her equally. He had to know that, be absolutely sure of it, and of her. The following week she sought out Gillian Taylor. She had got to know the girl quite well, particularly in the six months since Holger had come to join the Italians at Skinnerdale. She knew too that Gillian was carrying on an affair with Marco, one of the prisoners, and not only from Holger's accounts of his fellow prisoner's frequent absences from their quarters. The Land-Girl herself made little effort to hide her feelings for the Italian, and her friendly attitude towards Ruth and Holger made Ruth feel that she would prove a sympathetic ally. Nevertheless, it was far from easy for Ruth to bring herself to approach her.

Her face was red when she awkwardly broached the delicate subject she had in mind.

'Will you be out on Saturday night — for a few hours?' she asked abruptly. Ruth was already well aware that Gillian's flatmate, Eileen Dutton, was away practically every weekend, at her uncle and aunt's in Loftus, a few miles up the coast.

Gillian nodded quickly. 'Aye, I can be. No problem. You want to use the flat?' Ruth nodded ashamedly. The girl put her hand lightly on Ruth's arm for a second. 'You know what you're doing?' There was a wealth of meaning in the simple question, which both recognized.

Holger was surprised the following Saturday evening when Ruth led him to the front door in the corner of the courtyard. 'We do not go far,' he murmured. Ruth's face was pale. She glanced about her quickly, with a haunted look, and fitted the key into the lock. Then the door was shut and they were together, touching, in the tiny, dark space no more than a couple of feet square, at the bottom of the steep flight of stairs. Both were breathing heavily, caught in the sudden tension.

'Come on!' she whispered, and mounted ahead of him. The tiny cubicle of toilet and basin at the head of the stairs, the large, sparsely furnished living-room, to the left, looked both familiar and oddly different. Its present occupants had added their individual touches to try and create an atmosphere of home. Strange pictures on the white walls, strangers' photographs on window-ledges and mantelshelf.

She turned to face him. The long rectangle of late evening sunlight fell across the worn carpet, lit up her feet in the white strappy sandals. Holger could see the uncertainty, the fear, in the brown eyes as she gazed at him with shy resolution.

'Gillian said — I asked . . . ' She began to cry as he moved hastily to her, and they clasped desperately at each other.

They were on the lumpy sofa, she was stretched out, under him, one foot on the floor, the other bent awkwardly, knee raised, while he sprawled on top of her, their lips nuzzling and tasting feverishly. She felt his hand under her displaced dress, hard and heavy on the smoothness of her upper thigh.

'Gillian said — we could use her bed!' she

panted, when their mouths parted briefly.

He rolled off her, and she stood, shook the hem of her dress down, took his hand, pulled him to the small bedroom she herself had used when she stayed here.

She moved into the sun-filled room, felt the pressure of his resistance and stopped. His face looked drawn, beseeching almost. 'You want? You are sure?'

She nodded, felt the tears rolling down her face, nodded again, smiling. 'I want, Holger. I want, very much.'

Sacrificial virgin, sacrificial virgin! The phrase rang over and over in her mind, then was banished, when his hands moved, clumsy, frightening in their unsteady haste, so that she stopped him, and they stood facing one another while she drew the frock up over her head, then her best silk slip.

She was shocked, stunned sometimes, after that first frightening junction, at her own sexuality. It's love, love, she had to keep telling herself, for she wanted him so much, to see his body, to touch him. To have him touch her. There was a great fear of course that she would be pregnant. It's what I want more than anything, she told herself, and him, but they both knew it was neither lie nor truth, but something between, for it scared her half to death to think about what would happen if she was. What would they do to her if she did have his child? Probably shut her up.

She wasn't being melodramatic. Though girls were getting 'caught' all the time nowadays, it was no casual thing to have a baby out of wedlock. The girls talked of it often, the calamity it would present. Irene had told her of a girl she knew who had been put away in a nursing home, the family's doctor prepared to classify it as a form of dementia. 'Goodness knows when she'll be out, poor thing!' Irene lamented. 'They could keep her shut up in there for years!'

Holger suffered as much as Ruth. 'You'll have to get hold of some protectives,' Holger told her. He recalled his military days before capture. 'Can't you get them? Where you work?'

Ruth gaped at him in amazement, gave a scandalized little giggle. 'What? Good heavens, no!' She felt very much alone.

She longed to tell Irene of the great step she had taken, but somehow she couldn't bring herself to do so. Yet she was sure there would be plenty of girls who would be able to give her sound advice, doubtless from first-hand experience, on how to avoid getting pregnant. There was an expert back home, too, she reflected bitterly, but she would rather die than ask her sister. She could just imagine the resultant shrieking from the house-tops that would take place there.

It was Holger himself who solved the immediate problem for her. Immediate, that is, after the undoubted relief of discovering that her period was arriving on time.

'I have forgotten.' He smiled, patting the breast pocket of his battledress. 'My gallant allies from Italy. They have friends everywhere!' Ruth smiled, too, but blushed at the thought of facing the three dark-eyed prisoners the next time they met. It was bad enough with Gillian, who grinned knowingly, and winked at her after that first tryst. Thankfully, she did not seem particularly anxious to press the role of confidante. After all, she had her own absorbing affairs to took after, thank goodness.

Nevertheless, there was an uncomfortable amount of intimacy involved in their new friendship, for the flat above the stables became the chief and regular venue for the dramatic and permanent change in Ruth's and Holger's relationship. Neither of them liked the necessary furtiveness, nor the sense of obligation they felt towards Gillian. Though Gillian swore that she had told no one else of their secret, Ruth felt deeply uncomfortable in both the presence of the smiling Marco, and Eileen, Gillian's flatmate.

'She does not know what we do,' Holger tried to reassure her, but Ruth's reproachful look was eloquent enough as a protest.

'Oh come on! She wasn't born yesterday! She knows fine well what we do!' Ruth exploded.

But, in spite of all the pain and anxiety it caused her, Ruth was unshaken in her belief that she had made the right decision for both of them. Though the stress was still there, Holger's face reflected the solid certainty their action had given him. And Ruth felt that, for her, too, the commitment had been essential. She wanted him, wanted the solace of knowing him physically, as well as spiritually. There could be no going back now. She belonged to him, truly felt it. And that he belonged to her, too.

She sometimes felt that she lived only for those magical Saturday nights, the few precious hours when they could really be together in their exclusive little world, as the last full summer of the war slipped by. She wanted to share her happiness with others, wished that she could tell her family, Ernie and Maggie. One Sunday night, at the end of another harvest season, lying in her bed, her body still sore and bruised from the wonder of the loving she and Holger had enjoyed,

Ruth found herself whispering the truth into the darkness. There was a charged silence for a few seconds, then Irene whispered, 'I know. I knew ages ago.'

Ruth stiffened. How on earth ... ? 'Nobody's said anything,' the soft voice continued. 'No one needed to. It's been pretty damned obvious all summer.' There was a creak, then Ruth felt Irene's hand groping, searching for hers and she clutched at it tightly. 'Please be careful, darling.' Ruth knew that the dark-haired girl was deeply concerned for her.

She raised the hand to her own cheek, rubbed it gently. 'I will, love, I promise. But, oh God, Irene! I love him so much it hurts!'

The pressure of her grip was returned, then let go. Irene sighed, 'It's got to end soon, hasn't it?'

That very week Brussels and Antwerp had been liberated. But the previous day the first of the even more frightening V-2 weapons had fallen on London.

★ ★ ★

It took Heidi more than two days to travel eastwards across the country to reach the capital. It was a miracle that any trains managed to run at all, and there were many

364

times on the eventful journey that she wept and cursed her own foolhardiness in refusing to heed the advice of her parents and everyone else she came into contact with. At one point, she had to leap down from the packed carriage, rolling in the icy mud of a wet March day, then slipping and sliding down the embankment, huddled terrified with hundreds of others, while the enemy fighters roared over at rooftop height machine-gunning the train and the surrounding track.

She was glad that she had at least dressed sensibly, in trousers and thick underwear. By the time she arrived exhausted in the capital, she was covered in caked mud and grime, and badly in need of a bath and some proper food. Nevertheless, she had to wait another endless two hours when she reached the offices Gerhard's unit was using in Lichtenburg, sitting in the tiled, draughty vestibule of the old building, in which it seemed half the city's population was attempting to crowd.

There was another air-raid warning while she waited. Crying with weariness, she let herself be jostled and banged along with the throng that swept down into the dank, roomy cellar of the building.

'Come on, cutey!' She felt an arm slip round her padded shoulders and she was squeezed against the bulk of a chubby, unshaven man, of middle age she guessed, who was wearing the uniform of a railway official. He kept his arm about her, tried to pull her head, her blonde hair hidden by the checked scarf tied round it, down on to his chest. 'Don't cry! it'll be all right, you'll see. We're not done yet!' He leered, winked at her. 'Anyway, what's a beauty like you got to worry about? You've got better weapons than any bullets to see you through, eh?'

She thrust his arm vigorously away from her, and fought her way up off the narrow wooden bench.

'Get off me, pig!' The tears brimmed on her red, travel-stained face. 'My husband's a colonel here. I'll have you arrested, you oaf!'

The man looked suitably abashed but as she moved away another voice called out insultingly: 'And your farts smell of lavender, do they love?' She moved towards the stairs leading to the heavy doors and stood with the others clustered there. She gazed around her. A sense of panic seized her. They all looked so filthy, and gaunt. The place stank. In the dim lighting, the scene had the quality of a nightmare. All at once, the weight of hopelessness pressed down on her. They were finished, all of them. Germany was descending into chaos.

She felt better an hour later. She was lying stretched out in the porcelain bathtub, the scented water scummy with the dirt she had washed from her. Gerhard had just climbed out, and came back into the steamy room carrying two drinks. He was naked, and her eyes were drawn to the black curls above the dark hang of his genitals. In contrast, his body was white and frail-looking, the long shanks of his thighs scarcely filling out at all. She was almost ashamed of her own sleek frame, until she saw his eyes hungrily feasting on her, and she stirred with pleasure.

She rose as he came to her. Her body gleamed. She took the drink, their eyes met over the rim of their glasses. 'There now!' she breathed sensually. 'I'm fit to touch now. So come on. Touch me!'

But afterwards, the world was there, even as they lay in bed. They could hear the guns firing, the sirens wailed again, and Gerhard forced her to get up, drag on clothing. 'It's not just us, is it?' he chided. 'There's Inge. You've got to be there for her.'

The cellar of the living-quarters was much more comfortably appointed, for senior personnel and the staff who looked after them. Gerhard and Heidi were able to find a quiet corner, with easy chairs, and a supply of real coffee to make the long wait easier.

'We have to talk, darling,' Gerhard said, with quiet sadness, and Heidi felt that sinking despair inside her once more.

'I've arranged a place for you in a car, it's leaving tonight. It'll take you as far as Hanover. You should pick up a train from there.' He talked on over her rising wail of protest. 'There's no time! Things are falling apart, fast! The Yanks and the British are about to cross the Rhine in force. You've got to get back home as soon as you can. You mustn't get caught here. The Reds are heading for us. Berlin could be cut off soon. And you don't want to be around when those swine get here!'

She knew exactly what he meant. She hesitated. 'Can't you come — with me?' she whispered. 'It's all over, isn't it? It's hopeless.'

He smiled, bent forward, kissed her brow, just below her freshly washed yellow hair. 'I have to stay on. Duty. I'll do my best to get to you, you know that. You just survive. Take care of your folks — and Inge.'

He had her small case brought down. They went out into the rumbling, flashing dark straight from the cellar.

'You will come back to us? Promise? Please!'

'Yes! Go now!' He could hardly get the

words out. He had almost to push her into the car, was glad of the other firm hands reaching to drag her in. He stood back, watched the dim shape of the vehicle move out of the open gateway, into the darkness of the ravaged city.

Back upstairs in his room, he picked up one of the two glasses standing on the table and poured himself another generous drink. Soon he would go down one floor to the luxurious suite of rooms occupied by his superior. A select little group would meet there, to go over the details of their own complex contingency plans. It was knowing just when to leave, that was the crucial thing. Going too soon could be as bad as going too late. They had to slip out of the closing noose, but at the critical time, to enable them to get clear of Germany.

They knew it was no use surrendering themselves to the Allies. Any day now, news of the atrocities was going to shake the whole of the civilized world. The legitimate defence of 'we were only obeying orders' would not save them. The self-righteous howls for vengeance would drown out any other pleas. Bitterly, he reflected on the raids carried out on Dresden last month. St Valentine's Day! Over 100,000 dead in the firestorms that engulfed the city. There was a massacre all right! Innocents driven into the furnace.

The irony was, those damned Jews he had rounded up in Denmark were fine, as far as he knew. Sitting pretty in the camp at Theresienstadt. Not that it would help if he *did* fall into the enemy's hands, east or west. Well, if this escape-bid failed, there were always the cyanide pills they all carried. Certainly quick enough. Painless, he didn't know about.

He thought of his baby daughter, of Heidi, and his throat caught again, his eyes misted. Who knows? He might after all survive, might be reunited with them, some day. He moved, stared down at the tumbled bed, the covers flung back, the sheet still marked with the damp evidence of their loving. He fell forward, with a soft groan, driving his face into her pillow, absorbing the faint, lingering fragrance he found there.

★　★　★

Michael Bates glanced up from his slim pile of letters. A Jeep had bounced to a halt outside the tents, which had been rigged up for the field HQ. Now a young lieutenant was hurrying towards him, closely followed by Major Dewey, his own CO. His heart quickened a little at the look on their faces.

The lieutenant, whom he didn't know, looked ghastly.

'You're needed, Padre!' the major said tersely. 'Can you go right away? This is Lieutenant Evans. He'll explain.'

Even the young officer's voice sounded strained. He stared ahead, at the leather-coated back of the driver, didn't look at Michael.

'We've found a camp — a labour camp — one of those places. It's — grim.' He shook his head.

They came to a village — Bergen. It appeared to be deserted. Just outside, there was a long barrack-type building, surrounded by wire fencing, over to the left, well away from the road. Michael could see small, distant figures, standing at the wire, staring out. Most of them seemed to be dressed in pyjamas.

A little further on, they came to another high fence, stretching away on either side of the roadway, and an open gate-way, where several British soldiers were standing. As Michael climbed down, he noticed the smell at once. Sickly, sweet with rottenness. Sewage? An RAMC corporal hurried forward. 'You'll need this, sir. Typhus.' The sharp smell of DDT powder replaced the other smells as the corporal began to dust him thoroughly, shaking the powder over his clothing, up his sleeves, into his jacket. 'Pants, sir.' Bewildered, Michael undid his topmost buttons, pulled out the waistband of his trousers a little so that the powder could be dropped down the front. It rose in a cloud which made him sneeze.

He stopped, unable to take in what be saw. Outside the first hut, some figures were lying, others sitting. One or two were standing, some even tottered forward.

They're not human, Michael thought. Their knees, all their joints, were huge, joined by bones covered with grey or yellow skin. Huge, pale skulls wobbled on top of these grotesque skeletons. Eyes were huge and black, crusted mouths gaped toothlessly in wide grins which stretched the papery skin horrifyingly over the bone structure of the ruined features.

Some had a few rags clinging to them, most were naked. Dark trails of excrement marked their stick limbs. As he watched, one folded, like a puppet whose strings had been cut, collapsed in a heap, silently. The pale skull looked blue.

'They're dying all the time! Hundreds of them!' The lieutenant was staring. He had clamped his handkerchief to his mouth. Above it, his eyes stared in agony. He nodded at the hut. 'Please!' he gasped. 'Sergeant. Take the padre . . . '

He turned away, and, with a crawling sense of dread, Michael moved at the sergeant's side towards the ghosts grinning hideously on either side. A skeleton hand reached out, hesitantly, with fear, as though he might not be real, and brushed with dry-feather lightness over the sleeve of his uniform.

'Welcome!' came the hoarse whisper. 'Bless you!'

Michael thought for a second he would not have the courage to enter. The stench was a choking, nauseous cloud. Then in the dimness, he saw the tiered bunks, those round nightmare heads poking out, the stick arms raised, in greeting or supplication. The heaps of withered flesh that lay unmoving. The living and the dying lay with the dead, in a scene that Michael would never forget, and which would never cease to make him chill with fear all the thousands of times he recalled it in the years ahead. Somehow, he made himself walk the length of the hut, smiling as the tears streamed down his face. Some recognized the liberators and called out greetings. He entered other huts, all packed with dead and dying, though even outside corpses were scattered in profusion. A number died as he watched, using the last spark of life to drag themselves into the April sun.

Near what were clearly the administration offices, he found a medical officer and a handful of orderlies, grey with exhaustion, at work among row after row of bodies laid out on the earth. Even here, the scarecrow figures waved a feeble greeting, grinned their terrifying smiles at him. Some had red crosses shining on their foreheads. 'They're the ones that have a chance of making it,' the MO told him, his words muffled through the cloth of his mask. 'We're too late for most of them.'

There was a commotion at the end of the long, neighbouring building. Michael heard some high-pitched screaming, and frantic sobbing. There was a pile of rubbish bins, full of putrid waste from the kitchen. Beside it, an untidy jumble of naked bodies, heaped indiscriminately. A figure in khaki shirt and grey uniform trousers was kneeling in the dust, sobbing piteously. His short, greasy hair shone, his face streamed with mucus and sweat and tears.

A British soldier was standing over him, holding a Sten gun at the ready. There was a single stripe on his sleeve. A small group of the emaciated inmates were standing, silent, watchful.

'This bastard's a guard!' the Britisher said, his face working with emotion. 'They say he shot this lot!' He nodded at the pile of bodies. 'For stealing tattie peelings! I'm not taking the bastard in!'

The kneeling figure looked, saw Michael's uniform, perhaps recognized the dog-collar. He cried out wildly, lifted his clasped hands. The language he spoke was not German. Later, Michael learnt that Hungarians had formed the bulk of the guards at the camp. Michael looked, not at the sobbing figure on the ground, but at the British soldier. Their eyes locked in complicity and Michael turned away without a word. He was several yards away, jumped at the brief stutter of the weapon in the lance-corporal's hands.

★ ★ ★

By the end of the month, the horrors of Bergen-Belsen had been flashed around the world, in newspapers, magazines, and, most terrible of all, on the cinema screens, as stunned audiences watched piles of skeletal corpses literally bulldozed into the vast pits hastily dug to receive them. To Ruth it was the culmination of all her worst nightmares. Information came through, day after day, of other death-camps, but it was the hell of

Belsen which struck with most immediacy in Britain.

'You must leave me,' Holger said, in a voice that was lifeless. He sat slumped on his bed in the stable. Ruth sat beside him, weeping helplessly, unable to find any words to say, unable to offer the solace of her body.

Back at Allerton, at the evening meal in the dining-hall, Beryl Mills walked up to Ruth just after she had sat down with her plate, and spat with disgusting noisiness into her food.

'You Nazi tart!'

Ruth stood. She gazed round her. There was a shocking silence, nobody's eyes were lifted to meet hers, nobody spoke out in condemnation of Beryl's act. Ruth left the table, hurried out into the calm evening, shook off lrene's restraining arm and ran blindly for the gate and the solitude of the wood.

On the following Saturday, the day the news came that the German forces in north-west Germany had surrendered *en masse*, Ruth hurried down through the woodland path to the village. She had had a quick wash, changed into slacks and uniform jersey as soon as work had finished that afternoon. The girls said nothing. Several of them had gone out of their way to show their friendship after the incident at supper, and of course Irene had remained steadfastly and volubly loyal; incurring a measure of unpopularity herself from some quarters. But Ruth had felt increasingly anxious, without fully understanding why. She had not seen Holger since that almost wordless meeting in mid-week, when they had both sat smothered in the deadening unhappiness and despair which gripped them.

She half hoped he would be on the path somewhere, setting out to meet her, but there was no sign of him. She was almost running when she reached the stable yard. Marco and Tony were lying on their beds, and sprang up when they saw her. She stared at Holger's bed. The mattress was bare, the grey blankets folded neatly at its head.

'He has gone,' Marco said, his dark eyes eloquent with sympathy. 'There was trouble. He go outside. To village. Some of the local boys — they fight him, beat him. He is all right,' he added quickly, at Ruth's cry of alarm. 'Just-a bruises. But they take him. To camp. Near Malton, I think. Yesterday night.'

'But he — didn't he — say . . . ' There was nothing. No letter, no message for her of any kind. She sat down on his empty bed, oblivious to the two men's embarrassed presence, lost in the numbness of the disaster, his brutal rejection of her. She sank sideways, lay there, her knees drawn up to her breast, her face hidden in her arm. The men stared for a while, then quietly left her alone.

25

Ruth looked up at the craggy, patrician face opposite her. Though already silver-haired, and heavily scored with the lines of age, the features of Colonel Best were incredibly handsome. He ought to be an actor, a film star, Ruth thought distractedly. And he had the voice to match. Plum rich, with gravelly deepness, and that immaculate accent. She blushed again, suddenly seeing herself through his eyes. A common little tart, a Maxie Miller Land-Girl in her far from new uniform, hot for a Jerry flier. He probably thought she was pregnant already. Up the spout. Desperate.

She cleared her throat. Her eyes glistened with unshed tears, her lip trembled.

'I want to marry him.'

Colonel Best stared at her. He said nothing for a while. She did not lower her gaze, and at last he shook his head.

'My dear girl,' he said softly. 'I should imagine that's quite impossible.' He got up from behind his cluttered desk. 'But see him you shall!' His face broke into a warm smile. 'If we can find him for you. The camp's half empty, I reckon. We've got mostly Italians here. More like a hostel really. They come and go as they please, pretty much. And the war is over, thank God.'

Yesterday, Tuesday 8 May, had been officially declared Victory in Europe Day. At Allerton, the camp had been almost deserted. Nearly everyone had gone off for the weekend, just waiting for the announcement that the war was over. Irene had even asked her to come home with her. 'I can't bear the thought of you mooching about here on your own,' the dark-haired girl said passionately. But Ruth shook her head, embraced her fondly.

'No. I'm going to try to get over to Malton. He hasn't even written. All week. I've got to see him.'

And now it looked as though she had succeeded, unless he refused outright to talk to her. She was hardly sure of anything any more. His action in leaving her like that had shaken her badly. Whatever the reason, whatever the anguish he was going through, he should not have deserted her like that. It was a rejection of her, of their love; and it hurt deeply. She had felt utterly alone, like a ghost somehow, in the wild mood of celebration that had gone on all around her over the past few days.

On the train ride to Pickering, as the spectacular scenery of the moors slipped past her unnoticed, she tried to think clearly, to look ahead. Holger would claim that he had acted for her own good. *What is there for us?* He had said that more than once. *We love each other.* Her answer was always the same, rang out in her head even now, clear as ever. But what did it mean, in practical terms? They couldn't marry. He was an alien, an enemy. Permission would not be granted in Britain. Where could they go? Germany was an occupied territory, it would be ruled over by the Allies. British law would apply there, too.

Well then, she vowed to herself, she would live with him. What was marriage anyhow? Only the official acknowledgement of their feelings for each other. It made no real difference to the way she felt. They felt. People couldn't stop them from physically being together, from living as man and wife. Could they?

She didn't even know what was going to happen to Holger now. And that brought her thoughts back to herself once more. Full circle. She groaned inwardly, the vivid images of the atrocities drifting inescapably into her brain. Thousands upon thousands, women and children, babies, old people, gassed to death. She could feel the enormity of the horror. Holger, handsome in his flier's uniform, a young hero, his beautiful, golden-haired girl, smiling, waiting at home. And all the time, those camps — those factory places with their smoking chimneys, those poor creatures, worse than animals, dying . . .

But no! That wasn't Holger, none of it was his fault. She had seen him, held him, tasted his tears as he wept, appalled, just as she was. He could not — she would not let him — take the sins of a whole nation upon him.

When she came down the steps of the station at Pickering, the sun spilled with sudden brightness. The pub opposite was hung with flags, and though it was only just opening time, a crowd had gathered outside, glasses in hand. A small cheer went up and she glanced round, then blushed as she realized it was aimed at her, at her uniform. Many of the celebrants were in khaki, or air-force blue. 'Come and have a drink, luv!'

She gestured back through the portico at the large station clock. She smiled brightly. 'Sorry! Can't! Got to meet my boyfriend. I'm late!' The cheer went up again, louder.

It took her another hour to complete the eight-mile journey to the camp. There was a long walk along a narrow lane between farm fields to reach the gate, though she could see the turreted watchtowers at the perimeter, standing out against the white clouded sky from the main road, where she alighted from the bus. The country looked suddenly peaceful, rich. Gently undulating, so much gentler than the dramatic landscape of the moors she had left behind her.

Surprisingly, she had not waited long before being shown in to Colonel Best's office, and his sympathetic attitude had surprised as well as comforted her.

'Right!' he said decisively, at the end of their conversation. 'We'll see if we can track him down for you. Excuse me, Miss Palmer.' Alone, she glanced out of the window. She felt sick, her stomach churned, and rumbled. Should've eaten breakfast, she admonished herself. She was shaking badly, she realized. Her palms were sweaty and she wiped them on the thighs of her breeches. What if he did, after all, refuse to see her? It frightened her that she should even contemplate the possibility.

'Ruth!' He was there, and she forgot the colonel, the others in the outer office, staring curiously, as she flung herself with a lover's aggression at him, pulled him to her, thrust her mouth up demandingly to his. And felt his response, his desperate need, so that she trembled now with heartfelt gratefulness, clinging on to him, weeping.

'How could you do that to me?' she whispered against him. 'You bastard!' She didn't care, about swearing, about anything except being in his arms. Then she heard his smothered grunt of pain, felt the automatic little flinch, and she drew back, cried out at the dark bruising all along his cheek bone, the grazed skin at the corner of his eye, and temple, and knew that his body would be badly marked too. 'Oh, Holger!' Her hand moved gently to the bruise.

'Listen.' Colonel Best was smiling. 'Why don't you two take a stroll? Plenty of quiet spots round here. Just sign out at the gate.' He looked at Holger, still smiling, but conveying a clear message. 'Just make sure you come back,' he said lightly.

Holger nodded. 'Thank you, sir.'

They hardly spoke as they walked hand in hand out of the gateway. They didn't head in the direction of the main road, along which a steady stream of dark-bloused inmates of the camp made its way, but instead turned off along a path, then climbed a stile and edged along a green cornfield. They left the farmhouse comfortably distant, and after a while came across a grassy little knoll with a plantation of trees growing about it, and a shallow, rippling stream at its foot. They lay down, comfortably hidden from view, and moved into each other's arms.

Some time later, Ruth sat up, hunched forward. Under her jersey, her shirt was unbuttoned and her brassiere was hanging somewhere around her neck. She was very red and out of breath. 'Sorry, love. We've got to stop. Or go on. And I'm scared someone'll come.'

Holger had rolled over on to his stomach and lay still. He groaned and gave a small laugh. 'And I say to myself I will not see you again.'

She quickly fitted her breasts back into the cotton cups, restored her clothing, then put her hand on his shoulder.

'Why did you leave me like that? Why did you do it to me? Hurt me like that?'

His voice was thick. He kept his face averted, she could hear the tension in him.

'For you I did it. All those terrible things. They are between us. We cannot run from them. I wanted — to release you.'

'No! That's wrong. So wrong! We cannot run from this! From us! Can't you see that?' She flung herself at him again, thrusting her body the length of his, fastening almost savagely on his mouth, bearing down hard on him, and his lips parted, his hands came up eagerly to hold her.

* * *

'Any news yet?'

The steam of Ernie's breath rose on the frosty March morning. His nose shone cherry-red, his eyes were watering. 'Bit nippy, eh, lass? Let's start with summat to warm us up!' He turned back into the tiny hut and Ruth followed him. Her figure was thickened by the layers of clothing under the dungarees, she dragged her thickly socked feet clumsily in the Wellington boots. 'Just like old times this, eh?' He grinned, pouring out the black tea from the brown pot on the bench. It was, too, she thought. Working here in the gardens again, living back in her old room over the stables. In solitary luxury, too, as before. And yet there was a world of difference. In her world, and the world outside, too.

'Bad business, this. Think we'd be about due for a spot of good news after all we've had to put up with, wouldn't you?' He nodded at the folded copy of the *Daily Mirror* beside the teapot. The headlines blared out the weekend tragedy at Burnden Park, Bolton's football ground, where thiry-three people had been killed, and nearly 400 injured, when the crash-barriers had given way at the reinstituted FA cup game.

There seemed to be no end of shortages of just about everything, too. The euphoria which had swept through the country at the election of the new Labour government was rapidly draining away. There were even some who thought that the peace itself might not be long-lasting, including embittered Churchill who just last week, spoke over in America about an 'iron curtain' dividing Europe.

Gloom and doom all around, she thought. And within, certainly. Holger had been gone nearly four months. Repatriation they had called it. She had begged him not to go, to ask to be allowed to stay in this country. 'Is not possible,' he told her. Then he had added, 'I must go home. There is my mother,' and she had felt terrible, wept penitently. Afterwards the torturing thoughts had set in. He wanted to go back, wanted to have an excuse to leave her.

She kept seeing the image of that smiling blonde girl. She's married, she told herself angrily. She could even be dead, God help her! How could she be jealous of such an insubstantial ghost? It was her he loved, had told her so. He had proved it, shown her how much he loved her, in the bed where she lay now every night, waiting for him to come back. He had written, too, telling her of his unceasing efforts to get the necessary papers to return to England. Why was she so afraid?

The camp at Allerton had been virtually disbanded by the end of the summer last year, at least as far as the Timber Corps was concerned, the girls being replaced by the Forestry Department. That's why Ruth had been overjoyed when Ernie told her, the delight evident on his weathered face, that there was a job for her at the Hall. The autumn had been a brief idyll, with Holger allowed to spend the weekends away from the camp.

They had been as discreet as they could, though May, and several others from the Hall and the village, looked at her with thin-lipped disapproval and were scarcely civil. She would have to get used to that, and worse, she told herself. Like the reaction at home when she announced that she was 'engaged' to Holger, and was hoping to marry him as soon as they could get permission.

'A Nazi! A bloody filthy murdering Nazi?' Julia had screeched. Her display of outrage, extreme as it was, reflected the general feeling, of all except, as Ruth had known all along, her brother-in-law.

'Are you absolutely sure? You know what

you're doing?' Bill asked, with gentle sadness, and she had wept in his arms, overcome with tenderness for his innate decency. So much so that, before he left, she had got him alone, and kissed him, for the last time, with a passionate urgency, of love and a longing for his happiness which she expressed unashamedly with her body as well as with her heart.

Her father had looked stunned. They had known of her friendship with the German lad, but had clearly felt it was nothing more than her daft notions of pacifism which she had always spouted on about. But it was her mother's reaction which hurt Ruth most of all, for Alice, when she finally realized that Ruth was in earnest, had said with chilling and untypical calmness:

'You'll never be welcome in this house again, as long as you're with him.' Ruth had not been home, nor had she been in touch with any of them, since.

They heard footsteps, laughing voices from outside. The two youngsters, fifteen-year-olds who had just left school, were arriving for work.

'Best get out there,' Ernie sighed, putting down his chipped enamel mug. He shivered melodramatically. 'The sooner yon lad of yours gets himself back here the better!'

His words greatly comforted Ruth as she

followed him out into the bright early morning. She owed Ernie so much, a debt of gratitude she would always feel. It was he who had fixed things so that there was a job waiting for Holger. Once again he had persuaded Sir George, against a lot of opposition, she well knew.

'It's getting too big for me, lass.' Ernie shook his whitening head. 'I'll be glad when they get it sorted. Get themselves a proper manager, like. I tell you, if young Holger's patient, and sticks at it, there's a future here — for the pair of you!'

She believed him. There was. Her heart stirred with hope, and with a deep sense of thankfulness. But the lonely days, busy as ever, dragged on, and still Holger did not come back to her.

She hated herself for her dark thoughts when she got the letter telling her that he had seen Heidi, had actually gone to visit at her parents' home and found her there. Why? she asked herself, churning with emotion. Why had he even felt the compulsion to go back there, to try and trace her? She could just imagine it. How beautiful she would look, in her tragic role. Husband missing, in all probability dead. Heidi alone, with her little girl.

Stop it, stop it! she lashed herself, sick and

miserable at her thoughts. She could imagine so clearly all the pressures which would be brought to bear upon him. It was clear from what he omitted rather than wrote that his widowed mother was bitterly opposed to his plans. Ruth found herself even supplying the dialogue for the scene. *Going off to marry your father's murderer! Deserting your folk, your country! Traitor!*

The tears came, in the emptiness of her little bedroom, even though she despised herself for her weakness, her lack of resolution. Where's your faith? she asked herself wretchedly. Where's the love you both swore to each other, right here? She stretched out her hand, passed it lightly over the coverlet, her heart and her body aching with her need of him.

★   ★   ★

He came back in the middle of summer. This time he did not surprise her. That made the waiting worse, but at last they were together again, body and soul. They slept together, though he *did* leave her in the dawn to go down to the draughty bare room below, where he had slept with the Italian boys. It was a sop to convention which fooled nobody yet seemed to keep them, if not contented, less unhappy. 'We'll be married soon as we can,' Ruth told everyone, and she beheved it now.

Michael Bates came up to see them in August. Ruth had had difficulty in keeping track, had lost touch with him for long months at the end of the war. She and Holger were shocked at the change in his appearance. They knew he had been taken ill, and invalided out of the army some time the previous year. He was vague about it. *Exhaustion mainly, I think,* he had written almost dismissively to Ruth.

There was something about him, not just his careworn, rather crumpled appearance, but something else, more in his manner, and in his eyes, which had somehow a haunted quality. They kept darting away from Ruth's gaze, almost as though he couldn't bear to look at her directly for more than a second or two. It distressed and disturbed her. Almost as much as his announcement, which he made with an embarrassed abruptness, that he had quit the ministry of the Anglican church, was now taking up social work.

'Oh! We were hoping you'd marry us!' Ruth blurted, unable to hide her surprise or her disappointment.

'I'll be there, though!' he assured them heartily. 'Try and stop me!'

392

'I hope so. We'll need all the friends we can get!' Ruth smiled, making a joke of it yet knowing how true it was. She had not seen her family for more than half a year now. Only Bill had written to her. His former job was waiting for him, in Customs and Excise. *I've got a posting down south, in Southampton*, he wrote. *But I'll be on hand for the wedding though, that's for sure. Best man, or giving the bride away, whatever you want.*

His chance came on a blustery day in October. The red tape was finally done.

'I'm a Britisher now,' Holger smiled wryly. 'And you're responsible for me.'

'And you for me,' Ruth answered.

The day before the wedding the papers were full of the sensational news that Marshal Goering had cheated the hangman and committed suicide. 'So! My old boss has gone at last!' Holger quipped valiantly. Ruth saw the line of his clenched law quiver, and clung to him with desperate tightness.

'It's all over,' she whispered. 'It's all finished, all of that. There's only us.'

After they had talked with the vicar of St John's over at Kilbeck, he agreed to marry them in the church. Ruth didn't wear white, but a stylish tweed costume, and no one argued with her choice. The congregation was small, but the couple could feel the warmth of their hopes and their wishes for them.

Ernie gave her away, proud if uncomfortable in a starched collar and tie and dark suit. Bill had acted as best man.

'He's your family now as well,' she told Holger, aching with her love for him, and the loneliness she thought she could see lurking there in his eyes. 'Our family!'

And she had two bridesmaids. Irene, of course; Ruth had thought Bill would squire her gallantly through the day. They would get on like a house on fire, she knew it. But there was a second bridesmaid, totally unexpected until a couple of days before the wedding, for, in an about-face of magnificent effrontery, Julia declared her intention of being at her husband's side. 'You know me, kidder. Wouldn't miss a good knees-up for the world!'

They even had a photographer. He was calling out for yet another shot, while they stood huddled and shivering on the porch, when Ruth pulled away, and Holger followed at her bidding.

'Hey! You just promised to obey me, remember?' he laughed.

'Come on! It won't take a minute!' She led him off the path, through the yellowing, dead-looking grass among the old graves. He knew at once where she was going, and he followed her gladly. Out of sight of the others, they stood side by side, in front of the slab, which was beginning to show signs of weathering a little now. 'It doesn't look so new, does it?' Ruth murmured.

'It isn't.' Holger turned her, and they kissed, gently, then she stooped and laid her bouquet of white roses tenderly on the stone.

THE END

We do hope that you have enjoyed reading this large print book.

Did you know that all of our titles are available for purchase?

We publish a wide range of high quality large print books including:
Romances, Mysteries, Classics
General Fiction
Non Fiction and Westerns

Special interest titles available in large print are:
The Little Oxford Dictionary
Music Book
Song Book
Hymn Book
Service Book

Also available from us courtesy of Oxford University Press:
Young Readers' Dictionary
(large print edition)
Young Readers' Thesaurus
(large print edition)

For further information or a free brochure, please contact us at:
Ulverscroft Large Print Books Ltd.,
The Green, Bradgate Road, Anstey,
Leicester, LE7 7FU, England.
Tel: (00 44) 0116 236 4325
Fax: (00 44) 0116 234 0205

Antique dealing has its own equivalent to 'insider trading', as Charles Ramsay finds out to his cost. Offered the purchase of a lifetime, he sees all his ambitions realised in an antique jade cup, known as the 'Loot'. But as soon as the deal is irrevocably struck he finds himself stuck with it like an albatross around his neck — unable to export it without a licence, unable to sell it at home, and in a paralysing no man's land where nobody has sufficient capital to take it off his hands . . .

NO TIME LIKE THE PRESENT

June Barraclough

Daphne Berridge, who has never married, has retired to the small Yorkshire village of Heckcliff where she grew up, intending to write the biography of an eighteenth-century woman poet. Two younger women are interested in her project: Cressida, Daphne's niece, who lives in London, and is uncertain about the direction of her life; and Judith, who keeps a shop in Heckcliff, and is a divorcee. When an old friend of Daphne falls in love with Judith, the question — as for Cressida — is marriage or independence. Then Daphne also receives a surprise proposal.

SEARCH FOR A SHADOW

Kay Christopher

On the last day of her holiday Rosemary Roberts met an intriguing American in the foyer of her London hotel. By some extraordinary coincidence, Larry Madison-Jones was due to visit the tiny Welsh village where Rosemary lived. But how much of a coincidence was Larry's erratic presence there? The moment Rosemary returned home, her life took on a subtle, though sinister edge — Larry had a secret he was not willing to share. As Rosemary was drawn deeper into a web of mysterious and suspicious occurrences, she found herself wondering if Larry really loved her — or was trying to drive her mad . . .

THREE WISHES

Barbara Delinsky

Slipping and sliding in the snow as she walks home from the restaurant where she's worked for fourteen years, Bree Miller barely has time to notice the out-of-control lorry, headed straight for her. All Bree remembers of that fateful night is a bright light, and a voice granting her three wishes. Are they real or imagined? And who is the man standing over her bedside when finally she wakes up? Soon Bree finds herself the recipient of precisely those things she'd most wanted in life — even that which had seemed beyond all reasonable hope.